JIMMY
COATES:
REVENGE

Also by Joe Craig

Jimmy Coates: Killer
Jimmy Coates: Target

JOE CRAIG

JIMMY COATES: REVENGE

CAMILLUS

HarperCollins *Children's Books*

Thank you to:

Everyone at HarperCollins, particularly Stella Paskins,
Geraldine Stroud, Emma Bradshaw,
Gillie Russell and Sally Gritten.
Sarah Manson, Ann Tobias, Nicola Solomon,
Sophie, Miriam and Oli.
To Mary-Ann Ochota, *sine qua non.*

First published in Great Britain by
HarperCollins *Children's Books* 2007
Harper Collins *Children's Books* is a
division of HarperCollins *Publishers* Ltd
77-85 Fulham Palace Road, Hammersmith, London, W6 8JB

www.harpercollinschildrensbooks.co.uk
www.jimmycoates.co.uk

2

Printed and bound in Great Britain by
Clays Ltd, St Ives plc

About the author

Joe Craig studied Philosophy at Cambridge University, then became a songwriter. Within a year, however, his love of stories had taken over and he was writing the first novel in the *Jimmy Coates* series. It was published in 2005. He is now a full time author and likes to keep in touch with his readers through his website www.joecraig.co.uk.

When he's not writing he's visiting schools, playing the piano, inventing snacks, playing football, coaching cricket, reading or watching a movie.

He lives in London.

CHAPTER ONE - THE VISITOR

Jimmy's eyes opened before he even realised he was awake. His head was throbbing – another nightmare that vanished before he could grasp it. When he was asleep, his programming took over his brain completely. It grew like a vine, reaching into every part of his psyche. It spread dangerous knowledge and developed his amazing skills. Day by day Jimmy found himself becoming more lethal – and there was nothing he could do about it. Time was turning him into a killer.

What had woken him, he wondered. Judging by the eerie half-light it was the early hours of the morning. Jimmy didn't dare move his head from the pillow in case someone was watching him, but he listened, analysing every sound. He felt a familiar agitation in his chest – a paranoia he could never shake off. It was part of his nature now and he had learned to trust in it.

His right calf twitched under the duvet. Was that a

sign? It could be nothing. He realised that his muscles probably trained while he slept. How long had it been since NJ7, the most covert and advanced military intelligence agency in the world, had burst into his house to take him away? It felt like forever, but might not even have been more than a fortnight.

Since then, he'd had to live with the knowledge that NJ7 had manipulated human genetics to grow him – an organic assassin, designed to reach active-service capability when he was eighteen. It was crazy. Jimmy still thought of himself as a normal human boy. But he was far from normal. He was only 38 per cent human.

He pictured millions of tiny electric pulses emanating from his brain to the tips of each limb, making them ever more resilient. But the sensation he had now was something more than just his programming.

A drop in temperature. There was a draught from somewhere. The window had been shut when they went to bed. Jimmy was facing away from it now, so he couldn't check it. But how could anybody have broken the window without waking everybody?

He scanned what he could see of the room, his eyes quickly enhancing every shape, enabling him to see in the semi-dark. Three beds stuck out into the middle of the room, their headboards against the wall. In the bed next to Jimmy's, his friend Felix Muzbeke was fast asleep. A slow thread of drool trailed from his lips, glistening like a spider's web in the rain.

Out of the corner of his eye, Jimmy could discern the end of the third bed. His sister's feet made a reassuring bump in the duvet. *OK*, he thought, *so Felix and Georgie haven't been abducted. That's a good start.*

Jimmy was constantly aware that it wasn't just his own life under threat. As well as Georgie and Felix, there was Jimmy's mother. They'd all arrived at the Bed and Breakfast the night before, on the run from NJ7. Felix's parents, Neil and Olivia, had already been in hiding there.

Deep inside, Jimmy's human self was now starting to wake up. With this came a surge of anger, brought on by the thought of his own father – or at least the man he had always believed was his father. The man's words would never leave Jimmy's head: *"You're not my son."* To him, Jimmy was nothing but an enemy of the State. He had been ever since overcoming his programming and refusing to kill for NJ7. Now Ian Coates, the Prime Minister of Great Britain, wanted him eliminated.

Then Jimmy heard it. A sound so faint that Felix's drooling almost drowned it out. Immediately, an image popped into Jimmy's head that identified the noise – grease trickling down wood. It told him two things. One: the room had definitely been breached. Two: whoever had broken in was highly dangerous.

They've found me, he thought. Terror shook his entire body, but with it came a blast of confidence – the artificial self-assurance of his programming. It seemed to flick away the fear. Before he could even think about it, Jimmy exploded into action.

He kicked his right leg up and back, sending his duvet flying towards the window. It wrapped itself around an approaching figure. In the same movement, Jimmy flipped up into a handstand by his pillow – just in time. The intruder slammed the duvet back on to the mattress, then rolled to his feet on the other side of the bed.

Jimmy used his bare feet to push himself off the wall. He cartwheeled over and landed, standing, opposite his attacker. They had both moved without a sound. Felix and Georgie hadn't stirred. Now, for the first time, Jimmy was able to look at the person who had broken in. He was small – only just taller than Jimmy, in fact – and his physique was slight. His face was masked by a black balaclava, which matched the black combat uniform. On his chest Jimmy noticed three small vertical stripes. Even though his night-vision made it hard to distinguish colours, Jimmy knew that they had to be green – a green stripe was the emblem of NJ7. But why were there three of them? He shrugged off the inconsistency and noticed the contrast between the black military outfit in front of him and the Kermit pyjamas that he'd been forced to borrow from the B&B owners. He shivered, suddenly aware of his vulnerability.

Jimmy picked out the intruder's eyes – their pale blue was intensified by his night-vision. The eyes looked Jimmy up and down.

"They're not my pyjamas," Jimmy insisted. "I usually sleep in a T-shirt and..."

"What's going on?" Felix interrupted. His face was scrunched up like a new-born piglet and he was peering around blindly. For him, it was too dark to see.

Jimmy only glanced at him for an instant, but he knew straight away it was a mistake. In that split-second, the masked figure dived at him. Jimmy dropped to the floor and slid out of the way on his back. He went straight under Felix's bed and out the other side.

"Is that you, Jimmy?" Felix asked, with no clue what was going on.

The intruder landed with a roll, then sprang up and leapt at Jimmy again – right over Felix's head.

"Morning, Felix," Jimmy grunted, flipping himself up, feet first. He caught his attacker in mid-air – with his knees locked around the intruder's neck. "Bit of help would be nice."

The two fighters tumbled over each other across the floor. The noise woke Georgie.

"Jimmy, you OK?" she whispered frantically. There was no answer. She jumped out of bed and stumbled for the light switch.

Jimmy clung on to the attacker with every bit of strength he could muster. They twisted together, a flurry of limbs wrestling for control. Jimmy's programming was serving him well. He wrenched one arm free and clamped a hand down on top of his assailant's head. With one twist, he threw him off balance. The intruder's face hit the floor and the balaclava came away in Jimmy's fist.

Jimmy pounced, holding him down. Except, he gradually realised – it wasn't a him. There was a tickling sensation on Jimmy's lips. Stray hairs fluttered around his face. He spat them away, conscious of not loosening his hold. There was a strange smell in the air. Was that coconut shampoo?

Finally, Georgie found the light switch – but it didn't work. She clicked it on and off frantically. The room remained dark. Instead, she went for the door handle. In a burst of strength, the intruder performed a back flip so powerful it took Jimmy along too. She landed on him, knocking the wind out of him, and immediately launched herself at Georgie.

As Georgie pulled the door open a centimetre, the intruder slammed into the small of her back. The door banged shut, with Georgie's face pressed against the wood. She tried to scream for help, but before the breath even reached her lungs, she was pulled away and flung back on to her bed. The mysterious figure wrapped the duvet across Georgie's face and spun her over like a log down a hill. Georgie tried shouting again, but the bedclothes completely muffled the noise. She was rolled up so tight she couldn't move her arms from her side.

Jimmy was slightly dazed, but he shook it off and hurled himself at the base of Georgie's bed. It knocked into his attacker, throwing her off-balance. Immediately, Jimmy rolled under the bed, out the other side and slammed into her ankles. He tried to pin her to the floorboards again, but she spun like a break-dancer, planting a foot in Jimmy's face with each revolution.

Felix was out of his bed now, tentatively shuffling across the room with his arms outstretched. When he reached the wall, his hands felt about for the light switch, not knowing Georgie had already tried that. From inside her duvet-cocoon, she hollered and squirmed, gradually wriggling her way out.

"Don't worry, Jimmy," Felix announced. "I'm coming." Then, at the top of his voice, he yelled, "Help!"

"Quiet, Felix," Jimmy snapped, crawling backwards to avoid another kicking. The last thing he wanted was the neighbours arriving. That would give away their hideout to NJ7 in no time. "Get out and get my mum."

Felix went for the door, but the intruder turned to stop him. That was the distraction Jimmy needed. He flipped on his front and hooked his legs underneath the empty bed behind him. Then, with a thrill flooding his muscles, he bent his knees and heaved the bed off the floor. He lifted it right over his head with just his legs. It scraped the ceiling, then came crashing down in front of him. One leg snapped clean off and the frame smashed into splinters. The bed had landed upside-down – right on top of Jimmy's opponent.

Finally, Jimmy dragged her out. He dug his knee into her spine and his elbow into the back of her neck. She wasn't getting out from his hold this time.

"I'm on your side!" came her muffled shout. The tension in Jimmy's gut eased slightly, but he was far from relaxed.

"It's a trick," Georgie urged. She had made it out of the duvet at last.

"Who are you?" Jimmy demanded. It was becoming clearer by the second that this person was not part of an NJ7 assault team. She dipped her hand in her pocket. Jimmy clenched his muscles again, ready for anything, but his opponent pulled out nothing more than a small round piece of black plastic. It looked like the remote locking device on a car key. She clicked the button and on came every light in the room.

Jimmy felt her muscles relax. It was as if she was deflating slightly. The fight was over. She was giving up – for now. Jimmy stood up and slowly backed away.

For the first time, the intruder's face was revealed. Jimmy, Georgie and Felix let out a gasp. The person on the floor in front of them was a girl about their age. A flurry of auburn hair tumbled around her face. Jimmy was astounded. Felix was mesmerised.

"I've come to have a conversation with you," the girl said. Her voice was soft, with a very faint accent that made her sound slightly exotic.

Jimmy remained deadpan. "If that's what you call a conversation," he replied, "I can't wait for us to argue."

CHAPTER TWO - SEEDS OF RETRIBUTION

"Was I too rough for you?" the girl pouted. "I'm sorry. I was playing. I wanted to see what you could do." She stood up, moving with a strange elegance that didn't seem to fit someone so young.

"If I'd wanted you dead, Jimmy Coates," she continued, "you would never have even known I existed. I could have killed you quietly, quickly and from a distance." She moved towards him, almost gliding across the floor, her eyes never wavering from Jimmy's. "I think I would have done it painlessly though. You seem nice." Then she winked. Jimmy lost all feeling in his cheeks for a second. He was a picture of astonishment.

"My name is Zafi Sauvage." The girl held out her hand, which was covered in a black leather glove. In a daze, Jimmy shook it. The whole thing felt so bizarre. He wouldn't normally shake hands with anybody – especially not some strange girl, and *especially* not one who, only seconds before, had been trying to break his neck.

Felix brushed the others aside and shoved his hand in Zafi's direction. "Yeah, hi," he started. "I'm, like, delighted to meet you." Jimmy grimaced at the unusually posh accent Felix was trying on. "Frightfully delighted. My name is Felix. And may I welcome you by saying that, frightfully and awfully, you're, like, a knockout."

"If you're not here to try to kill me..." Jimmy interrupted. He didn't finish his sentence. There were too many questions all bursting to get out at the same time. Who did this girl work for? What did she want? How had she found out where Jimmy and the others were hiding? Above all the others was one question that repeated in his head like a siren. *Is this girl a programmed assassin like me?*

"I can't believe it," Georgie whispered, echoing his thoughts. "Another one. A third assassin."

"Aren't you going to ask me to sit down?" Zafi said, raising one eyebrow. Felix immediately ushered her to the end of his bed.

"Don't mind them," he blathered. "They've forgotten their manners. Hey, look what I can do." He pulled out his top lip and, with his thumbs, shoved it into his nostrils. He glared at Zafi like this until she let out a high giggle.

"My, how attractive," Zafi laughed. "Look what I can do." She pulled off her glove and pressed her palm flat against her eye. She twisted her hand, which made a weird sucking noise. Then she pulled her palm away and her eyeball popped out. It bounced around on the end of her optic nerve halfway down her cheek. She beamed with glee.

"Wow." Felix was so impressed that his voice quivered. Zafi calmly popped her eye back into its socket and flicked her hair behind her ear.

"Jimmy, look at this," Felix insisted. "It's so cool."

But Jimmy wasn't paying attention. He was examining the window to confirm what he suspected: the frame had been lubricated with some kind of grease. Zafi had opened the window expertly and with less noise than a shadow. But Jimmy didn't stop to admire her work.

He looked back at Zafi. Why did she look like she was about to smile, Jimmy wondered. Didn't she take any of this seriously? It was as if the corners of her mouth couldn't help curling upwards.

With the lights on, it was obvious that there was no green stripe on her chest. Instead, three vertical stripes formed an emblem just as powerful and just as proud. In his night-vision, Jimmy had assumed they were green, but one was blue, one white and one red. It was the Tricolore – the French flag. That seemed to answer the question of who she worked for.

Jimmy realised that because the French Secret Service, the DGSE, had helped him, relations between Britain and France were worse than they had been for centuries. In fact, both had threatened war. Jimmy was starting to see that if Zafi was an enemy of Neo-democratic Britain, she could be an important ally for him. His curiosity became urgent now.

"Hey, you two lovebirds," he began, "stop messing about. I need to know what's going on."

"Didn't you see what she did with her eye?" Felix panted. Jimmy ignored him.

"What's this 'conversation' you wanted to have with me?" he insisted. But before Zafi could answer, Georgie marched towards the door.

"I wouldn't bother fetching your mother," Zafi whispered. "She's a little drowsy at the moment."

Georgie turned to her with horror on her face. Jimmy felt a double layer of confusion – first was a lurch of panic for his mother's safety, but beneath it came a reassuring warmth. To his programmed side, it made perfect sense. Felix's cry for help. The crash of the bed on the floor – the other people in the house must have been drugged somehow to keep them out of the way. Assigned Zafi's mission, he would have done the same. As the thought ran through his head, Zafi explained it to the others.

"I sent some sleeping gas under the necessary windows before I came through yours."

Georgie looked at Zafi with a mixture of disbelief and anger. Then she marched out of the room anyway.

"Doesn't she trust me?" Zafi asked with a cheeky sparkle in her eye.

That was enough for Jimmy. *How dare she make a joke of it*, he thought. Didn't she realise she was playing with people's lives? And she hadn't even started to explain what she was doing there. Jimmy gripped Zafi's shoulders and held her down on the bed.

"How can you do all this?" he hissed, his eyes only centimetres from hers. His face was turning red, but Zafi's only reaction was to open her eyes wide and give a little smile.

"What a silly question," she replied, ever so gently. "The same way you can, Jimmy Coates. I'm a genetically programmed—"

"No, I mean, how can you bring yourself to do it?" Jimmy was really seething now. "Don't you realise that attacking innocent people, drugging them, even killing them – it's wrong."

"It might be wrong," Zafi whispered back, "but it's not me doing it, is it? It's nothing to do with me. I watch it happen. Maybe I'm sad about it, maybe not. It's not my responsibility."

Jimmy wanted to scream right in her face. He felt like tearing her to shreds on the spot, but instead his grip melted to nothing. He slipped off her. If he'd demanded any more answers, he might have had to admit to himself that he envied her.

Georgie came back into the room. She didn't look happy. "I can't wake Mum," she announced.

"What about my parents?" Felix asked.

"I can't wake any of them, OK? It's like they're hibernating or something."

"They'll be asleep for a few more hours," Zafi said, sitting up and flicking her hair behind her ear. "They'll be fine by lunchtime."

Jimmy wanted to get up and reassure his big sister, but he was still distracted by a small question at the back of his mind – what would he be capable of if nothing was his responsibility?

Georgie started the questioning again. "You'd better explain what's going on."

Zafi sighed. "But this is so much fun," she said, too brightly. "It's like a sleepover."

Felix almost laughed, but only because he was nervous.

"I work for France," Zafi continued with a shrug. "My government expects that Britain and France might be drawn into a war."

"What?" Georgie gasped. "Why?"

Jimmy cut in to explain. "Yesterday, the French sent a fighter jet into British airspace."

"Only after NJ7 bombed a French farmhouse," Zafi added.

"But that wasn't to attack France," Jimmy sighed. "It's where we'd been hiding. NJ7 were trying to get us."

"Well, all they've got for themselves is trouble."

Zafi and Jimmy stared at each other.

"I've come to invite you to join the right side," Zafi announced.

"You want me to work for France against Britain – in a war?" Jimmy tried to keep his voice as calm as possible. Zafi nodded.

"Who says there's going to be a war?" Felix asked. "That's rubbish. Nobody's loony enough to start a war."

Jimmy wished his friend was right, but he was far from sure. He walked over to the window. It was still open from when Zafi had sneaked in. For a second, he hesitated. Perhaps something in his head was suggesting he could escape into the night and disappear forever. It only lasted a second. He slid the window shut. It closed as silently as it had opened for Zafi, but to Jimmy it felt like the portcullis on a castle coming down to trap him inside.

Did she expect him to give an answer straight away? He had already put everybody he loved in mortal danger to avoid working as an assassin for one government. Surely it was madness of the French to think he would kill for them.

So why was he still thinking about it? And why was his hand shaking?

"I came to you before," he began eventually. "To the DGSE, I mean. When we needed your help. I offered to co-operate then."

"To co-operate?" Zafi questioned. "Or to join us?"

"I offered information. But Uno Stovorsky said he didn't need it. And he never suggested that I work for you."

"The DGSE didn't need you then, did we." Zafi explained haughtily. "We had me." At that she gave a sly chuckle. "But yesterday changed things. France needs you now."

Jimmy couldn't order any of his thoughts. "I don't understand," he started quietly. "I thought there were only two of us. Me and Mitchell. We're both English. How come you're also... like us, except that you're French?"

"I suppose you want a history lesson," Zafi sighed. "Well, the team of scientists that designed us fell out with each other twelve years ago. One of them was French and he escaped back to Paris when he realised there was going to be trouble."

"And he took you with him?" Felix gasped. His mouth was hanging open.

"Sort of." Zafi smiled at him fondly. "I wasn't born yet, was I. But he took with him all the files and the chip he needed to make me."

"So nobody at NJ7 knows about you?" Jimmy asked.

Zafi shook her head. "They've been looking for something called ZAF-1."

Jimmy recognised that name. He'd heard it inside NJ7 Headquarters, but he didn't know what it meant.

"You're... ZAF-1?" he suggested.

"You should pay attention more closely, Jimmy Coates." Zafi looked up at him and fluttered her eyelashes. "I said they're *looking* for ZAF-1. They think it's a Secret Service agency. But there's no such thing. There's only..."

"...Zafi." Jimmy completed the sentence for her.

"That's right – me!"

"They don't know anything about you," Jimmy exclaimed, the words tumbling out in his excitement. "I was there, in NJ7." He looked at Georgie, Felix and Zafi in turn. "I heard them talking about ZAF-1, trying to work out what it meant. They were scared of it, but didn't know what it meant..."

"Not yet," Zafi cut him off. "They will soon. They'll work it out from Dr Higgins' papers."

Dr Higgins – the scientist behind the original organic assassin project. The name still gave Jimmy an odd feeling. He wanted to hate the old man, but wasn't physically able to. The result was like being seasick, but enjoying it. Jimmy wondered where the doctor was these days. Higgins had gone on the run after doing some assassinating of his own. He could have been anywhere in the world. For all Jimmy knew, NJ7 had already found him and taken their revenge.

"I don't have any more time, Jimmy," Zafi said softly. She stood up and placed a hand on his wrist. "And nor do you." Jimmy tensed up. So did Georgie and Felix. "I did what I could tonight to help you," Zafi continued.

"What do you mean?" Georgie asked suspiciously.

"I created a diversion so they couldn't follow you out of London so easily." Zafi thought for a moment and smiled to herself. Jimmy couldn't stand the way everything seemed to amuse her. "I need you to come with me now."

Jimmy looked at his friend and his sister. He could see on their faces what they thought. The last thing they wanted was for him to leave them. But everything inside him was drawing him to go with Zafi. Surely he couldn't – up to now, he had done everything he could to avoid causing harm to anybody. The DGSE would almost certainly send him to kill. But who?

He closed his eyes and pictured Paduk, the huge Secret Service agent who ran the Prime Minister's 'Special Security'. He pictured Miss Bennett, who had pretended to be protecting Jimmy for so long as a fake form teacher at school. Then she had emerged as his most venomous enemy – Head of NJ7. They had stolen his life. They had tortured and tried to kill the people he loved. Was this the chance that he had wanted so badly? Was this the opportunity to get his own back and be working for a good cause at the same time?

Then Jimmy pictured Ian Coates.

"I'll do it," he rasped. His voice seemed reluctant to leave his throat. "I'll do it."

CHAPTER THREE - THWARTED

"Jimmy you can't!" Georgie shouted.

Jimmy was already moving towards the window. It was Zafi who stopped him.

"I presume we can leave by the front door, no?" she chuckled.

Jimmy felt himself laugh too, but it came out like a grunt. It didn't even sound like him. He turned to the door.

"Jimmy, stop," Felix ordered, grabbing his friend by the arm. Jimmy didn't look at him.

"Get off me," he growled.

"No way."

"Get off me, Felix," Jimmy said again. "You know I could snap you in two, don't you?"

"Jimmy, what are you saying?" Georgie yelled. She stepped between her brother and the door. Her face had gone white. "What's happening to you?"

"Let him come," Zafi insisted. "He wants to, can't you see?"

"No, he doesn't," Georgie countered. "It's not him." She seized Jimmy's face in her hands. "Come on, Jimmy, pull yourself together!"

Suddenly, Jimmy exploded with rage. "Get off me!" he boomed. He shook off his sister's hands and pushed Felix away. They both staggered back a step or two.

"It doesn't matter what you say," Zafi muttered. "He doesn't have any choice about it anyway. It's his destiny."

Jimmy felt the dark power inside him. It was the force that he thought he had learned to control. But it was always there and always growing more layers. It felt like a wild animal had burrowed even deeper inside him, devouring his soul as it went.

"Why are you doing this?" Georgie whispered. Jimmy looked at her and saw a horrible fear on her face.

"Are you winding us up?" Felix asked. "You are, aren't you?"

Jimmy didn't know how to respond. Felix's chirpy tone was completely out of synch with the weight of Jimmy's emotions.

"All right, tell you what," Felix continued, bouncing on the spot, "I'm coming too." Jimmy sighed. "Let's go," Felix insisted. With a flourish, he plucked one of the pillows from the bed and whipped off the pillowcase. Then he tied it around his neck. "Got to wrap up warm, cos, baby, it's cold outside."

"Felix, what are you doing?" Jimmy asked.

"I, my friend, am going to come with you and become a killer."

None of them knew what to make of this – least of all Jimmy.

"Felix, this is serious," he said.

"Yeah, serious," Felix echoed. "Seriously, I'm so serious. Let's go get serious with some Frenchies." He grabbed Jimmy's wrist again, but this time he was dragging his friend towards the door. "Come on, come on, haven't got all day. People to kill."

"Stop," Jimmy urged feebly. He pulled his hand away. "You're nuts."

"I'm nuts?" Felix mocked. "Oh, *I'm* nuts. Yeah, cos, funny thing is, we all thought you wanted to stick with us and get away from the fighting and the murdering. But some little French bird flutters in here with her little gadgets and her cool eyeball trick – that was so cool by the way," he quickly turned to Zafi and grinned. "And next thing you want to skip off to Paris to become an assassin, which is what NJ7 wanted you to be in the first place. But you're right – *I'm* nuts."

The others were stunned. If Georgie hadn't been so upset, she would have laughed. Zafi was the first to break the silence.

"Your friend is weird," she whispered.

"I know," Jimmy mumbled, "He's..."

"I like it."

Finally, a smile forced its way on to Jimmy's face. "Take off that pillowcase," he said. "You look ridiculous."

"So we're staying?" Felix asked. Jimmy nodded, and his sister plunged her arms around him.

"You're such an idiot," Georgie scolded Jimmy even as she was hugging him. "You have to think about these things more carefully. We're going to get out of here and be safe and normal again."

"It's a shame," interjected Zafi. "They said if you didn't want to come with me I should kill you." Jimmy's blood fizzed in his veins. Georgie gasped, her hand flying to her mouth. "Ha! Joking!" Zafi exploded into laughter. "Your faces are hilarious."

Felix and Jimmy both let out a huge sigh of relief.

"I don't think that's funny!" Georgie shrieked.

"It was *quite* funny," Felix suggested. "Not as funny as me obviously."

"So it's OK if I don't, you know..." Jimmy asked.

"Of course," Zafi replied, her voice light and almost squeaky. "You won't work for us, but that's OK because we know that you are no friend of NJ7."

"I'd never work for them, don't worry." At last Jimmy started to relax. He almost felt like himself again.

"But NJ7 won't have any distractions now," Zafi warned him. "I can't throw them off your trail any more. And if *I* can find you, *they* can find you. Get out of the country as quick as you can." She opened the door and was framed by the darkness in the rest of the building. "Maybe we'll meet again."

To his surprise, Jimmy was sad that this girl was leaving. There was so much she might have been able to tell him. He was suddenly overcome by the urge to know everything about her. Had she also grown up thinking she was a normal child? Or had she always known that she was only 38 per cent human? She seemed a lot happier with it than Jimmy was. Did she have parents? Were they, like Jimmy's, agents of the Government's intelligence services? And had they kept it a secret?

With all this blurring his thoughts, Jimmy found it hard to say anything – even a simple goodbye. Zafi reached into her pocket.

"I'll rewire the power supply outside on my way out," she announced casually. Her hand emerged holding the remote control clicker that had turned on the lights in the room. "Something to remember me by." She tossed it at Jimmy, who caught it in a daze.

"Don't you need it?" Felix called out, but Zafi was already floating down the stairs, making hardly a sound. She glanced over her shoulder, her hair catching the streak of light through the banisters.

"I'll make another one."

Jimmy, Georgie and Felix were unable to move. They were stunned. Zafi had come in like a whirlwind and left as much devastation. She had made so little noise – they didn't even hear the front door closing after her – and she displayed all the clinical killing instincts of a highly trained assassin. Yet her eyes had sparkled, her physique was delicate, her voice was soft and high, with a giggle that reminded Jimmy of the most annoying girls in his year at school.

While Jimmy was trying to fathom out how he felt, Felix reached across and swiped the gadget from his open palm. He clicked the lights on and off a couple of times.

"Cool," he muttered under his breath. Then he asked, "Do you think we'll, you know, see her again?"

Jimmy didn't answer. His gut was telling him that he hoped they would. But, at the same time, he could hear a stern voice in his head. It told him that if he ever did see Zafi Sauvage again, it could only mean that he was in trouble.

Jimmy, Felix and Georgie didn't bother going back to bed. There was no way any of them would have been able to sleep anyway. They were buzzing with adrenaline from Zafi's visit. Instead, the three of them took their duvets down to the living room. Felix turned on the TV.

"Chris will go ballistic when he hears about what happened tonight," he said.

"Do you think he's OK?" Georgie asked Jimmy. "And Saffron?" There was no reply. "Well? Do you?"

Jimmy exploded with frustration. "I don't know, do I? How is any of us meant to know?"

"All right, calm down, psycho." Georgie threw up her hands.

Jimmy mumbled an apology. He could picture Christopher Viggo's face as the man had driven off into the darkness the night before. With him had been his girlfriend, Saffron Walden, dying from an NJ7 bullet. Jimmy had already gone over and over it in his mind – hospitals were out because they were covered in security cameras, and they'd report a bullet wound to the police straight away. So unless Viggo knew a surgeon nearby who was also a so-called 'enemy' of Britain, Jimmy had no idea how Saffron was going to survive.

He curled up on the sofa, wishing his morbid thoughts would go away. Saffron and Viggo had done so much to help Jimmy. Viggo used to be an NJ7 agent himself, but he'd fled thirteen years earlier because of the evil of one man: Ares Hollingdale. From being Director of NJ7, Hollingdale had risen to become Prime Minister – but an undemocratic one. He'd used NJ7 to secure his position at the head of a dictatorship. And the population did nothing to stop him.

Sometimes, it seemed like Viggo and Saffron were the only sane people in Britain – at least, the only ones who were fighting for democracy.

Gradually, Jimmy's attention returned to the TV.

"The new Prime Minister, Ian Coates, is about to land in Washington DC to meet with the American President, Alphonsus Grogan." The newsreader was a woman with a vacant stare and a half-smile permanently on her lips. "The first item on their agenda will be American support for Britain in any possible military action against France, following French incursion into British airspace yesterday afternoon."

With every mention of the Prime Minister, Jimmy felt something rumble in his belly. He forced it down and told himself it was hunger.

"Ian Coates will first meet with the President at the White House," the newsreader went on, "before touring the cities of the East Coast of America. He will address the UN Security Council in New York in four days' time to present the case for Britain's legal right to retaliate against France."

Usually, the last thing Jimmy would have wanted to do was watch the news. But everything had changed. Now it was urgent that they all knew what the Government was doing. This was their enemy.

"I can't believe that's our dad," Georgie muttered.

Jimmy didn't answer. *Not 'our' dad*, he thought. *'Your' dad.* He felt a sting in his throat and wiped the back of his hand across his eyes. When he looked up, he saw his own face on the TV screen. It was the same old school photograph that Jimmy had seen on TV the day before.

"...still thought to be behind the murder of Ares Hollingdale," the reporter was saying, "and still on the run." The camera zoomed in on Jimmy's eyes.

"It's all right," Felix stated calmly. "You don't really look like that."

"It's all right?" Georgie exclaimed. "How is it 'all right' that they're telling the whole country that Jimmy murdered the last Prime Minister?" Jimmy shrunk into himself. He just wished they didn't have to talk about it.

In the last few weeks he had learned not to trust what came out of the TV. He could almost see the puppet-strings attached to the limbs of the newsreaders, and Miss Bennett somewhere, just out of shot, dictating every word that was said.

"Anyway," Georgie piped up again, furious, "NJ7 knows Jimmy didn't do it – because *they* did it."

"What?" Felix asked. "You think Miss Bennett sent someone from NJ7 to kill their own Prime Minister?"

"Maybe. Hollingdale was sadistic and cruel and probably crazy. Maybe they'd had enough and wanted Dad to take over."

Hardly realising he was speaking, Jimmy cut in. "He had it coming," he snarled.

All three of them looked at each other, shocked at what Jimmy had said, even if it was true. Was it him or his programming that was spitting out such venomous thoughts? Jimmy couldn't get any more words out of his mouth. He could feel his lips trembling, but there was nothing more to say.

The only sound was the drone of the television and the incessant ticking of a clock.

CHAPTER FOUR - DIAMOND IN THE ROUGH

The British Prime Minister stepped out of the White House's Oval Office to rejoin his assistants and his head of security, Paduk. The look on his face was far from optimistic.

"The President is considering our position," he announced.

"What does that mean?" Paduk asked. "You were in there with him for over an hour. It's not rocket science. Either he's on our side or he isn't."

Ian Coates' advisors huddled together in debate. He ignored them and threw himself into a chair of plush red velvet beneath a portrait of Hillary Clinton. He leaned his elbows on his knees and held his head. The quiet of the corridor was stifling and the cream walls seemed to be closing in on him. He felt like he was trapped inside a giant trifle. Somewhere, a clock ticked too loudly. Next to him, Paduk itched at his shirt collar.

"He can't keep us waiting like this," he grumbled. "Where's the respect?"

Ian Coates shook his head. "It's natural," he explained, trying to stay calm. "We're asking for their army to come and fight a war with us against France. That's not a decision that can be hurried."

Paduk grunted. "I remember when Americans were grateful to fight alongside us. Now they've forgotten everything. Most people in this country don't even know where France is."

"Most of them don't know where Britain is either, Paduk."

Suddenly, a door opposite them opened. They both shot to their feet and instinctively straightened their jackets. But it wasn't the President who emerged, merely one of his aides. She was a woman in her early thirties, with brown hair tied back in a tight knot. The shoulders of her business suit were just a little too wide to be stylish and there was too much red lipstick lining her fake smile.

"Current US policy is not to intervene in foreign conflicts," she announced. Her voice was clipped, with a clean mid-American accent. "But the President places great importance on the historical friendship between our two nations. Therefore, he would like to offer you a package of the finest military hardware the US industry has to offer."

"Weapons?" Coates spluttered. "You're offering me weapons?"

"Well, yes," replied the aide. "As well as hardware of all other types – trucks, planes, missiles—"

"I know what military hardware is," interrupted the Prime Minister. "So how much will this package cost?"

"Eighty billion dollars."

Ian Coates let out an incredulous laugh. "I knew it," he scoffed. "Grogan needed just enough time to phone the bosses at the arms companies, didn't he?"

"I can't answer that, sir," replied the aide blankly.

"Tell Grogan I came to meet a President – not an arms dealer." Coates spun on his heels and marched away, with Paduk and his own aides following close behind.

As they were escorted out of the White House, Ian Coates tried to contain his anger. He tried to imagine how he'd behave at the press conference that was coming up in a few days. How could he put a brave public face on this and pretend to be friends with the President of the USA? He also had to go through the motions of meeting with the UN in New York. But none of that ruled out the drastic action he could take in secret.

"Call Miss Bennett," he hissed under his breath. "I'm approving the Reflex Plan."

"The Reflex Plan?" Paduk gasped. "Are you sure?"

The Prime Minister nodded.

* * *

Mitchell checked the platform clock again. It was just habit now. He didn't need to know the time – he wouldn't even have remembered what it was if anybody had asked him. But every few minutes he looked up at the clock. His fingers tore and twisted at a paperclip he had found on the platform the night before.

It was days now since Mitchell had faced Jimmy, but not for a second had the confrontation left him. Every possible thought had blasted through his brain. And, like a high-powered water jet wearing down stone, his torment had reduced his mind to dust. At least, that was how it felt.

Your brother's still alive.

Mitchell could still hear Jimmy's words in his head. He had repeated them to himself so many times that they had almost lost all meaning. Another teenage boy walked past. He was probably a couple of years older than Mitchell – fifteen or sixteen. In Mitchell's hunger and fatigue he saw his brother's face on the boy, just the way it had looked when Mitchell had beaten it senseless. He shook his head hard and rubbed his eyes. The other boy was gone, but for Mitchell, the image of Lenny Glenthorne lying limp on the floor was as vivid as ever.

He could still feel the horror of being told that he had murdered his own brother. With that power over him, it had been easy for NJ7 to make Mitchell their assassin. They'd quickly sent him after his first target –

Jimmy Coates. But when the moment came to complete the job, Mitchell was defeated – not by a stronger punch or some secret gadget, but because Jimmy had claimed that Mitchell's brother wasn't dead after all.

Since then, Mitchell's survival instinct had forced him below ground. He had wandered through the Underground network, easily hiding from the overnight workers when the network closed in the early hours of each morning. He'd broken into the staff toilets to find water. He'd slept only a few hours at a time in any one place, continually moving on, sometimes walking through the tunnels and always avoiding the District Line – the line represented on the map by the biggest green stripe in London. His clothes and hands were black with dirt.

He could feel NJ7 all around him, watching. Not just in the thousands of security cameras, but in person. He'd seen those figures waiting for him – shadows that hovered on the platforms and by the exits. Agents of the Green Stripe were everywhere. He knew they could pick him up any time. They'd implanted a tracking chip in his heel. But that didn't matter. Mitchell knew he was going to go back to them eventually. NJ7 was his life now. And it was a life that seemed to suit him well. The incident with his brother had led him to these things – training, purpose and something that could almost have felt like happiness.

Now he didn't even know whether he *wanted* his brother to be alive or not. The possibility didn't fill him with joy. His brother had beaten him up countless times. Maybe Lenny didn't deserve to die, but he certainly didn't deserve Mitchell fighting *for* him. Whether Mitchell had killed him, or NJ7 had just made it look that way, what difference did it make? Either way, Leonard Glenthorne was out of his life. Even if it turned out that NJ7 had killed him, there was nobody left in the world who was going to take revenge. *Least of all me*, Mitchell thought.

He looked up at the clock again. He didn't even know how much time had passed. It was a good feeling to know that it had passed at all. He gave his paperclip a sharp kink with his thumb. A commuter strutted by, glancing at Mitchell's face. All he saw was grime and suspicion. He looked away quickly, like everybody else did, and clutched his briefcase tighter.

Is this what I've become? thought Mitchell. *No. I'm better than this. I'm different. I work for NJ7.* He pushed himself off the bench and marched along the platform. He was still as strong as ever, despite so long with hardly anything to eat. After these days of confusion, he was ready for the truth. He was ready for NJ7.

Halfway along the platform Mitchell dropped to his knees. There was a square in the platform floor that looked like some kind of trapdoor. He had seen dozens of these all over the tube network. Each one was about half a metre square, with a tiny keyhole.

Hardly aware of what he was doing, Mitchell opened his fist. There was his paperclip, bent into a strange and intricate shape. *Of course*, he thought to himself, *there must be easier ways to reach NJ7 than walking through the streets.*

He jabbed his paperclip into the keyhole. All this time, his programming had been fashioning the perfect key. In one fluid movement, he hauled open the hatch, threw himself in, feet first, and pulled the door shut over him. He didn't even bother opening his eyes.

Instead, he surrendered himself completely to the intelligent force that drove him. He had landed on his back in a dank crawlspace. He immediately rolled a few metres to the side, feeling the platform floor just a whisker above him. Without knowing why, he counted the rolls – one, two, three, four – until eventually his body stopped itself dead. His hands shot up and, after only a second to feel around, he again pressed his paperclip key into a hole. He gave it a quick turn, then punched open another hatch door.

Mitchell emerged beneath bare strip lights that warmed his face. Around him were grey concrete walls covered in loose wiring that looked like a rainbow on a glorious day. This was no longer London Underground. Mitchell was back at NJ7 Headquarters and he wanted some answers.

He snapped his paperclip in two and flicked it to the floor, then broke into a sprint. It felt as if every muscle was thanking him for the chance to run again. He still felt as if he was watching somebody else's actions, but it was a show he enjoyed watching. He swelled with pride to see himself move with such authority.

He tracked his progress through the labyrinth with ease. There were no features to mark his route, just miles and miles of grey concrete tunnel. They were like the veins of his own body. He just needed to look inside himself to see where they led.

In some places the corridors were broad thoroughfares; in others they were barely wide enough for Mitchell to squeeze down. There were no doors of course – NJ7 Headquarters were designed so that if it ever became necessary to evacuate, the whole complex could be flooded by the Thames in 120 seconds.

The constant pad of Mitchell's feet was virtually the only sound, but he ran on his toes, keeping the noise to a minimum. Then he heard something from round the next corner – tapping on a keyboard. In an instant, he made the calculation: just one person. A man. Sitting down. Facing the entrance of a room with no other way out. As he approached, he made more deductions based solely on the sound of the person typing: left-handed. Not a trained fighter because the arms weren't strong enough, so a technician, not a field-agent.

Whoever it was, he was about to meet Mitchell Glenthorne.

Mitchell whipped round the corner. In front of him was exactly the scene he had pictured – a lone man, typing at his desk. The light from his computer screen picked out the whites of his eyes, which were stretched out in astonishment, and a green stripe on his lapel. A diamond twinkled in the man's left earlobe. There was no time for him to cry out. Mitchell moved too fast, diving over the desk. He rocketed into the man's torso, forcing him backwards over his chair. As they landed, one on top of the other, Mitchell's fingers homed in on the earring.

With a vicious twist, he ripped it straight out of the man's ear, bringing half the lobe with it. Now the man found the breath to cry out in agony. His hand snapped to the side of his head. Blood splattered over his crisp white shirt.

Mitchell held him down with one arm across his neck. They were face to face. Mitchell hadn't seen this man at NJ7 before, and though he looked young, he didn't seem inexperienced. There was a sinister confidence in his expression that said he knew situations like this.

"Where's Miss Bennett?" Mitchell hissed.

"Mitchell, it's a pleasure to meet you," the man replied calmly. His accent was faintly Irish. "But I don't believe you have an appointment."

Mitchell was outraged by the lack of fear. He brought the earring up to the man's face and examined the sharp tip at the back. "I'll appoint this in your eye unless you tell me where Miss Bennett is."

The man didn't flinch. For a second the only movement was the throbbing of a vein in his temple. "She's in a meeting." A smile crept up the man's cheeks.

Mitchell pretended to stab the earring downwards, but stopped short. The man blinked and tried to pull away, but he was at the mercy of a thirteen-year-old boy. Mitchell felt the man's breathing quicken.

"Try again," Mitchell hissed. "I won't be pretending next time."

The answer came almost straight away, but in a smug whisper: "Dr Higgins' old office."

Mitchell rolled to one side and pushed himself up, launching into a run. He wove through the tunnels again, with a diamond earring in his fist and blood covering one arm.

"Did you lie to me?" he barked as soon as he turned the corner into Dr Higgins' office. Miss Bennett was facing away from him, pencil and notepad in hand, studying one of the charts on the wall. The room was lined with computers and in the centre was a large empty desk. Miss Bennett's curves were silhouetted against the wall. There was a green stripe down the back of her stilettos.

"Welcome back, Mitchell." She sounded almost bored and didn't turn round. "Been sightseeing?"

"Where's my brother?" choked Mitchell. "Is he alive?" He edged round the room towards her and at last she turned to face him. The smile on her face offered no comfort.

"What do you think?" she asked.

Mitchell couldn't hold back his temper any more. "Tell me the truth or I'll rip you apart."

"You've made a very basic mistake," Miss Bennett stated clearly.

"My mistake was trusting you."

"It's worse than trusting me, I'm afraid." For an instant, her cheeks seemed to flush with excitement. "You've underestimated me."

Still staring at Mitchell, she reached behind her and tapped a key on the keyboard of a computer. Suddenly, a blinding strobe light flashed from the monitor. Mitchell's hands rushed to his face, but it was too late. He was temporarily blinded. Then he felt a vicious stab on his forehead. It knocked all sense of balance out of him. He tumbled to his knees. After a few moments, he could see again, but he just dropped his head and looked to the floor.

Miss Bennett took a deep breath. "Mitchell Glenthorne, I don't respond well to threats. In future you will raise all your enquiries with the appropriate courtesy." Mitchell made no response. Miss Bennett bent down low. She placed a finger under Mitchell's chin and raised his face to meet hers. Her perfume coated Mitchell's nostrils. "I mean you'll say please and thank you," she whispered. To Mitchell it felt like the most terrifying telling off he could have imagined.

He couldn't believe it. With such a powerful assassin inside him, surely he could have sprung up and taken control. He heard a distant calling in his head, urging him to resist. But the fight was gone from his heart. He had no real reason to challenge Miss Bennett. She was one of the few people in his life who had treated him well.

"If we hadn't told you your brother was dead," she explained gently, "you would never have agreed to work for us, would you?" Mitchell shook his head. "And that would have been the real tragedy, wouldn't it? Because, you see, this is where you *belong*."

"So *you* killed him, not me?" Mitchell asked meekly. A release of energy surged through him – was that relief?

Miss Bennett took him by the shoulder and helped him to his feet. "No," she replied. "Nobody killed him."

Mitchell's relief froze. The news should have made him happy, but it didn't. Instead, he could feel anxiety creeping through him, stiffening every muscle.

"You came close," Miss Bennett went on, "but NJ7 doctors are keeping him alive for their own purposes."

Mitchell felt a jolt of anger. His cheeks grew hot and

his hands trembled slightly. But it was anger at himself. How could he have behaved like this? He was an assassin working for the finest espionage organisation in the world. It was time to annihilate his old feelings. He clenched his teeth and forced himself to stand tall, looking straight at Miss Bennett. This was his family now.

"You sent agents after me," he said, holding his voice steady. "Just now, when I was hiding on the Underground, I mean. Why didn't they bring me in?"

"I knew you'd come back," Miss Bennett countered, obviously trying to sound casual about it. "You're not like that other one, Jimmy Coates. I had agents keeping an eye on you just to make sure you didn't cause any trouble, but I thought you deserved some time to yourself. You've worked very hard. Now, isn't it good that I trusted you?" She smiled a feline smile, then pulled out a mobile phone from her suit jacket and punched a few keys.

"But while you've been away, some of us have been working," she added. "There's someone you need to meet."

A few seconds later there were footsteps in the corridor. Then in walked a short man in his mid-twenties, who had a blood-soaked rag clutched to his ear and a look of deep resentment on his face.

"This," Miss Bennett announced grandly, "is the man who is going to end the Jimmy Coates affair and bring order back to Britain's Neo-democratic project." She held out an arm in welcome. "Mitchell, meet the new head of NJ7's technological team, Ark Stanton."

"Yeah," grunted the man. "We already met, thanks."

CHAPTER FIVE - THE REFLEX PLAN

Mitchell couldn't help laughing. This was clearly a man who liked to be smartly turned out. There's only so much you can do to look good when there's blood pouring out of one ripped earlobe. Apart from that, he looked like an artist had sculpted his head out of olive-brown clay and stuck on two flints of slate for his eyes. It was a perfectly proportioned face, even down to the impeccably neat layer of stubble.

"What the hell happened to your ear, Stanton?" Miss Bennett asked.

"Just an experiment that went wrong." He glared at Mitchell, his Irish accent a little stronger than before.

"I think this belongs to you," Mitchell announced casually, holding out a diamond earring. Ark Stanton pocketed it abruptly.

It didn't take long for the man to find some bandages and patch up his ear properly. Then he pulled a mirror from Dr Higgins' old desk and wiped most of the blood from his face. His shirt was almost completely red, blending in with the worn, leather worktop.

"Well?" barked Miss Bennett. "What have you got for me? I've been told you're a genius." Before Stanton could even smile, she added, "I never trust what I'm told."

In response, Stanton could only sneer. When he started his explanation, there were daggers in his voice.

"As you know," he began, "Jimmy Coates doesn't transmit a signal." He pulled out a pile of papers from a drawer and slammed them down in front of him on the desk. "He was designed that way so that no enemy could trace him. Unfortunately, it means that we can't trace him either. So I wondered whether, instead of *transmitting* a signal, he could *receive* one. He wasn't designed to receive signals electronically, but I studied Dr Higgins' old notes and I believe that if we transmit a series of strong enough images, bombarding every frequency, it could be enough to jam Jimmy's programming."

"What do you mean, jam his programming?" Miss Bennett scoffed. "He'll just fall over and melt?"

"No, he won't even realise it's happening, but we could force him to do certain things he would never usually do, or go places without knowing why. All the time, he'd feel like it was his programming compelling him to act. But it'll be us."

Mitchell looked across at Miss Bennett's blank expression. He wasn't great with computers, but this seemed like technical talk that was fairly simple to understand.

"You mean it'll be like hacking into him and giving him a virus." He tried to sound casual about it, but really he thought Stanton's idea was one of the most fantastic he had ever heard. Miss Bennett glanced at him. He didn't look back, but couldn't hide his proud smile.

"Yeah, that's sort of right," Stanton replied. His ear may have been bandaged now, but he hadn't forgotten about his run-in with Mitchell. He glared at him a moment longer than was necessary. "Except that we can't just email it to him," he went on. "We need to transmit it through the airwaves and force it on him. So it's everywhere around him – in the very air he breathes."

"But we don't know where he is," Miss Bennett interjected. "We'd need a transmitter strong enough to cover the whole country."

"Or a network of transmitters." Stanton let his full lips curl into a smile. His eyes twinkled like the earring Mitchell had ripped out.

"You look like a man who has something in mind, Ark," Miss Bennett cooed.

"Mobile phone masts."

"Yes, of course," Miss Bennett gasped, leaning back in her seat. Her eyes seemed to go misty for a second or two and her words were faint. "Even if we can't find him," she whispered, "we can control him."

"The signal might periodically jam some other electrical systems," Stanton interrupted, "but nothing serious."

"Like what?" Miss Bennett asked suspiciously.

"The power supply, air-traffic control, TV reception."

"Air-traffic control isn't serious?"

Stanton shrugged. "Were you thinking of flying somewhere?"

Miss Bennett stroked her chin for a second, then also shrugged.

"What about me?" Mitchell asked. "Won't I also, you know, pick up the signal?" He squirmed a little – referring to himself as if he was a radio didn't come naturally.

"Forget about it," Stanton told him. "You might get headaches or muscle cramps, but the signal's designed for Jimmy's psyche, not yours."

Mitchell nodded uncertainly.

"So," Miss Bennett cut in, "apart from control over every phone mast in the country, what else do you need?"

"I need to know everything there is to know about Jimmy," Stanton gabbled, delighted that his plan was being taken seriously. "For maximum impact I'll need a psychologist, a graphic designer, and a complete behavioural and emotional profile of the target."

"You need to know how Jimmy behaves and feels?"

"Yes – I need to get inside his head. Will I have any chance to interview the Prime Minister? He would know him best, wouldn't he?"

"No time for that," Miss Bennett murmured. "He's in America."

She thought for a moment and looked sideways at Mitchell. He always assumed he had done something wrong when she did that, but he held his chest out, not wanting to seem uneasy.

"Eva Doren," Miss Bennett announced suddenly. "The girl's known him for years through his sister. Recently she was even living with him. She must have observed something. I knew that girl would be useful to this organisation." Miss Bennett jumped up, full of excitement.

"What about her family?" Stanton asked. "Are they still looking for her?"

"Unfortunately, yes. They're a nuisance."

"What if they find out she's here and take her away? I don't want to lose Eva halfway through the project. I'm not so worried about her parents, but those two brothers of hers are angry. I heard they were smart too. They could cause problems. And Eva's intelligence will be integral to this project."

Miss Bennett raised an eyebrow. "Is she that clever?"

"This isn't a joke, Miss Bennett. You know I mean the vital information she can provide us about the target."

Stanton's expression was becoming more fraught. Miss Bennett raised a hand to calm him down.

"I'll deal with them," she said softly. "Her parents and her brothers. Don't worry. But wait a minute, if we're going to control Jimmy, we have to decide what we're going to make him do..."

Stanton smiled, relaxed once more and leaned forward to conspire closer.

"Actually, I have designed some rough images ready for transmission. I thought this would be the perfect way to implement the Reflex Plan."

Miss Bennett seemed to freeze. This was the first time Mitchell had seen her remotely close to being dumbfounded, but he had no idea what this 'Reflex Plan' was. Gradually, Miss Bennett's expression melted into one of utter glee.

"Well, that would mean I could assign this young gentleman another mission." She was almost talking to herself, but Mitchell knew she meant him. Then she leapt up and her words reverberated around the bunker. "Well, what are you waiting for? We can improve the images as we go along. For now – start transmitting the signal."

"Miss Bennett," Stanton smirked, "we already are."

Jimmy knew not to look the checkout girl in the eye. But his new appearance made him seem older than nearly twelve, and he could think of a much more natural way for a teenage boy to act. When he took his change he lifted his head and smiled.

"Thanks, love," he grunted. Then he winked and swaggered away.

His hair was bleached blond now, and spiked. It wasn't inconspicuous, but it was certainly different to the pictures of him on the news. His new look, combined with his confident demeanour, meant there was no way that checkout girl would connect him to the boy everyone was after.

Jimmy moved briskly down the street. Since Zafi had left them, they had spent three days in hiding at the Bed and Breakfast place. *Too long*, Jimmy thought. Despite Zafi telling them to move on straight away, they had stayed put, waiting for Christopher Viggo. But now, even in this short walk back from the corner shop, Jimmy saw threats on every side. Every shadow twitched; every sound was a cocked rifle; every passer-by was an NJ7 agent about to pounce.

Jimmy pulled his hoodie over his head and quickened his stride. His heart picked up its pace as well. There was something wrong. It was in the rhythm of his steps – they had an echo. Somebody was following him. He stopped dead. One step later, so did whoever was following. Jimmy pretended to be looking in a shop window. He studied the reflection, comparing every shadow to what he could remember of the street behind him. What had changed? He could feel his gut churning, but was it his programming preparing for a strike, or his fear?

A breeze sent a chill through his body. He couldn't stay standing in the street like that. It was too exposed. Should he run? *I shouldn't have come out at all*, he thought. Even though it was starting to get dark, he felt far too visible. He knew the others were just as vulnerable to an ambush by NJ7. Any of them could be recognised, but Jimmy was the only one equipped to deal with the danger, except for his mother. She had once been a fully trained NJ7 operative, but she'd already been out for a pile of second-hand clothes, the bleach for Jimmy's hair and basic food supplies. It was too risky for the same person to go out again and they'd needed to replenish their stock of fresh groceries.

Jimmy's eyes flicked from side to side, checking for even the slightest hint at the presence of the Green Stripe. *Am I imagining things?* he wondered. Noises, shadows, suspicions – was this the only evidence he had that he was being followed? The hairs on the back of his neck prickled. *Get back*, he ordered himself. *Quickly.* His instincts were screaming it.

When he turned to carry on walking, he was sure he caught a glimpse of a figure crouching behind one of the cars. *Attack me*, he urged inside his head. *Please, attack.* At least if they did, Jimmy would know that he wasn't going mad and then maybe this whole thing could be over. But no attack came.

Eventually, he was back inside the refuge of the Bed and Breakfast.

"We've got to move on," he shouted out. One by one the others emerged into the hallway. "This is crazy. They know we're here. I can feel it."

"Calm down," his mother reassured him.

"You're the one that's crazy," added Georgie. "If NJ7 knew where we were they would have come to get us."

"Somebody was following me out there." Jimmy looked at the faces of the others. Each of them was more filled with doubt and fear.

"Are you sure?" his mother asked. Jimmy didn't answer. He knew he couldn't be sure, but he was almost overwhelmed by that jittery feeling. His programming was warning him that there had been somebody else out there in the street. And Jimmy had learned that when his programming told him something, he should trust it – without question.

"We have to wait for Chris," Helen Coates insisted.

"Why?" Jimmy snapped back. "Why do we have to wait for Chris?"

His mother was astonished. "What do you mean?"

"If this were an NJ7 operation," Jimmy went on, "would we wait for Chris? Would we? I'm telling you, it's the wrong decision. We're running out of money already, and for all we know Chris might not be back for weeks. What if he can't find a doctor who will help Saffron in secret? What if—"

"We have to give him every chance," his mother cut in. "Otherwise we're abandoning the one man who's done most to help us, aren't we?"

"Is that really why we're waiting for him, Mum? Because he helped us?" Jimmy dropped the groceries and rubbed his eyes. "What good does it do him if we wait here? Does he need us? Or do we need him? Do *you* need him, Mum?"

Everybody stared at him – Felix and Georgie, Felix's parents, and Jimmy's mother. Even the couple who used to run the B&B shuffled down the stairs to see what the shouting was about. Jimmy longed to know what was going on in his mother's mind.

"What if he doesn't come back at all?" he whispered.

Everybody in the hallway took on a look of horror. But gradually, Jimmy realised none of them was looking at him any more – they were staring straight over his head.

Jimmy spun round to see a black silhouette in the frosted glass of the door. Before he could move, the door handle slowly turned. With a click, the door opened just a crack, and four fingers curled around the wood. The wind swept in, bringing with it the words, "You shouldn't leave the door unlocked."

With that, Christopher Viggo was back.

CHAPTER SIX - TWENTY-SEVEN LIVES

Eva stepped into the spotlight with a heavy sigh. The panel had allowed her a break, but it had seemed like only a few seconds – one deep breath and it was over. She had no idea what time it was because the room was one of NJ7's concrete bunkers, completely enclosed from the outside world. When she turned to face the panel again, she felt like they had been going so long and worked so hard that they had pummelled time itself out of existence.

Her reddish-brown hair was tied back in a pony tail. Her head was spinning and her eyes throbbed from the hours under the intense illumination. She couldn't even see the people interviewing her from here, though she knew it was a man called Ark Stanton, a psychologist called Dr Amar and a graphic designer. The designer had a clipboard on his lap and the sound of his felt-tip pen scratching against the paper ground at Eva's nerves. A bead of sweat tickled the back of her neck.

"Let's return to Jimmy's temper," Dr Amar began. His voice was high-pitched – a smug, Scottish whine. "If a wasp stung him, would he respond a) with indifference, b) by saying 'ouch' and frowning, c) in some more physical manner or d) by chasing after the wasp and trying to kill it?"

Eva wiped her brow. "I don't know," she whimpered. "I told you, I don't know things like that. This whole thing is ridiculous."

She couldn't see the panel, but she could feel them glaring at her even more intensely than the 400-watt bulb that shone in her face. She knew she had to help NJ7 so that she could keep pretending to be on their side. They mustn't suspect for an instant that she was still loyal to Jimmy and, of course, her best friend Georgie. In the long run, she was sure that it would turn out to be the right decision – she could do her friends more good as a spy within NJ7 than if she'd also escaped. But that meant she could never refuse to co-operate with the Government. If they suspected her deceit, she would be finished.

But today, they had taken a sudden extra interest in her. They'd subjected her to these strange and intense conditions, then interrogated her with hardly a moment's pause. Hours and hours, with more and more questions – all about Jimmy. Surely this meant they had found her out.

"We need to know, Eva," Ark Stanton said firmly.

"Erm…" Eva squirmed and fought back the tears. Any second she knew she would break down and confess everything. She could picture herself doing it and a huge part of her longed to give in.

"Make your best guess," Dr Amar insisted. "Is it a, b, c or d?"

Eva was genuinely trying to work out the answer, but could hardly remember the question. Her thoughts were continually invaded by memories of her friends. She missed them all even more than she missed her own family. The feeling was so strong it made her feel sick. She peered into the light, shielding her eyes with her hand.

"I'm sorry about the extreme conditions, my dear," the psychologist added. "They are necessary so that we can scrutinise your physical responses as well as your verbal ones. We need a thorough psychological profile of the target."

"The target?" Eva repeated instinctively. She did her best to hide her distress, but how could she conceal anything under this much scrutiny? The light burned into her forehead. The designer's pen tapped against his clipboard, and each tap pounded through Eva's head. *They know*, she thought. *They know I'm a traitor. Admit it and they won't kill you.*

Her breathing was rapid. Each breath felt like sandpaper in her throat. A tear dripped through the sweat on her face. She opened her mouth, about to spill everything, but suddenly… blackness.

Stanton had switched off the spotlight. Eva's eyes took several seconds to adjust to the normal light of the room.

"I think we've got as much out of you as we can for today," Stanton muttered. "You've done well. Thanks, kid." Eva couldn't speak. She choked back a scream and looked around her, dazed.

"We can carry on tomorrow," Stanton continued. "Thanks, doctor." He signalled to the psychologist and the graphic designer. Both nodded, gathered their notes, and left. On his way out, Dr Amar took the film from a camera that had been trained on Eva the whole time. Then she was alone with Ark Stanton.

"That was tough, wasn't it?" he started, his soft voice coming like an embrace to Eva's ears. "Your intelligence is vital, you know. Dr Higgins would have had all the answers, but he's gone. Miss Bennett knew Jimmy well as his form teacher, but that's old data now. You are the last person to have spent time with Jimmy. The last person on our side anyway. You can tell us how he thinks, how he acts and how far his capabilities have developed."

"Maybe it would help if I knew what all this was for," Eva suggested. If she knew what was going on, she might be able to help Jimmy.

Stanton thought for a second, then nodded. "Let me show you what we're going to use it for. You deserve it. You've worked hard."

He dashed out of the room and came back cradling a cat in his arms. Its fur was black and ragged, sticking out from a tough, wiry frame.

"Say hello to Miles," Stanton announced, shaking the cat's paw in Eva's direction. "This used to belong to Dr Higgins. He left it here when he deserted."

Eva was so confused she didn't know what do with herself. Seconds before, she thought she was going to be exposed as a double agent – now she was being introduced to the staff pets. She could feel her knees quivering and had to consciously try to relax them.

"This isn't an ordinary cat though," Stanton explained, placing the animal carefully on the floor. He pulled his chair up behind his desk and tapped a few keys on his computer. His eyes were still on the screen as he spoke. "When Dr Higgins and his team were designing the organically programmed assassins, they needed a prototype."

"A prototype?" Eva gasped, slowly pulling herself back together.

"To test the technology," Stanton replied, still focused on the computer. "So they built a cat."

Eva couldn't believe what she was hearing. She stared at the creature at her feet. It curled round her ankles and peered up at her, purring.

"This cat is… an organic assassin?" She could hardly contain a laugh. It was as if she'd slipped into a weird dream.

"No," tutted Stanton. "The cat's not an assassin. They couldn't programme that sort of intention into a cat. Miles is just tougher, stronger and faster – plus he's survived to be about three times the age of any cat that ever lived."

"A cat with twenty-seven lives," Eva mumbled, reaching down to stroke it.

"What was that?"

"Oh, nothing." She felt its warmth on her hand. "Poor thing."

"*Useful* thing, you mean," Stanton insisted. "Thanks to Miles I can test out my theory about Jimmy Coates." Then he reached forward and set up what looked like a grey plastic stick on a little stand – an aerial. There was a broad smile on his face as he tapped one final key. He leaned back, a glint in his eye, and whispered, "Watch this."

Eva didn't know what he was talking about at first. Stroking the cat was the most relaxing thing she'd done in all the time she'd been at NJ7. She was quite happy to lose herself in that feeling, but suddenly the cat pulled away and hissed. Eva jumped and drew her hand back sharply. For a second, she was terrified that the cat was going to attack her. But it didn't.

Instead, the creature lurched sideways as if an invisible train had hit it – then slammed against the concrete wall. Eva let out a yelp of disgust. The cat slid down to the floor. But that wasn't the end of it. Eva could only watch as Miles shook off the pain, crawled a few metres, then hurled itself against the wall once more. This time it crashed head first and a smear of cat blood followed it to the floor.

"Stop that!" Eva screamed. "He's gone mad! He's going to kill himself!"

"Ha! Don't worry," Stanton laughed. "He's tough. It would take hours of this to kill him."

"Stop it!" Eva cried again, her hands over her face. "Stop it now!" Her whole body was trembling at the horror of it. She staggered forwards to grab hold of the cat, but it hissed at her with murder in its eyes, then dived at the concrete again.

"Enough!" Eva yelled, her words barely audible through her tears.

At last, Stanton tapped the space bar. "Looks like Miles was receiving my signal all right," he chuckled.

Eva felt she never wanted to open her eyes again, but she couldn't stop herself watching the cat. Its self-destructive passion had gone. It was reeling about as if it was drunk, and licked its paws to start slicking back its fur. Then it limped out of the room.

"You're going to do *that* to Jimmy?" Eva panted. The blood on the wall burned into her eyes. It was the only colour in a room full of grey.

"No, no," Stanton replied. "He might be a kid, but he's smarter than that cat. Jimmy will destroy himself in a much more sophisticated way. I'm designing the signal now."

Terror seized Eva's body. She had guessed what Ark Stanton was going to say next.

"And Eva," he declared, "I couldn't do it without you."

CHAPTER SEVEN - KILL ZAF-1

Viggo walked into a scene of stunned silence. He smiled his small smile, nodded his head to Helen and ruffled Jimmy's hair as he walked past. He went straight through the hall and into the living room without anybody stopping him. His stubble seemed a little coarser than when he had left them and there was a cut healing along the right side of his imposing jawbone. It looked a couple of days old to Jimmy.

"So, like, what?" Felix blurted out. "Did I miss something? Are we not speaking to him any more?"

"I think we're just pleased to see him," said Felix's mum glancing at Helen Coates, who sighed wearily.

"I suppose I better put the kettle on," she said.

"Great," chirped Felix. "Any biscuits in those bags, Jimmy?"

Unfortunately, as soon as Helen flicked the kettle on, the lights went out.

"See what you did, Chris?" she called out, trying to

make a joke of it. "You turn up and there's a power cut."

"Looks like the whole block," added Felix's mum, pressing her nose up against the window.

It was a few minutes before they found candles and some matches. Eventually they crowded round Viggo in the living room.

"You know what?" he announced. "I actually missed all you ugly mugs."

"I bet you thought we couldn't survive without you," Jimmy chuckled.

Viggo broke into a broad smile. "Without me," he said, "I thought you wouldn't even be able to wipe your—"

"That'll do, Chris," Jimmy's mum cut in, placing a hand on his shoulder. Felix tried hard to stifle his laughter, and Jimmy felt his tension dissolve. But there was still a dark question on his mind. It was Georgie who asked it first:

"How's Saffron?"

Viggo's mood suddenly changed. He sucked some air in through his teeth.

"She's going to be OK," he said. Everybody sighed with relief. "I found someone who could help and she's being looked after. I think she's safe."

"And she's recovering?"

"It was touch and go when I left, but more touch than go."

"Wait, which one's good?" Felix chipped in. "Touch or go?"

"What I mean is," Viggo explained, "she seemed to be getting better. But slowly – her recovery will take time. And unless Jimmy has developed the power of a Delorean, time is what we don't have."

"What's a Delorean?" Jimmy asked, his face screwed up. Georgie and Felix were pulling the same expression. Felix's dad let out a deep, explosive laugh.

"It's from an old movie," he chuckled. "Don't worry about it."

"Shouldn't you have stayed with Saffron?" asked Felix's mum.

"I wish I could," Viggo replied. "But she's safer without me there – apart from Jimmy, I'm NJ7's most wanted. As soon as I can, I'll go back for her or get her to join us. But for now, we've got a great opportunity to escape. And we have to take it quickly. It looks like the only reason NJ7 haven't found us already is because something threw them off the scent."

"That was Zafi," Jimmy said firmly.

"Zafi?" spluttered Viggo. "Who or what is Zafi?"

"ZAF-1," Jimmy replied, feeling the words stick slightly. He'd never said this out loud before. "She's the French version of me."

"Bloomin' brilliant," muttered Viggo, rubbing the back of his neck. "This gets better and better, doesn't it? Well, you don't have to worry about what this Zafi person told you. I've got some new contacts of my own. It's a huge chance for us. They're going to help us get out."

"Out of the country?" asked Georgie.

"That's right – out of the country and into hiding."

"We're running out of money," Helen interjected. "And I can't exactly withdraw cash from my account. You realise that, don't you?"

"Don't worry." Viggo dismissed her concern with a wave of his hand. "It's all taken care of." Helen raised an eyebrow.

"Where are we going?" Jimmy and Felix asked at almost exactly the same time,

Viggo couldn't help smiling now – and smiling properly, with his teeth glinting. He stood up, stretched, then took Jimmy by the shoulders and announced, "New York City!"

Jimmy, Felix and Georgie were overjoyed. The boys jumped up and down, punching the air, nearly knocking over some of the candles. Georgie let out a tiny scream and slapped her hand over her mouth.

Jimmy had heard so much about the USA. It was the place where all the great products came from – the best games, the best clothes, the best music. But most of it was only available in the UK if it was imported illegally. Ares Hollingdale had gradually made it harder and harder for foreign companies to sell their products in Britain. He'd hated anything that wasn't British. Even American TV shows were heavily censored – sometimes the jokes didn't even make any sense, although Jimmy realised that might not have been to do with the censoring. In any case, that had been the only way for him to learn about the USA. He had never imagined that he would have the chance to go there.

Jimmy's mother was more subdued. She moved closer to Viggo and asked under her breath, "Who are these new contacts, Chris?"

"I'll explain later." They stared into each other's eyes for a second before Viggo finally looked away. "Everything's arranged. There's a van outside – the one I came here in. In the morning we're all driving to Heathrow. These guys will get us through customs and everything."

"Must be pretty powerful contacts," muttered Helen. Only Jimmy noticed her unease. Everybody else was celebrating. An extra cheer went up when the lights suddenly came back on. In the split-second before anybody had adjusted, Jimmy caught sight of Viggo's face. Why wouldn't he explain who these contacts were, Jimmy wondered. He could feel his insides shifting like quicksand. There was something wrong here. What bargaining had Viggo conducted to set up such an easy escape? And what sacrifices was Jimmy going to have to make in order to fulfil that man's side of the deal?

"We'll leave early," Viggo proclaimed. "Everyone should try to get a few hours' sleep."

It was only on his way up to bed that a new worry hit Jimmy. America was where Ian Coates was. The Prime Minister of Great Britain, the man Jimmy now referred to, in his head, as his "ex-father", was in Washington to meet the President and the US Senate.

Am I cursed? Jimmy thought. *Do I have to follow that man wherever he goes?* At least his ex-father would be in a different city. There was some comfort in that. Nevertheless, Jimmy went to sleep with one fear – that if the two of them ever met again, Jimmy didn't know what his instincts would make him do.

"Miss Bennett, I don't get it." Mitchell was hunched forward at his desk in one of the briefing rooms at NJ7. He was alone in there with the director of the agency. The surroundings were as bare as they could be – slabs of concrete for walls, with a few exposed wires snaking their way around. This briefing room, like all the others, also had a few desks and an overhead projector attached to a laptop. Mitchell noticed that the logo on the back of the laptop didn't belong to any huge American corporation. It was a simple green stripe.

"Why aren't you sending somebody else instead?" he went on. "I'd understand that. But there's nobody going after Jimmy Coates at all."

Miss Bennett was busy at the laptop, but after a few seconds she looked up at Mitchell.

"Oh, you'd understand it, would you?" she said sarcastically. "If I sent somebody else to kill Jimmy Coates? After you were in a position to kill him twice and failed? That's so *understanding* of you."

Mitchell hadn't been to school in a while now, but that feeling of being the least significant person in the world flooded back. He bowed his head and stared at his desk.

"Oh, cheer up, Glenthorne," Miss Bennett insisted. "You're still the best thirteen-year-old, genetically programmed assassin we've got." She laughed, and after a couple of seconds Mitchell did too. He buzzed with the excitement of being back in the briefing room. It could only mean a new mission. And if it wasn't Jimmy Coates, Mitchell had no idea what it could be.

The overhead projector flashed to life. Emblazoned across it in massive letters was ZAF-1.

"ZAF-1," announced Miss Bennett.

"Yeah," Mitchell muttered, "I can read."

Miss Bennett glared at him. He shrunk into his chair. Clearly, sarcasm was a one-way street.

"Dr Higgins' papers seem to suggest that for over a decade, the DGSE, the French Secret Service, have had access to the assassin technology that built you."

Mitchell tensed up. Suddenly, he was paying closer attention. Miss Bennett went on, her voice sounding just like a teacher explaining part of some textbook.

"At first we thought ZAF-1 referred to a second French intelligence agency. Now we've realised, of course, that there's hardly enough intelligence in the whole of France for one agency – let alone two."

Mitchell chuckled.

"Our current theory," Miss Bennett went on, "is that 'ZAF-1' refers to a French assassin. The oldest he could be is about twelve, and if he were any younger than nine he would be almost completely ineffective." She pressed a button on the laptop to flick to the next screen. Nothing happened.

"Oh, blast," she exclaimed. "I hate PowerPoint."

"I'll show you," sighed Mitchell, pushing himself up. His chair leg screeched on the floor, but not as loud as Miss Bennett yelled at him now.

"I don't need showing, thank you!" She slammed the lid of the laptop shut. "The rest is simple. Find the French assassin. Kill him before he kills you."

"What do you mean, 'before he kills me'?"

"What do you think I mean? If the French could steal the assassin technology, they could also know about you. Pretty soon we're going to be at war with France. We know that and they know that. So, just like us, the first person they will want to eliminate is their enemy's most powerful assassin."

Pride rushed through Mitchell. Miss Bennett wasn't being sarcastic about his abilities any more. He sat at his desk with his chest upright and broad. "Where do I start looking?"

He had never expected to be sent on a mission where so little was known about his target – what he looked like, where he was or even whether he definitely existed. But somehow, all of that doubt added to the feeling of responsibility. It certainly added to the excitement. Mitchell could feel the tips of his fingers tingling.

"Paris," Miss Bennett explained. "I have a support network spread out across France right now and several agents in the process of infiltrating the DGSE as moles. They should have information for you in a few days. Start your own investigations in Paris and I'll arrange for you to meet with one of these agents as soon as they have something for you. Good luck. Britain is depending on you."

Mitchell's face stretched into the biggest smile of his life. The trials of the last week were behind him now. The boy in him had set aside his confusion. He was an assassin again – time to find his target.

CHAPTER EIGHT - I DREAMED

Heathrow airport was full of armed police. It always was. Jimmy knew that. But he still couldn't force down the feeling that every one of them was staring at him. CCTV cameras peered into every corner of the terminal building.

Suddenly, there was a bang. Jimmy jumped. He sniffed for the smell of cordite and swivelled round, expecting the black nose of a machine gun to be pointed straight at him.

"Calm down," Felix hissed. "It was just that guy dropping his suitcase."

Jimmy said nothing. He marched on through the terminal. There weren't many people about – it was before the midmorning rush, and in any case, not that many people travelled in and out of Britain these days. The light glared off the lino floor. The sounds of people getting on with their business mixed with the squeaking of their shoes and the ticking of the terminal clock.

In Jimmy, every muscle was ripped tight. He and Felix had been paired off together, while the others spread out around the terminal. Each group was to check in at a different desk and at a different time, though every now and again Jimmy caught a glimpse of one of them through the crowd.

"*I* should be tense," Felix carried on. "Not you. They could bring *me* down by sneezing too hard."

But I'm the one they're after, Jimmy thought. He checked the back pocket of his jeans again. The corners of the fake documents dug into him. Another false identity. Another new life he'd destroy as soon as it was finished with. He'd examined them in the van on the drive to the airport. He'd looked as hard as he could without getting car sick, and they seemed good – too good in fact. The more pieces of this operation Jimmy saw, the more he was worried about who these new contacts of Viggo's might be. Still, he had no choice now but to go along with the plan and remember his false details: Sam O'Shaughnessy, from Acton.

Suddenly, he let out a yelp of pain and pressed his fingers to the point where his right ear joined his skull.

"What is it?" gasped Felix.

Jimmy's head felt like someone was firing lightning bolts at him. And it wasn't the first time it had happened that morning. Felix quickly realised what was wrong.

"Again?" he asked. They stopped and Jimmy bent

double, holding his head. "It's like Harry Potter and that stupid scar, isn't it?"

"Yeah," moaned Jimmy sarcastically. "It's *exactly* like that." That was the fourth time in the day already. Each attack hit in the same spot on Jimmy's head and with the same pain – a precise and piercing stab that lasted thirty seconds or so, then dissipated to nothing. He took a deep breath and pulled himself upright.

"You OK?" Felix asked. Jimmy nodded and squeezed out a smile.

"So what's wrong with your head?" Felix said as they reached the queue for check-in. Jimmy didn't know how to answer. It wasn't like anything he'd experienced before. His only explanation was that it must have something to do with his programming developing.

He liked to think that he was more comfortable with his programming now – that he knew roughly what it was capable of and almost how to control it. But really he had to admit he had no idea. It was like an alien growing inside him. More than that – the alien *was* him, and it was more him than the human part.

"Dunno," he shrugged, trying to sound casual about it. The truth was, the pain wasn't the only new phenomenon Jimmy had woken up with. There was something else. Something much more worrying to him. He had tried to bring it up a couple of times – with Felix and with the others too – but each time he had stopped himself because it sounded so insignificant.

The last thing he wanted was more attention on the tiniest detail of his development.

Jimmy and Felix – or Sam O'Shaughnessy and Billy Gutman – handed over their passports. They nodded their heads obediently at all the questions – small lies that went towards the bigger one of escaping the country. The whole process went smoothly, but that was just the first step of a long journey. Jimmy couldn't relax.

As they walked away from the desk, he took a deep breath. He had to get something off his chest.

"I dreamed something," he muttered.

"What?"

"I dreamed," Jimmy repeated, louder this time. "And I remember it. Bits of it anyway. Images."

"So what? It's just a dream. I had this dream once – oh my God, it was so real. I dreamed I was looking out of my bedroom window and this giant porcupine landed – it was from space, obviously – and all these cartoon characters came out..." Felix rattled on and Jimmy let him. He needed to gather his strength to explain what was on his mind. "...and they were like an army and they took over the garden and then I looked down and I was wearing this T-shirt and it had this logo on it and it was, like, the head of a cartoon character cos, get this – I was *on their side*!"

"But I *dreamed*," Jimmy insisted. "Don't you think that's odd?"

"It's just a dream," Felix said. "Don't tell it me. Other people's dreams are dull."

"You don't get it!" Jimmy shouted, then immediately regretted it and lowered his voice to a whisper. "I don't have dreams. I've never dreamed in my life. I train. My training is telling me something."

Suddenly, Jimmy's programming swirled in his stomach like a bad fry-up. His senses magnified everything around him. The sounds of the terminal intensified, as if he could hear every word of idle conversation within a 200 metre radius. The scent of metal polish and bleach filled his head.

"What's up now?" Felix whispered.

"Keep walking," Jimmy ordered under his breath. "Keep looking straight ahead." In his mind he replayed the images that had put him on alert. He knew he'd spotted something. Was it a silhouette darting round the end of the check-in counter? Could he be sure? Yes, he was beginning to form a picture now – it was two figures, in fact, outlined against the lake of white light reflected in the floor. Why had they moved away from Jimmy and Felix so sharply and without their shoes squeaking?

"We're being followed," Jimmy muttered.

"You've got mental problems," Felix countered. "But all right, I'll play along."

They moved towards passport control as normally as they could, but Jimmy felt the desperate drive to get there quicker.

"Come on," he urged. By the time they handed their passports to the security officer, Jimmy was virtually dragging Felix by the arm.

"Let go," Felix insisted. "We're not married."

Perhaps it was the humour in Felix's comment. Perhaps it was Jimmy's conviction that there were two strange figures following them. Whatever it was that distracted them, Jimmy and Felix didn't notice when the security officer smiled. He always found aliases amusing. He nodded to his colleague at the x-ray machine.

The two boys were still anxiously glancing behind them for two phantom shadows when they were waved through the security checks. From then on, their passage on to the plane was easy. Far too easy.

Thin horizontal strips in the colours of the rainbow. Splashes of red and yellow against a dirty cream background. A white number 53 on a green background. The letter K, bold and black on a bright white wall.

Jimmy forced himself to focus on these images, bringing them into the forefront of his mind, stronger each time. They were the images he'd seen in his sleep – fragments of the first dream he had ever remembered when he woke up. He closed his eyes. The plane hadn't even taken off yet and he was already driving himself mad with these vivid pictures in his head. It even overshadowed the excitement of being on a plane for the first time.

He pulled out a set of felt tips and a notepad he'd bought in the departure lounge shopping centre. He gripped the pens and tested each colour. Then he started to draw. At first all the images fitted on one page. Then he turned to a clean sheet and drew bigger, bolder – one image per page: horizontal strips in the colours of the rainbow. Splashes of red and yellow. The number 53 – but this one was white, so he drew a green outline and coloured in the outside space. Finally, a thick K – black on white. Then his concentration was broken by an announcement from the captain over the loudspeakers.

"Good afternoon, everybody. I apologise for the short delay..."

"What are those pictures?" Felix asked, at last looking up from his in-depth study of what was going to be showing on the TV during the flight.

Meanwhile, the captain continued over him: "...We were experiencing minor interference with our computer systems. There must be an electrical storm on the continent. But there's nothing to worry about..."

"They're stuck in my head," Jimmy rasped. His throat was suddenly dry.

"It's easily fixed," the captain droned on, "so we'll make up the time in the air and should be landing at JFK on schedule."

The flight was turbulent, but nevertheless Jimmy was determined to get some sleep. He wasn't really tired, but he knew he wouldn't be happy until he found out whether he was going to dream again. He half expected that he'd imagined the whole thing and convinced himself that these images were inside his head – just like he now doubted whether there really had been two people following them at the airport.

It wasn't until several hours later, when the stewardess was handing round the immigration cards for US customs, that Jimmy finally dropped off. His card sat on his lap, unnoticed.

Jimmy only woke up when the plane touched the ground at John F Kennedy International Airport, New York City. All the excitement about coming to America was gone. There were just four things in Jimmy's head: thin horizontal strips in the colours of the rainbow. Splashes of red and yellow against a dirty cream background. A white number 53 on a green background. The letter K, bold and black on a bright white wall.

Jimmy reached for his pens.

CHAPTER NINE - FATAL THUMBS

Jimmy's first experience of the United States was waiting in line at customs. He felt a little woozy from the flight, but kept a constant check on his surroundings. He deliberately stirred up his programming every few seconds so that it was never far from the surface.

"Hey," Felix whispered, sidling up to him. "Is your immigration card already filled in?"

Jimmy glanced down at them, clutched in his fist. Before he could check, Felix pulled them towards him to see for himself.

"Isn't that a bit weird?" he asked.

Jimmy didn't know what to say. Had one of the stewards on the flight been Viggo's contact? Were they being smuggled into the US by a renegade airline company? For Jimmy, nothing seemed too ridiculous after everything he'd found out in the last few weeks. He peered further back in the queue, where Viggo was waiting with Helen and Georgie. Viggo gave Jimmy a slow nod of reassurance, but it did nothing to calm the boy's nerves.

"I don't trust any of this," Jimmy muttered. Anger infused his voice. A surveillance camera swivelled over the crowd. Jimmy dropped his head.

"Take it easy," Felix urged. "We've made it, haven't we?"

"You really think that? Look up there." Jimmy nodded to the head of the queue, where the customs officials waited in their high-sided booths. "First those guys will scan our passports. Then they'll check our forms. All the time we're on camera. The computer is already comparing our faces against a database of the faces of millions of criminals. Then they'll take our thumbprints using an electronic reader that automatically scans the database for matches."

"But—"

"Exactly – NJ7 probably put all our fingerprints on that database. As far as Interpol is concerned, *we're* criminals. We've got perfect passports and documents. We even look a little different from usual, but Felix – we don't have fake thumbs. And what about retinal scanners? Even with your eyes closed, the laser can read the identity that's imprinted on the back of your eyes. Ask Chris how his 'contacts' are going to fix that."

Felix was silent, staring at his thumbs. As they shuffled together up to the desk, the fear in them both grew deeper. Jimmy closed his eyes and rolled his thumb over the electronic reader. His head drowned out the clatter of the hall. All he could hear was his own breathing and the ticking of the custom man's watch. His fear connected directly to that darkest point, somewhere behind his stomach. It sent a vibration up the side of his body, which then wrapped around his brain.

Against his will, he started visualising his escape. *Wait until the last possible second*, he could hear something saying inside his head. He screamed at it to stop, knowing that if he tried to run, he would feel the thud of a dozen bullets in his back. But the instructions became stronger as the time ran out – and more violent, until Jimmy's imagination was drowned in a savage but efficient bloodbath. Any second he would burst into action, unable to control the destructive cravings that would surely cause nothing but his own death.

Finally, his swirling thoughts were pierced by the coarse twang of the customs official. "Thank you, sir. You can go."

From customs, they made their way separately to a rank of hire-cars, where a mini-van was waiting, while Viggo picked up the keys. Moments later, they were all on their way to Manhattan.

"Now can you tell us what's going on?" Jimmy exclaimed as soon as the van door was shut.

"You know what's going on," Viggo replied. "Your life is being saved and so are the lives of the people you love." He slammed his foot down on the accelerator. Jimmy's mother was sitting in the front passenger seat. She put a hand on his shoulder.

"Calm down," she said softly. "We're all just relieved, that's all."

"Well, a bit of gratitude would be nice," Viggo grumbled.

"Gratitude?" Jimmy exploded. "I thought I was going to get shot back there. Why didn't you tell me someone had hacked into the airport computer? Or however else they got us through. How about sharing a little information about what's going on?"

Viggo could barely contain his anger. "Do you think I'm an idiot?" he seethed. "Do you think any stage of this operation hasn't been completely thought out in advance? I told you they'd get us through customs. You've got to trust me. Have a little faith in the people we're working with."

"But we don't know who we're working with!"

To that, Viggo gave no answer. Jimmy shrank back into his seat. He looked around at the others in the back of the van: Neil and Olivia Muzbeke, Georgie and Felix. Nobody made eye contact. Surely they agreed with him?

Jimmy couldn't help thinking that after the amount of trouble these contacts must have gone to, they would eventually want something in return. It was so frustrating that his fate was completely in the hands of people he knew nothing about. Jimmy had lost control over his own life again. Of course, he was grateful that these people weren't trying to kill him, but that seemed almost irrelevant now. Whoever they were, they had stolen control.

"Maybe you could just tell us where we're going," Helen Coates suggested.

"OK," Viggo sighed. "As long as you understand that what I don't tell you, it's best that you don't know." He paused and wiped his forehead with the back of his sleeve.

"We're going to Chinatown," he explained. "We're meeting a Mrs Kai-Ro. She doesn't know who we are or anything about us. But my contacts say she can be trusted and she doesn't ask questions."

Jimmy tried to imagine Chinatown, but he had no idea what it would look like. And wouldn't they stick out if they weren't Chinese?

"That's it," Viggo insisted. "There's nothing more to know. Once we get there I'm going to meet with my contacts again and discuss the next step. But for the time being, I can't think of a better place in the world to hide than Chinatown."

CHAPTER TEN - STORM IN A TEACUP

Mitchell pulled his coat tight around him. Spring must have been late in Paris this year. Surrounding him were tower blocks that seemed to lean out over the pavement. They turned the streets into concrete tunnels that channelled the wind so it blew the litter around his ankles and the dust into his face. This wasn't the picturesque, historic Paris that so many millions of people love. This was Fontenay-aux-Roses, a filthy and forgotten *banlieue* on the edge of town. It was also Mitchell's rendezvous.

He crossed into a park and headed towards a garish funfair. It was a flashing, blaring mess, spewing out a cloud of fast-food wrappers and stray helium balloons. In ten minutes, he was to be at the candyfloss machine to receive information on his target. NJ7 contacts had been investigating at the DGSE offices nearby.

Mitchell sneaked through the temporary fencing and pretended to smile at the kids who were doing the same. Then he discreetly checked his watch. Early. He walked slowly around the edge of the fair and ended up in the queue for one of the rides. He was killing time.

All around him was the unnecessary noise and fake excitement of a modern funfair. There was no charm to the place and the promised thrills of the rides meant nothing to Mitchell now. He watched some older kids hiding round the back of the burger vans. *That's where I'd be*, he thought, imagining how things would have been different if he'd been born in Paris. Then he realised there was no luck involved in where he had been born. He had been designed and created. All of his existence had been set out for him. But it still felt right. It still thrilled him to be doing his job – and to be doing it well.

Mitchell saw one of the kids throw an empty can at an unsuspecting passer-by. The others let out a chorus of laughter and, for some reason that he couldn't explain, Mitchell wanted to laugh too. But it felt as if the laugh itself was weighed down by a block of granite in his chest. Mitchell couldn't remember the last time he had just hung out like that. He could hardly even remember the boys who used to be his mates.

He was pulled out of his thoughts by a nudge from behind. He spun round to see a boy who must have been only about five. The child's face was nothing but congealed ice-cream and a disgusted frown. Mitchell realised he had reached the front of the queue. He glanced at his watch again. It wasn't time yet. In any case, he didn't want to arouse attention by deciding not to get on the ride after all.

It was a giant waltzer – eight huge teacups, each on the end of a metal tentacle. Mitchell carefully stepped into his compartment and pulled the restraint over his shoulders. There were three seats in each cup so the five year-old stomped in as well, staring at him, still not smiling. The third seat was left empty.

"Where's your mum?" Mitchell grumbled. The child stared. A dribble of snot crept down his upper lip, mingling with the ice-cream. Mitchell grimaced and looked away.

Slowly, the machinery chuntered into action. In the centre, where the spokes met, there was a cramped booth. In it, a scruffy young man leaned on a set of levers. But he wasn't paying attention to the ride. He was looking out for any girls walking past.

The giant cups lifted high into the air. Four of them, including Mitchell's, kept rising once the others had stopped. He looked out across the fairground, trying to ignore the breeze that chilled his neck. Then the machinery gave a heavy KERCHUNK and the tentacles starting going round. The four higher ones went in the opposite direction to the cups beneath. Then all of them started spinning.

It was slow at first, but Mitchell's view of the fairground quickly became a blurred smear of colour. The kid next to him started screaming his head off. The wind blasted into Mitchell's face. Then French pop music started blaring out from a set of huge speakers. It all blended with the drone of the machinery to make a truly hideous sound.

The only thing Mitchell could see properly were the people in the three other compartments that were whirring round at the same rate. It was then that he noticed the girl.

His first sight of her sent a shudder across his skin and something forced him to look for her again. His cup spun on its own axis, faster and faster. Every time Mitchell was facing the right way, there she was: staring at him from the teacup opposite.

She looked like she was about twelve. Her hair was a sleek auburn and she had wide blue eyes. She wasn't blinking. Despite being hurled round in a never-ending circle, this girl had an air of stillness, as if she had slowed down time.

There was a smile on her face, but not the wild enjoyment of the kids around her. They were getting their kicks from the ride. This girl was happy about something else – and Mitchell got the feeling it was something nasty. He couldn't help staring back, craning his neck to see her every time the ride spun him round the wrong way.

Then he heard it. At first, he thought it was the wind, the music, the machinery or the screams of the child next to him.

It flew into his ears as a whisper: "Mitchell."

He looked for the girl. She was still staring at him. It sent blades into Mitchell's chest. His programming whirred round his belly. This girl was bad news. At last he saw her move.

She took in a deep breath and yelled at him over the din of the ride: "I know about you, Mitchell." Her voice was high, piercing the racket. She had a very faint French accent. "I know what you're looking for. I've seen your agents investigating at the DGSE."

She grinned at him. Her teeth glinted in the neon light. In his shock, Mitchell tried to stand up before he realised that the safety restraint was locked in place. Mitchell pumped that extra strength into his arms and there was a click as the hinges snapped.

Mitchell's head was spinning as fast as the teacup he was sitting in. He looked around, frantic. Surely everybody in the fairground could hear the secrets this girl was shrieking at the top of her voice. But nobody else seemed interested. If they could hear at all, they probably didn't speak English.

"Who are you?" Mitchell shouted.

Slowly, he raised the restraint off his shoulders. The boy next to him stopped screaming and tried to raise his restraint as well. When he couldn't, he took up screaming again, with even more vigour.

Mitchell twisted, trying to keep his eyes on the girl, but now her seat was empty. He scanned the other compartments. She wasn't there. He looked down at the four other teacups, spinning in the opposite direction. They were rising now.

After a second, Mitchell's compartment jolted to a halt and immediately started hurling round the circle the other way. He was thrown off his feet and smacked his chin against the floor. The metal scraped off a layer of skin and his jaw jarred into his head.

When Mitchell staggered to his feet, all the teacups were spinning the same way. He looked round the circle. There she was – in a compartment two along from Mitchell's. Suddenly, she leapt up, rolled over in mid-air and landed in the next teacup.

It was only now that the young man in the charge of the ride noticed that something was going on. Panic twisted his face. He waved his arms about, desperate to remember how to stop the ride in an emergency. He hauled on a lever, but the ride sped up. Everybody's screams went up a notch in intensity. The man's face went white and he scrabbled for his walkie-talkie.

"I know what you're looking for!" the girl shouted again. Then her teacup lifted with three others and changed direction. Mitchell lost sight of her again. He stared at the teacups whizzing around above his head, trying to catch another glimpse of her.

He was only faintly aware of the ride slowing down and the crowd of funfair staff. The music stopped and the screaming stopped with it. The drone of the machinery gradually came down from its insistent pitch.

Does she really know what I'm looking for, Mitchell asked himself. *How can she? How can she know who my target is?*

At last, he heard her whisper again: "It's me."

Mitchell shuddered. He couldn't see where the voice had come from. Then, on the other side of the ride, he caught a glimpse of a shadow. It was a figure that leapt from the top level and rolled in mid-air. As soon as she landed, she was gone. If any normal person had jumped off a moving fairground ride like that, they would have broken limbs. That's how Mitchell knew for sure.

He jumped up and caught the edge of the teacup above him. The kid next to him was left stunned, licking ice-cream off his cheeks. Mitchell gently swung round half the circle. The ride had almost stopped now, but he used what momentum was left to heave himself off again.

The ground came to meet him with a surprising bump. Mitchell smiled as his programming cushioned the pain. He just hoped none of the other kids were stupid enough to try and copy him.

He knew he was too late to chase after the girl. He knew she would be racing away at a pace too fast to catch. For now. Instead, he jogged in the direction she had gone, away from the fairground, across the park and back into the urban jungle of Fontenay-aux-Roses.

Mitchell didn't need to meet his NJ7 contact any more. He had just met ZAF-1.

"Having a nice little Parisian holiday?" Miss Bennett asked sarcastically. She and Mitchell were on a bench in the Place des Vosges, both huddled against the cold. The geometric lawns were precisely trimmed and the canopy of leaves above them dappled the whole square with shadows. The trees clearly thought it was early Spring, though you would never have guessed it from the temperature.

"I found ZAF-1," Mitchell announced. He wasn't in the mood for Miss Bennett's teasing. He had a job to do. "She's a girl."

Miss Bennett raised an eyebrow. "How's her health?" she asked. She kept her voice low, while three or four metres in front of them a lone child was building a tiny castle in the sandpit – or was it a chateau? Meanwhile his mother stood by, desperate to get back indoors.

"She's not dead, if that's what you mean," Mitchell replied.

"So you know where to find her?" Mitchell paused. "What happened?" Miss Bennett went on. "You gave her your number but she's not calling? Is that it?" There was a cheeky smile playing on her lips. Mitchell decided he didn't like this playful side to Miss Bennett. He preferred the way she acted back in the bunkers of NJ7.

"I'll track her," Mitchell insisted. "She knew I was looking for her, so she came to check me out. I think she enjoyed the risk – as if it's a game to her."

"A game?"

"Maybe. That might be her weakness."

"Interesting." Miss Bennett thought for a second, then added, "So you've called me out here because you need access to the imagery intelligence for the time after she got away from you, correct?"

"Sort of. You're right – I need to see what the satellite saw, but not for the time after she got away. She would have been prepared for that and made sure she couldn't be tracked by satellite."

"So what do you want me to do?"

"Track her backwards," Mitchell explained. "Find the point when I saw her, then work backwards so I can see where she was before then – not where she went afterwards."

"You intrigue me, Mitchell Glenthorne. What have you got planned?"

In front of them, the little boy had finished his sandcastle. Now he smashed his fists into it, mashing sand into the fibres of his mittens. His gleeful giggle echoed round the square.

"Wherever she's been," said Mitchell, "she'll go again – sooner or later. And when she does, I'll pick up her trail. No matter how clever she thinks she is or where she goes, I'll track her. There'll be nowhere on earth she can go to get away from me. Then we'll see whether she likes playing *my* kind of games."

CHAPTER ELEVEN - STAR OF MANCHURIA

As soon as Jimmy saw Chinatown, he knew that Viggo had been right. He couldn't imagine anywhere else on earth where they would be better hidden – not a cave in the middle of a desert, and not halfway up a mountain in Outer Mongolia. He'd never seen so many people crowding in the streets – even in the centre of London. They all bustled against each other, shoulder to shoulder across the width of the road.

Viggo had abandoned the mini-van a few streets away and now they were all following him. Every other step, Jimmy was delighted by a thick and exotic smell that he didn't quite recognise. Above him, the night air was illuminated by a million neon lights in every colour. It was mostly Mandarin lettering, but with some Korean and Japanese. Suddenly, Jimmy realised that for the first time in his life he could tell the difference.

He picked a word at random. To his eyes it was just

a collection of lines and squiggles, but he heard himself sounding it out under his breath:

"*Mian tiao*," he whispered. "Noodles!"

"Where?" Felix blurted out. "I'm up for noodles. But shouldn't we follow Chris?"

Jimmy shook his head in wonder. He knew his programming gave him the ability to speak French, but he never imagined he would be able to read and understand Chinese.

He felt himself starting to relax. Surely there was no way NJ7 could find them here. But he couldn't allow his concentration to wander. *In a crowd, a killer can come out of nowhere*, he thought. He deliberately tightened his shoulders. Every time the lights reflected off a watch or a mobile phone, he flinched, imagining it was the blade of a knife aimed at his throat.

"Don't worry, mate," said Felix. "We'll go for noodles later. Or *dum sum*. "

"Do you mean *dim sum*?" Georgie chuckled.

"Yeah, whatever, we can get some of that as well if you like."

Gradually, Jimmy noticed how different New York was to how he had expected. The streets were as dirty as they were at home, and a few of the shop fronts were boarded up – not as many as in London, but some. Jimmy had imagined it would be a place where everything was clean and everyone was successful.

"America's not like it is on TV," he whispered to Felix. "It's as miserable as England. If this is a *real* democracy, it looks just the same as a *Neo*-democracy."

"Yeah," Felix agreed, "but they have real Coke here. I think that's the difference."

Viggo stopped beneath one of the only English signs in the street. It was a bright orange neon announcing the 'Star of Manchuria'.

"Is this us?" Felix shouted above the hubbub of the crowd. Viggo nodded. "Awesome," Felix went on, clenching his fist. "We get to stay in a restaurant." He pushed past Jimmy and opened the door. It rang a little bell as he entered and a venetian blind clattered against the glass. Before Viggo could stop them, Jimmy followed.

The smell hit them first. It was almost overpowering – so much stronger than it had been in the street, but utterly wonderful. Every face in the room turned to stare at them. One man had a string of noodles still dangling from his mouth. Even the immense carp in the fish tank next to them seemed to have paused to examine Felix and Jimmy.

"Er, hello," Felix announced meekly. He grinned, revealing the gap between his two front teeth and stretching the faint freckles on his cheeks into fat oblongs. Then a face appeared on the other side of the fish tank. The water magnified it and warped it into a hideous mess of distorted features. It rose from the depths and emerged over the other side of the tank as the face of a small Oriental lady.

Her wrinkles looked like scratches, as if a cat had once attacked her face. But the only thing that had really attacked her was time. She immediately started screeching at the top of her voice. It was a passionate tirade of incomprehensible sounds. Jimmy felt like each syllable was attacking his brain. His mind was trying to keep up, throwing up the meanings of odd words but moving far too slowly. Each phrase echoed in his head, obscuring the next one, until all he could hear was a babble of disjointed English, mixed with every foreign language in the world.

His head was swimming. He staggered to one side and held himself up against the fish tank.

"OK, OK!" It was Viggo, waving his hands about, trying to put this woman at ease. But she didn't stop. Jimmy took a deep breath and again tried to piece together some of what she was saying. He couldn't keep hold of any of the words long enough to string them together.

Viggo bundled Jimmy and Felix out of the restaurant. The others were waiting, confused about what was going on.

"Come on," Viggo whispered. "We're not staying *in* a restaurant; we're staying above it."

He hurriedly pulled out a key from his pocket and unlocked the door right next to the restaurant entrance. This one had no window, no menu and no 'open' sign. Behind it was nothing but a grimy staircase covered in a stained brown carpet. It was torn at the edges, where the dirt blended into the walls. There was no light.

Without hesitating, Viggo marched up the stairs. Felix was next in line, but was unsure whether to follow. Jimmy gave his friend an encouraging shove from behind.

"All right," Felix moaned, scrunching up his nose. "I'm going. But I prefer the smell of the street."

"You would," Jimmy quipped. They all followed Viggo up the stairs, to the rooms above the Star of Manchuria.

"Why was that Chinese lady shouting at us?" Felix whispered when they reached the second floor.

"That's Mrs Kai-Ro," answered Viggo. "She runs this place. She's agreed to hide us for a while."

"She is one angry lady."

"She's not Chinese," Jimmy blurted out suddenly.

"What?" asked Felix.

"You said, 'that Chinese woman' but..." Jimmy paused, surprising himself with his own certainty, "...she's Korean."

Felix stopped and turned to stare at him. His mouth hung open. Jimmy smiled sheepishly. Finally, Felix unfroze and exploded with excitement.

"Oh my God," he gushed. "YOU SPEAK KOREAN! That is SO COOL!"

Jimmy tried to explain that he still needed a bit of practice before he'd really be able to speak to Mrs Kai-Ro, but that didn't dampen Felix's enthusiasm.

"All right, Felix," said his mother. "That's enough."

Viggo unlocked another door and they filed into the second-floor rooms. They were as dingy as the staircase: a living area with a beaten-up couch, an old TV and one corner that had been converted into a tiny kitchen; a bedroom with no furniture at all, just a couple of mattresses on the floor; and a bathroom that looked like a cave made of damp and rust. It smelled like one too. The small square window opened on to a fire escape at the back of the building. Beyond that was a tiny courtyard where the bins were kept.

"We've got the next floor up as well," Viggo announced, flicking on the light – a bare bulb in the centre of the room. "Neil and Olivia, why don't you take the room upstairs, and then..." He cut himself off. He and Jimmy's mother were standing awkwardly by the door to the remaining bedroom. They glanced at each other and Helen's face went red. So did Viggo's. "Erm, no, wait..."

"How about girls upstairs, boys down here?" Neil suggested quickly.

Everybody murmured their agreement. Georgie, Helen Coates and Felix's mother, Olivia, dragged themselves up one more flight of stairs.

Suddenly, Jimmy clasped the side of his head and cried out in pain.

"What is it?" Viggo demanded.

"My head," Jimmy gasped. His eyes were watering and he could hardly speak. "It's that pain... ah! In my ear..."

"This happened to him this morning as well," Felix added. "He should see a doctor."

"The last thing we want is a civilian doctor examining him," said Viggo. Then he turned back to Jimmy. "Are you OK?"

Jimmy wiped his face with his hands. "Yeah," he said wearily. "It's gone now. It's always the same. It's like a stab right here." He pointed to the side of his head, where his ear met his skull, but at that moment, the light flickered and died. The room was pitch black.

"Jimmy," Felix whispered. "You caused a power cut."

"No way," Jimmy protested. "It's not my fault. I didn't do anything, did I?" He searched his programming, terrified that it really had been him that had caused the darkness.

Gradually, a noise filtered through to them from the restaurant below. It cut through the building almost as much as Jimmy's strange headache had pierced his brain. It was the furious rant of an old Korean woman whose restaurant had been disrupted by a power cut.

"She is definitely one angry lady," Felix whispered.

"The whole block is out," came the deep tones of Neil Muzbeke. "I don't think it could be you, Jimmy." He was standing at the living-room window, overlooking the street. His voice always came as a comfort to Jimmy, and even more so now.

"Let's just sit tight," Viggo suggested. "I'm sure this is nothing to do with us." Jimmy appreciated him saying it, but there was still a note of doubt in the man's voice.

"Everyone OK down there?" Jimmy's mother shouted down.

"Yeah," Viggo yelled back. "All good."

With the lights off, time seemed to stretch so that every second lingered in the air, refusing to pass. Jimmy looked over the faces of the others. They were lost without the light, frozen still. Only Jimmy had night-vision, of course, and yet he was wishing harder than any of them that the wait would be over. In those moments, he imagined what it would be like if he could control time. He could make these minutes of darkness flash past in a single blink, so nobody would notice them. Then he could slow everything down, stretching the hours into years so that he would never reach the age of twelve.

Jimmy tortured himself with that single thought. If he never reached twelve, he would never reach thirteen. Then he would never reach eighteen, and his powers would become no stronger than they were now. He could stay as human as he would ever be. The assassin in him would die before it was ever fully born. But that was just a fantasy. Every second Jimmy breathed, even here and now while the lights were out, his programming grew inside him. It hurtled him towards his fate: total submission to the assassin inside.

CHAPTER TWELVE - PREMONITION

The lights flickered back to life. Then, through the window, came the dazzling colours from the neon mess outside. They cast strange, colourful shadows on everybody's face.

"It can't be a coincidence," Felix insisted. "There was that power cut back in England and then, as soon as we arrive, they start happening here too."

"But it wasn't me, OK?" Jimmy tried not to sound too upset, but really he was terrified. He hated the idea that he could somehow cause something like this and not realise. A simple power cut didn't seem too dangerous, but what if he could also do worse, without intending to? Could he be blamed for it when he had no control over it?

Felix's father smacked the side of the television a couple of times. The screen was scrambled. "Come on," he insisted. "What have I got to do to get a picture?"

Meanwhile, Viggo was dashing in and out of the rooms. "Right," he announced, "everything seems secure. I'll go and have a look round upstairs. Then I've got to go out." He looked at his watch, studying it a little longer than usual. "What's the time difference here?" he asked.

There's no difference, Jimmy thought to himself. *It passes at the same rate wherever we are.*

"By the way," Viggo went on, not waiting for an answer, "they left a little cash for us." Everybody turned to look at him. "You know, so we could eat."

"Yeah, but who's 'they'?" Jimmy asked.

Viggo turned away. "I'll tell you when I know it's safe," he mumbled. "Meanwhile, get yourselves some food. Don't go out in pairs. One person should go, alone, then come straight back." He picked up one of the cushions on the couch and unzipped the lining. His hand came up clutching a bundle of ragged dollars.

"Once you've eaten," he ordered, "get some sleep." He slammed the money on top of the TV. It sprang into life, suddenly showing a clear image for the first time.

"Don't worry, Chris," said Neil Muzbeke. "I'll take care of things here." Viggo nodded uncertainly, then, without making eye contact with anybody, he marched out.

"He's a bit grumpy, isn't he?" Jimmy asked.

"He's always a bit grumpy," Felix replied.

Jimmy shrugged. He was thinking back to the first days he had known Viggo. In the short time since then, so much had happened that they had all changed. But with Viggo, something seemed wrong.

"He must be upset about Saffron," Jimmy suggested.

"I think you're right, Jimmy," Felix's father answered. "We all are, aren't we? And it must be hardest for him."

Jimmy nodded. Of course Viggo was sad about what had happened to Saffron. But the stiffness in Viggo's face didn't look like sadness. His gruff attitude, his short temper and his secrets... *It looks like he's angry*, thought Jimmy. *Angry and impatient.*

"Anyway," Felix chirped. "Noodles all round?" He snatched the top few bills off the bundle and dashed to the door. "Back in a sec!" he shouted.

"Hey, where are you off to?" yelled Neil Muzbeke, pulling himself to his feet, but Felix was already out on the landing.

"Yo, ladies!" he yelled. "Say 'no' if you don't want noodles."

After a half-second pause, Felix's feet hammered down the stairs.

His father ran out after him and shouted, "You go for food then come straight back, OK?" There was a distant holler from Felix, then his father peeked his head back round the door.

"Back in a sec, Jimmy," he mumbled. "I'd better watch Felix. It's not that I don't trust him, but he does tend to get distracted."

Jimmy laughed, but it was half-hearted. He was mesmerised by the love and care that Neil Muzbeke had for his son. He couldn't help trying to remember the way his own father had acted towards him. *This is the way things seemed*, he told himself. *But it was all fake.*

"So far there has been no explanation from the energy companies for the sudden disruption in electricity supply that has struck across the nation at various times in the last few days." Jimmy was crouched by the window, deliberately avoiding the TV screen. It was hard. American news bulletins seemed a lot more colourful than British ones, even though they didn't seem any better at providing information.

"They're not telling us anything," exclaimed Neil Muzbeke.

Jimmy ignored him and stared at the rain. He chomped through another mouthful of noodles, while Felix gulped down more Coke. Jimmy had never really liked Chinese food – especially if he had to use chopsticks. But the cardboard container in his lap was almost empty and most of the food had gone in his belly, not down his front. Either American Chinese food was very different or Jimmy's tastes were changing with time.

"Meanwhile," the news continued, "let's return to our top story: President Grogan's announcement, ahead of the UN Summit tomorrow, that he'll be seeking to ease the diplomatic tension between Great Britain and France." On the screen, Grogan was smiling and waving to a crowd. He was a large man, with round, bulging cheeks that were surprisingly pink for a man in his mid-fifties. Beneath his eyes were the grey sacks that come with running a country.

"Can we turn it off, please?" Jimmy asked.

Neil hauled his bulky frame off the sofa and hit the switch. The picture cut to black just as President Grogan was replaced on screen by an image of Ian Coates.

"I don't want to see that man," Jimmy rasped, turning back to the window.

"He doesn't deserve you," Neil reassured him, gently. "He betrayed us all, and he doesn't even deserve you being upset about it."

On the outside, Jimmy smiled and nodded. But his heart was infected with anger. Neil's words sat in his head: *'He doesn't deserve you.'* Jimmy wanted to scream: *What does he deserve?* But he stayed silent.

Jimmy snapped out of his sleep. In less than a second he was fully awake. He lay still, his eyes open. His head was throbbing. A multicoloured neon haze seeped through the tattered curtains. The light was boosted by his night-vision, giving everything a blue tinge that made it look almost like being underwater.

The street still sounded busy, but obviously far less than it had been earlier that evening. Its noises were drowned out by Neil Muzbeke's snores and the ticking of the clock. Jimmy turned over. They'd pushed the two large mattresses together to give them as much sleeping space as possible, but now there was a dip sucking Jimmy towards the huge mound of Neil Muzbeke. Another body twitched and wriggled every few seconds, and was much smaller: Felix. He was kicking at the makeshift sheets – some coats and old cushion covers they'd found in a closet. Everything smelled bitterly of damp.

Jimmy guessed it must be the small hours of the morning, though he couldn't be sure – the clock didn't seem accurate and Jimmy's own sense of time was more confused than ever. However late or early, Viggo clearly wasn't back yet. Whoever his contacts were, Jimmy thought to himself, they must have a lot to discuss. But that was far from the only thing on his mind.

Jimmy sat up and wiped his eyes. Sweat matted his hair, even though it wasn't hot in the room. It was the images. The pictures from his dreams had returned stronger than ever. In the half-light, even objects in the room took on the shape and colour of his dreams:

Thin horizontal strips in the colours of the rainbow.

Splashes of red and yellow against a dirty cream background.

A white number 53 on a green background.

The letter K, bold and black on a bright white wall.

Jimmy crawled out of bed and reached for his notebook. Flicking through the pages, he found everything that he had just seen in his sleep. They were even more vivid in his head this time. The colours were brighter. The outlines of the shapes were sharper. What did they mean? It wasn't just the images. It was the feeling that went with them. Jimmy heard his pulse pounding inside his head. With each beat, it intensified the terror in his gut.

He threw down the notebook. It landed with a big black K staring up at the ceiling. Jimmy shuffled towards the bathroom. The bare floorboards sent a welcome chill up through his bare feet. There was a draft coming through the bathroom window. Jimmy breathed it in, grateful for some freshness, despite the fact that it smelled a little of the restaurant's refuse. He splashed water on to his face. It came out of the tap in a dribble and was ice cold. There was no towel, so Jimmy just leaned on the sink, letting drips run down his neck.

He stared at himself in the mirror. His bluish vision exaggerated how different he looked now from the Jimmy who had jumped out of his bedroom window, trying to escape two mysterious men in suits. He didn't like it. If there was one thing Jimmy wanted above anything else, it was to go back to before that time. But he knew it was too late. Despite his strength and speed, despite the instincts of a lethal predator, time still travelled only in one direction.

He closed his eyes and tried everything he could to relax. Gradually, the images faded from his mind. With a few more deep breaths, the feeling of doom subsided as well. Then he heard a click.

His eyes shot open. In the mirror he caught sight of his pupils dilating rapidly. A shiver ran over his skin. His muscles tensed. A warm current surged through him – his programming swooping into action. Something was wrong. But Jimmy was ready to deal with it.

CHAPTER THIRTEEN - CLEAN STRIKE

Jimmy stayed absolutely still. Could the noise have been Viggo coming back? The bathroom door was still open. Jimmy glanced in the mirror, waiting for the living-room light to come on or Viggo himself to appear. He counted the seconds. Nothing changed.

He couldn't even be sure where the click had come from. The front door of the apartment? The bedroom? The fire escape? Very slowly, not making a sound, he turned round. He peered at every detail of the apartment. Night-vision is never crystal clear, so Jimmy had to analyse each outline to work out whether anything had changed.

CRASH!

Something slammed into Jimmy's back. The wind was knocked out of him. He fell forward and smacked his chin against the wall. He tasted blood, but didn't have time to do anything about it. As soon as he hit the wall, he spun off it again. Just in time – a fist plunged down at him, aiming a knife at exactly the point where the back of his neck had been. The blade scraped against the tiles.

Jimmy looked up to see two intruders. Both were covered head to toe in black. Their faces were obscured by balaclavas with tiny slits cut for their eyes. The one furthest from Jimmy pushed the bathroom door shut. Then he flicked on a torch and shone it right in Jimmy's eyes.

"Is that him?" he whispered.

"That's him."

Their voices were muffled by their headgear and in any case, Jimmy didn't have time to analyse how they sounded. The closer man raised his fist above his head. A sliver of moonlight outlined his knife. There was nowhere for Jimmy to go. The bathroom was barely big enough for one person – let alone three.

With the torch in his eyes, all Jimmy could see was the flashing of the knife blade. Without thinking, he felt his arm snap out to the side. He snatched two toothbrushes from the sink and pulled his hand back. His programming was in control now, but that was exactly what Jimmy needed to stay alive.

Squeezing the toothbrushes together in his fist, Jimmy pushed them towards his attacker. He caught the knife blade between them. With a twist of his wrist, he plucked the knife from the man's hand. It spun into the air and both men made a grab for it.

They both missed and scrabbled on the floor to find it.

Jimmy used one man's back as a springboard, climbing over him to jump up on to the sink. He nearly slipped, but steadied himself with a hand against the opposite wall. He stood with one foot on either side of the basin. He had to bend his head forward to avoid hitting the ceiling.

Before the men could even gasp, Jimmy smashed his heel against a bottle of mouthwash. It exploded in a minty-fresh cascade of foamy liquid. The combination of the mouthwash and the splinters of glass all over the floor made it impossible for either man to find the knife. The torchlight danced around frantically.

Jimmy took a breath to yell for help.

"He—!"

The sound was cut off before it had even started. The two men grabbed one of Jimmy's ankles each and yanked him down. It was an awkward fall. Jimmy jerked his head to one side to avoid smashing his skull on the porcelain. There was a tumble of bathroom items all about him. He landed on the floor with a bump. The men loomed over him, both bending down to strangle him.

"Wait," Jimmy gasped. "You left the toilet seat up."

With the punch of a heavyweight boxer, he slammed the toilet seat down on the torch man's head. It rang out like Big Ben. With his other hand, he splashed mouthwash into the second man's face, then grabbed at something from the floor.

He was moving too fast even to know what he was doing. In no time he had yanked out a metre of dental floss. He spun it round the knife man's ankles, then flung one end over the rail that held up the shower curtain. When he caught the end again he heaved on it with his whole weight. The man was completely upended. His limbs flailed about and he landed in a splat on his back. Jimmy dusted himself off, gritted his teeth and quipped, "Always floss."

By now the torch man was rubbing his head and staggering to his feet. Jimmy gave him a firm push that sent him tumbling backwards into the bath. The man grabbed hold of the shower curtain, but it couldn't take his weight and ripped down with him.

Finally, Jimmy ran his arm across the shelf by the bath. It sent half a dozen bottles of shower gel clattering to the floor. Some looked like they had been there for years gathering mould. Just as one of them hit the floor, Jimmy stamped his bare foot down on it. Bright green gel burst out of the top. It was aimed perfectly – right in the knife man's eyes.

Now Jimmy had a chance to call the others. He drew in a breath, but stopped himself. Another click. More attackers? A million thoughts rushed through his head. He glanced at the two men writhing about the bathroom in pain. Neither one was capable of making any effort to hurt Jimmy now. These weren't trained men, Jimmy thought. This whole confrontation had been too easy. But if these men weren't from NJ7 – who were they?

Jimmy reached for the knife man's balaclava, snatching a roll of toilet paper with his other hand, ready to shove it into the man's mouth to keep him quiet. But there was somebody in the living room. Jimmy's programming surged up again, reaching a level of intensity he never realised was possible. He kicked open the bathroom door and dived into a combat roll.

He leapt up and seized this new attacker by the collar. The momentum carried them both to the other side of the room. Jimmy pressed him up against the wall. This one had no balaclava. In Jimmy's night-vision, his face was a blurred pattern of blue light. Jimmy hurled the toilet paper across the room. Perfect aim – it flicked the light switch on.

Jimmy turned back to the man. He was eyeball to eyeball with Christopher Viggo.

"What's going on?" It was Neil Muzbeke, rushing from the bedroom in his boxer shorts. His belly wobbled and his knees shone in the light.

Jimmy jumped back to let Viggo pick himself up. For a second, they were both speechless. Jimmy put all his effort into forcing his programming away. *It's over*, he urged himself. *The fight is over*. Inside him it felt like there was a wild beast reluctantly turning back to its cage. When Jimmy spoke, it came out like a growl.

"Bathroom," he blurted, pointing in that direction.

Viggo and Neil Muzbeke rushed over to the open door. Jimmy turned, expecting to find out at last who had attacked him. But the bathroom was empty. All he saw was the moon reflected off the windows of the apartments opposite, shining through the broken pane and reflected again in a lake of mouthwash. The shower curtain fluttered in the breeze. Jimmy shivered and moved closer.

Blood was splattered across the bath, the floor and some of the tiles on the walls. The knife was gone and so were the men.

"Looks like he escaped the way he came in – the window and the fire escape," Viggo muttered, sticking his head out into the night.

"There were two of them," said Jimmy. His voice was croaky, still having to fight its way out through the swirling energy in Jimmy's lungs.

"Tell me what happened," Viggo ordered.

"It wasn't NJ7," Jimmy started. "They were strong, but with no combat skills."

"Wait," Viggo interrupted. "Slow down. Just tell me what happened. They came through the window, yes?"

"If they weren't NJ7," Jimmy went on, ignoring what Viggo had said, but staring straight at him, "who were they?" His anger rose up, forcing him to shout, "Who were they, Chris?" Viggo stared back, shocked at the violence in Jimmy's voice. But Jimmy wasn't finished.

"There's us in this room and there's them upstairs!" he shouted. "Who else knows we're here?" Viggo finally realised what Jimmy was suggesting.

"This has nothing to do with my contacts," he insisted.

"Who are they?" Jimmy yelled. "Who are these people that you trust so much? And why did they send two men to kill me?"

Jimmy felt like his gut was about to bubble up and burst out of his mouth. He couldn't take any more lies. His programming twisted through his body, pulsating up his neck and taking over his brain. For a moment, it threw up the echo of Jimmy's very first mission – kill Christopher Viggo. Jimmy heard unfamiliar thoughts whipping through his head. He despised himself for thinking them, but at the same time, the sensation of hearing them felt wonderful. His eyes saw nothing but Viggo. *Lie to me and I'll kill you*, said a voice in his head. *Even if you're my father, I'll kill you.*

Jimmy let out a cry of anguish and shuddered at the notion that had just gone through his head. He squeezed his eyes shut and clenched his fists, wrestling to take control of himself.

"My contacts are protecting us," Viggo insisted, "not attacking us."

"Well, they're not doing a very good job, are they?" Jimmy whispered. He had no more strength to shout. "We have to get out of here." He dashed round the room, gathering the few items he had brought, including one of the toothbrushes that had saved his life tonight. He was determined not to stay in that apartment any longer.

"No," Viggo insisted. "Jimmy, stop!" He rushed over and seized Jimmy by the shoulders. "You're not thinking. Do you know how long it takes to find secure rooms? Do you know what went into setting up this place? There's nowhere else to go. NJ7 has satellite surveillance covering the entire globe. As soon as we step outside these walls, we're in danger."

Jimmy pulled himself away. Viggo's words were beginning to get through to him.

"I'll go to meet my contacts again first thing tomorrow," the man went on. "I'll ask what they know about these two people who broke in tonight. I'll insist on extra protection. They'll sort it out." He brushed his hair out of his face and sighed heavily. "Besides, if these two men came to kill you, they didn't do very well, did they? You don't look dead to me. Dead grumpy maybe, but not dead."

Jimmy tried to compose his thoughts. At last, his blood was cooling. Maybe Viggo was right. Jimmy had easily seen off the two intruders, and relocating to another apartment now would just be inviting new dangers – far more threatening ones.

"The best way to find out who they are," Viggo continued, calmer now, "is to stay here and wait for them. If they really want you dead, they'll come back. And when they do, we'll be waiting."

CHAPTER FOURTEEN - FACE OF POWER, FACE OF DEATH

"What happened?" It was Felix. Jimmy hadn't noticed him come out of the bedroom. Then a knock on the door brought Jimmy's mother in as well.

"Everything OK down here?" she asked. "We heard shouting."

Jimmy didn't know where to start – but he didn't have to.

"Everything's fine," said Viggo. "We'll have to talk about it in the morning."

"You're sure this is still a safe place?" Jimmy demanded.

"This is the *only* safe place," replied Viggo.

Helen shot a puzzled glance at Viggo, who discreetly nodded towards the bathroom.

"Oh no!" Helen gasped, looking over the mess and piecing together what must have happened. "Jimmy, are you OK?" She rushed over to crouch beside him and took him by the shoulders. Jimmy dropped his eyes to the floor.

"I'm fine," he mumbled.

"Woah, Jimmy," Felix said, staring at the bathroom floor. "You completely trashed the bathroom. What were you doing in there?"

"Come on," said Felix's father gently. "Let's all get some sleep."

Felix ignored him and plonked himself down on the sofa.

"Well *I'm* going to bed," grumbled Viggo. Neil Muzbeke gave a deep chuckle and followed him into the bedroom.

"Don't stay up long," he whispered, giving Felix's hair a ruffle on his way past.

Jimmy, his mother and Felix were left in the living room.

"I'm glad you're OK," said Helen, pulling her son into a hug. Jimmy squirmed with embarrassment. Normally he would never have let his mum do this in front of his friends. But after a moment or two, Jimmy realised how much he needed the reassurance. In that instant, he wished he could tear his heart open and rip out all of the troubles that had built up inside him. Even in his mother's arms there was doubt – he felt comforted, but how could he relax completely when she wouldn't tell him who his real father was? He pulled away.

"What's the matter?" Helen asked.

Jimmy didn't know how to answer.

"He saw the images again," Felix said quickly. "And he keeps getting those, like, pains in his head, or his ear, or wherever. You know what I mean."

Jimmy's mother turned him round and looked into his face.

"Are they getting stronger?" she asked, managing to hide the depth of her anxiety. Jimmy nodded. "And they're always of the same things?" All Jimmy could do was nod again.

"Show her your notebook," Felix cut in. "Oh, sorry," he added. "I, like, read your notebook." For a second, Jimmy felt the overwhelming urge to share his fears with Felix. He hadn't told his friend yet that Ian Coates wasn't his real father. He hadn't even told Georgie. He opened his mouth and his tongue quivered, waiting to form the words. But they wouldn't come. Instead, he gulped down his anguish.

"I'll get it," said Felix. His voice was bright and even now, in the dead of night, he had so much energy it almost made the walls buzz. He dashed into the bedroom to fetch Jimmy's notebook. Jimmy was alone with his mother. He looked into her face.

"Your eyes are bloodshot," she whispered. "You need some sleep."

"I need to know who my father is," Jimmy snapped. In his eyes was a challenge. Before Jimmy's mother could react, Felix was back.

"Here you go," he said, flicking through the book. "I thought you were better at colouring in than this,

Jimmy." He handed the book to Jimmy, open to a page in the middle with a picture of a dark black K.

Jimmy wasn't paying attention. He was scowling at his mother, whose eyes were welling up.

"Maybe you should draw how you see them now," Felix suggested. Jimmy knew what Felix was doing. It was obvious that something was going on between Jimmy and his mother, but Felix was trying to ease the tension. Jimmy was thankful that he was there.

He took a pen from Felix's hand and started scribbling on the next page in the notebook. Felix had only brought the green felt-tip, so Jimmy started with the outline of the number 53. He was hardly concentrating though. He only glanced at the paper every now and again. His head was down, but his eyes were watching his mother.

When Jimmy had coloured in the whole page in green, leaving white spaces for the numbers 5 and 3, he flicked the page over and carried on drawing.

"It's not just the images," he explained quietly. "Or not what they look like anyway."

"What do you mean?" Felix asked, fascinated by every move Jimmy's pen made.

"It's how they feel." He was still watching his mother, letting his pen move without checking its progress. His hand wandered freely over the page, scrawling with such confidence that it looked as if his fingers didn't need the rest of his body. Every move was definite. Every mark was strong. "I see these pictures in my head and I've no idea what they're pictures of. But I know they represent something horrible. As if someone is in, like, terrible danger. It feels like if I put all the images together, somebody will get killed. I think my programming is trying to warn me, instead of train me. It's like there's going to be a murder and I have to stop it, but I can't."

"So someone is trying to kill you?" Felix asked. "We knew that already."

Jimmy's mother turned away and wiped her eyes on her sleeve.

"No," said Jimmy. "It's not me that's going to get killed. But I don't know who it is." He flicked to the next page and went straight on drawing, even faster. The pen flew across the paper in a fury.

At last, Helen drew in a couple of deep breaths and summoned the strength to join in the questioning. But she remained facing to one side.

"How would your programming know all this, though?" she asked.

Jimmy shrugged. "Maybe I've seen something or heard something. Maybe we all have. But we just don't realise the importance of what we've seen and heard. Maybe an assassin could, you know, put all of the little bits of information together and come up with the big picture."

"Big picture?" Helen repeated. "So why is it giving you lots of small ones? And when is it going to tell you exactly who is in danger?"

"Erm," Felix murmured, "I think it just has." He snatched the notebook out of Jimmy's hands. Slowly, he turned it round and held it up. Jimmy looked at it, amazed. On it was a new image. It wasn't one of the pictures that had been flashing round his head. It was an image he had never realised was in his mind. But there it was – instantly recognisable.

Jimmy looked at his hands, then back at the picture. He had drawn it without paying attention to what he was doing. It was a sketch of a man's face. The cheeks were round, and the hair was thinning. Under the eyes there were dark bags. This was a far better drawing than any of the others, and better than anything Jimmy had drawn before in his life. It was a superb portrait of the President of the United States, Alphonsus H Grogan.

The next morning, Jimmy was cramming cookies into his mouth one after the other, straight out of the box. His jaw was so tense he almost cracked his teeth every time he bit down. Next to him on the couch was Georgie, while Felix was leaning round the open door, trying to hear what was going on in the other apartment.

They were on the floor above, while beneath them the adults discussed what was going on. Except it sounded more like arguing than discussing.

"Keep quiet," whispered Felix.

"I'm not saying anything," protested Jimmy. "I'm just chewing."

"Well, chew quieter."

Jimmy dusted the crumbs off his lap. "It's no good," he announced, munching on his last cookie. "They don't believe me."

"What do you mean?" Georgie asked. She was tucking into a cinnamon bagel that was almost the size of her head.

"I mean," Jimmy replied, "that if they believed me about the President being in danger, they'd have taken this." He plucked his notebook from the arm of the sofa and waved it about in the air. "And they would have gone straight to the police to warn them."

"Warn them?" Georgie scoffed. "About what? A dodgy portrait artist drawing pictures of the President in green felt-tip?" She snatched the notebook and flung it to the floor.

"So you don't believe me either?"

Georgie threw her hands up in despair.

"What is there for me to believe?"

"That the President is in danger. There's an assassin after him. I can feel it."

"Jimmy, people get 'feelings' about the President being in danger every day. Some of them keep quiet about it. They live happily ever after. The others go to the police and claim they have images in their head telling them it's certain the President will be dead before the weekend."

"And what happens to them?" Jimmy mumbled, pretending he didn't know exactly what the answer was. Georgie sighed and held her head in her hands.

"What I'm saying," she went on, "is that *of course* the President is in danger. He's *always* in danger – he's the President. But he has security, doesn't he? And maybe your 'images' are to do with him, but maybe they're not. And even if they are, we can't do anything about it. If we tried, we'd all get locked up in a loony bin."

"And then Miss Bennett would definitely find us," added Felix. "I reckon she's got a subscription to Loony Monthly Magazine."

"Don't you start on me as well," Jimmy begged.

"I'm not starting," Felix replied. "I believe you."

Jimmy forced himself to smile. He knew he could always rely on Felix. It wasn't much of a comfort today though. The worst thing was that he was filled with doubt himself. When he thought about it rationally, he knew that everything Georgie had said made sense. The images in his head could mean nothing except that he was slowly going crazy. Telling the authorities would only put them at a massive risk of being found by NJ7. And yet that feeling was so strong inside him. It swallowed the rational, sensible thoughts, reducing them to nothing but a squeak.

The images had come to him again in the night. They had been so strong this time that Jimmy could close his eyes at any moment and see them, scorched into his eyelids. The face of the President was there too, more clearly now than ever. With it came that same terror. It felt as if Jimmy was looking at the face of a dead man, but one with his eyes open, able to breathe and plead for Jimmy's help.

Too late. The man's time had run out.

Jimmy heard the click of the door of the apartment below, then feet on the stairs.

"Chris is leaving," Felix whispered. He was leaning so far out of the door, Jimmy wondered how he didn't overbalance. "He must be going to see his contacts about what happened last night."

Jimmy had been so focused on the puzzle inside his head that he hadn't had time to worry about the two men who had attacked him. It was almost enough to make him laugh – he wasn't scared of killers with knives who came up the fire escape, but he was terrified of the pictures in his own imagination. The images were nothing – not even air – and yet his fear of them twisted his mind into knots.

Georgie got up and went to peer round the door as well, but Jimmy jumped to his feet and snatched a few dollars from the table.

"What are you doing?" Felix whispered. "Your mum's coming up. Don't act crazy."

Jimmy ignored him and dashed towards the bathroom. The footsteps came closer, making their way up the stairs. Helen Coates pushed open the door to the apartment.

"Jimmy," she announced, "I need to talk to you." She looked up just as Jimmy disappeared through the bathroom window. The clang of the metal fire escape rang out.

"Jimmy!" Felix yelled. "Quick, we should go after him." He ran to the window and was about to climb out. Helen gently pulled him back.

"Let him go," she said.

"What?" Felix turned round and saw the sadness in her face.

"What do you mean, 'Let him go'?" It was Georgie, standing by the bathroom door. "You can't let my brother just wander off into New York. There are maniacs and muggers and Government agents out there!"

"It's OK," Helen explained. "He'll be fine. He's gone after Chris, hasn't he?"

The others nodded, not understanding what could possibly be going through Helen Coates' mind. Then she doubled their confusion.

"He thinks Chris is his father."

Georgie and Felix both jolted slightly.

"Has he gone mad?" Georgie asked. "In fact, have you *both* gone mad?"

Helen sighed and finally looked her daughter in the eye.

"Jimmy is your half-brother, Georgie," she replied.

A gust of cold air through the window sent shivers over Georgie's skin. Her face fell first into shock, then quickly into thought. She looked like she was doing a complex mathematical sum in her head.

"Who is Jimmy's father?" she asked angrily.

"It doesn't matter," Helen replied.

"Of course it matters!" Georgie exploded. Her fists were clenched and her face was twisted with anguish. "You can't keep secrets from us. It's not fair!" She looked across at Felix, who had gone red with embarrassment and was trying not to make eye contact. On the other side of him was the open window. Georgie looked out, grappling with her thoughts.

"You said he's gone after Chris," she said, more calmly now. "Is Christopher Viggo Jimmy's real father?"

Her mother turned away and gestured to Felix. "Come on," she said. "We should let Jimmy do what he has to. He'll catch up with Chris and be perfectly safe." She pulled the window closed and tried to usher the others out of the bathroom, but Georgie refused to move.

"Jimmy's father is dead," Helen announced. "That's all that matters."

CHAPTER FIFTEEN - KNICKERBOCKER

The jumble of lights and smells of Chinatown was almost too much for Jimmy's senses to take. He wasn't used to being outdoors during daylight hours. *Don't look up*, he heard a voice inside him whisper. *The satellites will see your face.* He twisted and ducked his way between the crowd, moving fast to catch up with Viggo.

Jimmy hunched his shoulders against the cold and the light drizzle. At Canal Street subway station, Viggo trotted down the stairs. His long coat rose up behind him like a cloak and he disappeared into the darkness. Jimmy pelted down the steps after him. He had to weave between the tourists and the commuters, who seemed to move in slow motion.

By then, Viggo had already swished through the turnstile. Jimmy ducked behind a corner. He could see Viggo standing on the platform, looking furtively from side to side, mentally noting the features of the people around him.

The luminous yellow numbers on the platform clock quivered to the next minute. How long until the next train? Jimmy gritted his teeth and fumbled for money to buy a ticket. His nerves were so on edge he could almost feel the electricity in the air.

Then came the rattle of the tracks. Behind him, a train swept into the station. The dust in the air swirled round him, making the hairs on the back of his neck stand on end. All Jimmy could hear was every noise the train made magnified a thousand times. He never noticed anything unusual about the two men in black leather gloves, purchasing a ticket from the next machine.

The train stopped. The doors slid open. At last, Jimmy grabbed his ticket and charged towards the turnstiles. The train doors were closing. The back of Viggo's head disappeared into a crowded carriage.

Jimmy swiped his ticket and surged forwards. This burst of speed sent him flying through the crowd. He slipped between the doors of the train, scraping his nose on the rubber seal. *Made it*, he thought with a smile, leaning against the door to catch his breath. He was in the carriage next to Viggo's.

Two tall lean men were left behind on the station platform. One tapped a black umbrella on the concrete.

"Best not to do it in public anyway," he mumbled.

His companion put his fists back in his pockets, discreetly putting away his knife.

"His time will come," he grunted. "Sooner than he thinks."

Both men had refined English accents.

Viggo stepped off the train at Times Square, so Jimmy did the same. There were enough people on the platform to keep Jimmy hidden as everybody made their way towards the exit. But Viggo took a different turn. He quickened his step and broke away from the crowd, heading down a tunnel signposted 'Shuttle'.

Jimmy waited a few seconds, then turned the same corner. Viggo had disappeared round a bend in the tunnel, but Jimmy picked out his footsteps, echoing against the tiles with a regular tap. Suddenly the noise stopped. *Is this the meeting place?* Jimmy thought. If it was, he had to get a look at who Viggo was meeting. He edged round the corner, holding his breath. There was no sign of Viggo.

Jimmy held himself still. A minute went by, maybe more. To Jimmy it seemed like forever. Nobody passed him along the tunnel. The place was deserted and eerily quiet. It was as if Christopher Viggo had disintegrated to dust – except there was a door.

It was an old door, with white paint peeling off in some places and stained almost brown in others. Around it, the wall was smeared with an extra layer of muck. There were large patches of damp where the tiles had long since fallen off and smashed. The smell of this part of the tunnel was thick – like meat after it's been left out of the fridge too long. All these were the marks of time. Jimmy reckoned this must have been one of the oldest parts of the subway network.

The door looked completely ordinary except for one thing – above it was a space with no tiles where the stone wall was exposed. And carved into the stone, in capital letters about fifteen centimetres high, was the single word KNICKERBOCKER. The word was so worn by time and dirt that at first glance it was hard to make out. But now that Jimmy had seen it, he couldn't take his eyes off it.

What could it mean? he wondered. Was it some kind of code? What possible reason could there be for this dilapidated old door, labelled KNICKERBOCKER? Jimmy gingerly pressed against it, but it didn't budge. No surprise there, he thought. But there was no keyhole either – there wasn't even a handle. For a second he considered breaking it down, but he knew in his gut that was the wrong option. He needed to get through quietly, and without being observed.

Jimmy turned his brain inside out, trying to work out how to get through. Then he spotted something. Just above the first R of KNICKERBOCKER, tucked in where the letters touched the ceiling, there was a small white box. It was about five centimetres square and as grimy as the rest of the door. Out of one side of the box came a thick white cord – some kind of electrical wire, Jimmy assumed. It ran down the edge of the doorframe and disappeared into the wall at floor level.

Jimmy felt his insides rumbling – his programming was churning, then it sent a rush up Jimmy's spine that swooped through his neck and gripped his brain. In a flash so strong it nearly knocked him sideways, Jimmy knew what he had to do.

He took one step back, then a running jump at the door. In mid-air, he stretched his arm up and gave the box a tweak. It clicked round by a millimetre, then snapped back into its original position. Even before Jimmy landed he could picture the current surging down the wire and releasing the electromagnet that kept the hinges locked in place.

He was dazed by his new-found understanding of simple electrical systems, but he had no time to lose. Straight away, he leaned on the door. There was no resistance. It didn't even squeak. A door that looked this old, yet opened without a creak? That's when Jimmy was sure he was on to something that people weren't meant to know about.

He carefully closed the door behind him and stood in the darkness. His eyes itched for a moment as his night-vision kicked in. Directly in front of him was a short staircase. He crept up it until he could see over the top step, then lay flat on his stomach. His nerves hummed inside him. This place was far from welcoming.

Jimmy was looking into a large carpeted room, with a complex arrangement of corridors, pillars and an incredibly high ceiling. Nothing was very clear though – his night vision could only give a guide to outlines; everything looked blue and fuzzy.

There was a something in the middle of the room that might have been a desk or a bar, and behind that was a huge staircase. It swept round in a grand curve, leading to a balcony. That was bad news for Jimmy. As if there weren't enough hiding places in the room already, from the balcony anybody could be watching, waiting to ambush an intruder.

The place was cold and smelled a bit like the toilets at school, but the last thing Jimmy wanted to do was leave. He stayed flat on his front and pulled himself forwards on his elbows. His eyes roamed the room, taking in the swirls that ran up and down the walls.

Then he started picking up sounds, impossibly quiet but unmistakable: footsteps creeping round the room. They came from everywhere. Jimmy tried to work out the positions of the other people or even how many there might be. *One on the balcony*, he thought. *No, two. And one in the corner up ahead. No, wait, the opposite corner.* The noises seemed to shift like the whispers of a ghost.

Then came a sound that ripped through the darkness and stunned Jimmy's ears: gunfire. It came with an explosive flash. Then there was another. Jimmy felt a cloud of dust fly into his face. Like a panther, he launched into a sprint. In less than a second he was sheltered round the corner of a partition wall.

Another flash. Another blast from a machine gun. As soon as it came, Jimmy ran to a pillar and wrapped his limbs around it. His only chance to avoid getting trapped was to keep moving and to head towards whoever was firing. Who could these people be? Then he had a sudden thought – these contacts were on his side, weren't they? They were only firing because they didn't realise the intruder was him – Jimmy. One of the gunmen could even be Viggo himself.

"Hold your fire!" Jimmy yelled. "It's me – Jimmy Coates! It's Jimmy!" As he shouted, he kept climbing. His fingers dug into the plaster and his arms strained to pull him up, metre by metre. At last he was able to grab the balcony and haul himself over.

Then came another shot. This one slammed into the top of the pillar he'd just left. A block of plaster crumbled away and crashed down to the floor.

"Stop!" Jimmy shouted – he had to give it one more try, in case they hadn't heard. "Chris! It's me – Jimmy!" Whoever it was, they had heard. And Jimmy was giving away his exact position.

Another peal of machine-gun fire – Jimmy dropped flat on the floor. He felt the bullets graze the back of his T-shirt before they tore chunks out of the wall next to him. If he stayed where he was, the next shot would be aimed a centimetre lower. *Who are these people?* screamed a voice inside his head.

Jimmy pushed himself into a forward roll and came up running. He moved as swiftly as he ever had, panic jarring through his muscles – but it wasn't swift enough.

In the next instant there was another flash and another machine gun roar. Jimmy felt a smack in the back that came with the force of an elephant impaling him on a tusk. He stumbled forwards. The air seeped out of his lungs. His vision faded to a purple blur. He reached out for something to hold on to – anything. He found the railing of the balcony, but the momentum of the shot sent him straight over the top of it. He tried to hold on, clutching at the cold metal like it was life itself.

The strength in his fingers evaporated. Jimmy tumbled through the air, head over heels. Time stretched as he fell, tormenting him with the chance to remember the first day he had discovered his strange abilities. *I've fallen before*, Jimmy heard himself thinking. *I can survive. I must survive.* But at the same time he knew it was the bullet, not the fall, that could bring him down forever.

CHAPTER SIXTEEN - COLONEL KERYS

Despite the carpet, Jimmy's landing was unforgiving. He wished he wasn't strong enough to stay conscious – the pain in his back quadrupled when he slammed into the floor and bounced. Every bone seemed to judder. For a second, he kept his eyes closed, waiting for the pain of the bullet wound to take him over completely.

But it didn't. Instead, as it spread from the point of impact, it faded. Very carefully, Jimmy rolled his shoulders. His joint clicked, but there was no jab of pain. The moment of agony had passed. Then he noticed something else. He felt around with his hands. The carpet beneath him was dry – no blood.

He was surprised to find the breath flowing back into his lungs without any discomfort. He knew he was strong, but surely being shot in the middle of his back by a machine gun should have caused more damage than this?

At last he found the confidence to roll on to his side. The gunfire around the room had stopped and before Jimmy could get to his feet, the lights came on. Jimmy blinked.

"Thank you, gentlemen," came a shout, echoing around the hall. "This exercise is over." It was a deep American boom, with a coarse texture that suggested it came from an older man.

"A bit late now," was the response – in a familiar English voice. "You've already shot Jimmy." It was Viggo.

"Chris?" Jimmy called out. "Why did you let them shoot me?" He was shocked to hear his own voice coming out so clearly, and that he had no shortness of breath. Had he really been shot at all or had he imagined it?

He peered into the murky corner of the hall where the voices had come from, his head still on its side. Even sideways, though, he was able to recognise Christopher Viggo running towards him.

"I told him to stop them," Viggo said in a rush, "but he wouldn't. Are you OK?"

"I was shot," Jimmy said softly, not able to believe what he was saying.

"Ha!" Behind Viggo marched a stocky man of about sixty. He was dressed in dark blue army uniform, with a chest so covered in ribbons and medals it looked like a patchwork quilt. His shoulders were broad and he carried his cap under one arm, which exposed his thinning hair. "Ha!" he laughed again, throwing his head back to show off his speckled and wobbly chin. "Are you dead?" Jimmy didn't know what to say. "Are you dead, Jimmy Coates? You don't look dead to me! Ha!"

The man reached where Jimmy was lying and tilted his head to examine Jimmy's face.

"Step down, gentlemen," he called out, without turning away. Looking over the man's shoulder, Jimmy saw two huge men un-strap machine guns from their shoulders, unclip night vision goggles from their helmets and salute.

"Sir, yes, sir!" they shouted as one, then marched smartly away.

"You should have stopped the exercise as soon as we saw him come in," Viggo insisted.

The American shrugged. "I wanted to see how my men would cope when an unexpected element gatecrashed their party," he snarled.

"And how did they cope with this 'unexpected element'?" Jimmy asked, anger bubbling over in his voice.

"Very well," came the reply. "They shot it. Ha!" The soldier threw his head back again, then ran a hand over his skull, smoothing down what little hair he had left.

"Oh, I'm sorry, Jimmy," he said when his cackle had died away. "Perhaps this wasn't the best way for us to meet, eh? I'm Colonel Keays." He held out his hand and fixed Jimmy with a stare.

Jimmy looked at Viggo, whose expression was almost pleading. It was several seconds before Jimmy reached out to take the Colonel's hand. When he did, the man hauled Jimmy up with hardly any effort. He may have looked old, but it was immediately clear to Jimmy that Colonel Keays had led a life where strength meant everything.

Straight away, Viggo turned Jimmy round to examine his back.

"Is it bad?" Jimmy asked, rolling his shoulders again to see whether it hurt. It didn't.

"That's amazing," Viggo gasped.

"Told you," Keays muttered. "Not a scratch."

Jimmy and Viggo both looked at him as if he had landed from another planet.

"Top-secret, state-of-the-art technology," he explained. "We call them 'laser-blanks'. We're still testing them, but so far it looks like they're perfect for training exercises."

"Laser-blanks?" Jimmy repeated, bemused. "I don't understand." He squirmed at the thought of a laser going into his back.

"Each shot is actually a photon-cluster – basically, a packet of energy that's designed to mimic exactly the behaviour of a real bullet. You can use them with regular guns, they don't leave shells on the ground, or make a mess like that ridiculous paintballing, and, best of all, they hurt like hell when you get hit. That means that even in training there's a genuine desire to avoid getting shot – which is a good habit to have in combat." He paused to brush some dust off his cap, and polish the eagle insignia with his sleeve. Jimmy was still too shocked to start thinking about who this man was or who he worked for.

"The difference is," the solider went on, "with laser-blanks, you're up on your feet again in no time. Now, with a regular target there'd still be considerable pain after the event and some nasty bruising the next day, but I've heard you're no regular target." He stroked his chin and looked Jimmy up and down, a strange smile on his lips.

Jimmy didn't know how to react. He'd never expected to encounter the US army and especially not in such unusual surroundings. He was about to ask Viggo what was going on, but he was cut off.

"You shouldn't have followed me," growled Viggo. "Why did you do it?"

Jimmy was taken aback by Viggo's anger and tried to avoid his glare.

"To find out who your contacts were," he snapped.

"I said I'd tell you when you needed to know."

"Well, I needed to know now, OK?" Jimmy couldn't hide the frustration in his voice. The two of them stared at each other, fuming. Jimmy wasn't going to back down.

"Hey, hey, take it easy," Keays urged, placing a hand on Viggo's shoulder. "Don't be mad at the poor little killing machine." He winked at Jimmy. Jimmy felt like his face had been slapped. How could this man call him that and then find it funny? Jimmy's eyes burned. But it was worse than just a cruel description – it revealed how many of Jimmy's secrets Viggo had shared.

"He was following his natural instincts to make sure he and his family were safe," the Colonel went on and patted Jimmy on the back. "Well, you're safe now, Jimmy. You're with the CIA."

"The CIA?" Jimmy gulped.

"That's right, buddy." The Colonel blasted out another raucous laugh and rocked his head back. "The Central Intelligence Agency – defending the land of the free by any means necessary."

Jimmy quickly ran through the events of the past few days. It seemed obvious now. Only an organisation with the power, the expertise and the budget of the CIA would have been able to get all of Jimmy's group out of Britain, through US immigration and into a safehouse in Chinatown. But why would they go to so much trouble? There was suddenly so much running through Jimmy's mind. He stared at Viggo, full of doubt.

"I had to keep it secret," Viggo said, still furious. "You should be thanking me. Do you know the risks I took to get in touch with the CIA? You can't just call their fugitive hotline, you know."

Jimmy felt a heat building inside him. He fought to keep control and hear Viggo out.

"It was the best thing for you," Viggo went on. "And would you have come to America if I'd told you my contacts were another government agency? No way – you'd have refused to get involved with them. I know you don't have a lot of trust left for governments."

Jimmy's anger jumped up in his chest, but then he realised Viggo was right. First, they had gone through the terror of escaping NJ7, then the French Secret Service had let them down to serve their own ends. The last thing Jimmy would have done was willingly put himself in the hands of a third country's Secret Service. And so far, it looked like Viggo had done the right thing by getting the CIA to help them.

"OK," Jimmy mumbled, dropping his eyes to the floor. "But you should have..." He didn't even bother finishing his sentence. There was far too much for him to worry about. He didn't want to waste his energy in endless arguments with one of the few men he could trust.

"Good, that's good," Colonel Keays announced, nodding his head and smiling. "Now that we're all friends again – welcome to the Knickerbocker Hotel."

"What?" Jimmy exclaimed. For the first time since the lights had come on, he allowed himself to look around the place. Dust covered every surface and even seemed to clog the air. The walls were a deep red, with golden swirls decorating the corners, all the way up to the ceiling. The banister of the staircase was gold as well, and incredibly ornate. Jimmy's mouth dropped open when he looked straight up and saw the biggest chandelier he could have imagined. It was draped in giant cobwebs. All around him was a scene of faded glory, frozen in time.

"In the 1920s this was a popular place," the Colonel explained, striding towards the stairs. "The guests were so well looked after they even had their own door straight on to the subway so they could avoid the weather outside. That's the only entrance these days." He climbed as he spoke, waving his cap around at the surroundings. "Look at the place! The Knickerbocker is perfect for simulating warfare in an urban environment – the balcony, the pillars, even the elevators. It all makes a fascinating challenge to a Secret Service commando unit."

Jimmy imagined teams of soldiers securing positions all around the vast lobby.

"The other great thing," Keays shouted, his voice echoing down from the balcony, "is that they converted the upper floors into a cinema. We can make as much noise as we want; test weapons, explosives – anything. Everybody assumes it's Dolby Surround Sound. Ha!"

Jimmy tried to smile with the Colonel, but he just wasn't in the mood.

"What does he want from us?" Jimmy whispered. Colonel Keays was too far away to hear now.

"He wants to find a way to relocate us," Viggo replied, glancing sideways at Jimmy. "That's what we've been discussing: going into hiding with false identities."

"But what's he doing it for?" Jimmy insisted. "All this money and help he's given us. What does he want in return? Me?" He almost choked on the word.

Viggo looked up at Keays nervously, but it was OK – the Colonel was strolling about the upper level, still proclaiming about how clever the CIA was to use the Knickerbocker.

"He wants the same thing we want," Viggo whispered. "To smash NJ7."

Jimmy felt a jolt of shock. It looked as if there was suddenly a demon in Viggo's eyes. *That's what you want*, Jimmy thought. *I just want to be left alone.*

"Look what they've done to us," Viggo went on. "And to Britain."

Jimmy didn't know how to respond at first. From the aggression all over Viggo's face, it didn't look like he was thinking of Britain – or even himself.

"The CIA isn't helping us because they care about Britain," Jimmy suggested.

"So what? They're on our side now. It's our chance to grind NJ7 into the ground – for everyone they've lied to, for everyone they've betrayed, and everyone they've shot in the back."

Viggo turned away and hid his eyes with his hand. "Let's make them pay," he muttered under his breath.

"But we came here to hide," Jimmy countered, "not to fight back. We might be able to get away to somewhere they'll never find us."

"Wake up, Jimmy!" Viggo yelled. The Colonel had seen they were talking and was coming back to join them. "There's nowhere to hide," Viggo continued. "Any ten-year-old kid can search Google and watch live satellite feeds of every centimetre of the earth's surface. Can you imagine what NJ7 is capable of? With billions of pounds diverted from British industry and welfare to pay for military technology?" He drew in a heavy sigh and rubbed his face. "They could find a gnat on the back teeth of a sardine at the bottom of the Indian Ocean. So wake up to reality. It's time to be as smart and as devious and as cruel as they are. Maybe that's going to be nasty – violent even. Maybe it could even cause a war. I don't care any more."

Jimmy was staggered by the violence in Viggo's voice. He had never seen him so passionate.

"They've done enough!" Viggo bellowed. "They have no feelings. They kill without question. It's time we stopped feeling too." A tear crept down the side of his nose.

Jimmy could hardly breathe, he was so stunned. A part of him wanted to console his friend, but his feet were rooted to the spot and his voice had died in his chest. Then, inside him, came the rumbling of his programming. It was like a sleeping monster, stirring at the noise coming from the entrance to its cave. It longed to kill.

Was it really time to stop feeling and kill without question, Jimmy wondered. *But feeling is the part of me that's human*, protested a quivering voice inside his head. But that voice quickly faded away.

CHAPTER SEVENTEEN - BLOODPRINTS

Suddenly, Jimmy stumbled to one side and clutched his ear. He cried out in pain. It felt like a drill was forcing its way into the side of his head.

"What's the matter?" Viggo asked urgently.

Jimmy couldn't even speak.

"Same as last time?" Viggo asked.

Jimmy nodded, breathing deeply. He leaned on a pillar to support himself. After less than a minute, the attack passed.

"What's this about?" asked Keays.

"I don't know," Jimmy said softly. He wiped his face with his hands and found they were shaking.

"He's been like this for days now," Viggo said with concern. "And he sees strange images too. Is there a CIA doctor who could take a look at him?"

Jimmy knew at once that a doctor wasn't going to help. His programming was sending him a powerful message. He felt like the only way to deal with the attacks and the images was to respond to what it was telling him.

"I don't need a doctor," he blurted out.

"Are you sure?" Viggo started. "Before, you said that..." But Jimmy cut him off.

"Someone's going to kill the President."

Jimmy knew they would probably think he was crazy, just as Georgie had warned him. But he was face to face with a senior officer from the CIA. Jimmy felt he had to say something. If he didn't, the consequences would be his responsibility.

Viggo and Keays were both taken aback. "Can you predict the future now?" Keays quipped.

"Jimmy, you're not thinking straight," said Viggo. "Is that what you think the images in your head are telling you?"

Jimmy refused to let Viggo make him feel stupid. "I *know* it's what they're telling me," he insisted. "And they're getting stronger. If I close my eyes I can see the President's face, and I know there's an assassin being sent to kill him."

"How could you possibly know that from what you see in your dreams?" asked Viggo, exasperated. "You're being ridiculous."

"Ridiculous?" Jimmy could hardly hold back the anger that bubbled in his gut. "How's this for ridiculous – I thought I was a normal kid. Now I can see in the dark and breathe underwater. How come that's not ridiculous, but this is?"

Viggo and Keays looked at each other, unsure what to say.

"I'm telling you," Jimmy went on, "someone's going to try and kill President Grogan – and soon. My programming must have noticed something, maybe from the news, or maybe it just knows how NJ7 works." Now there was panic in Jimmy's voice. He shifted from foot to foot as he spoke, unable to contain the energy buzzing through him.

"NJ7?" Viggo repeated. "So you're saying you think it's NJ7 that will send someone to kill the President?"

"I can just feel it," Jimmy said weakly. He dropped his eyes to the floor, suddenly embarrassed that he'd brought up the subject at all.

"Why would NJ7 want to kill President Grogan?" Viggo asked. "He's their ally. He can help them if there's a war against France."

Jimmy shrugged. He could hear how outrageous he must have sounded. He had no evidence to go on, just his faith in his own instincts. Even that was beginning to weaken.

Keays cut through the awkward silence. "Actually," he said quickly, "that's the information that was given to the public."

"What?" Viggo asked, shocked. "Grogan has suddenly become an enemy of Britain?"

"Not quite," Keays explained. "But it's very unlikely that the President will get US troops involved in another expensive foreign war just to help out the British. Especially since Britain closed its doors to American businesses."

"So, what are you saying?"

"I'm saying that if Grogan refuses to help, and NJ7 thought there was anybody else who would be more sympathetic, then they'd have every reason to try and eliminate the current President. It's one of the scenarios we've had to consider in my department."

Jimmy felt his faith in himself cautiously returning. Then Keays snatched it away.

"But that's exactly why the President is safe," the Colonel insisted. "We've already thought of this and covered every possible angle."

Jimmy searched his mind for some indication of what to believe. How could he know what was a justified fear and what was paranoia?

"Hey, look," Keays began again, "it can't have been easy you telling me this." His eyes twinkled at Jimmy, like drops of ink drying on parchment. "But you can relax. The President is perfectly safe – he's at the United Nations right now, which is one of the most secure locations in the world. This afternoon he has a press conference with the British Prime Minister, and there's no way anybody could harm him there. For a start, nobody except the Security Services even knows where the press conference is going to be until I announce it in an hour's time. After that," he paused and Jimmy thought he saw a smile flicker across his face. "Well, let me show you."

Colonel Keays marched quickly away, disappearing into the darkness at the other end of the hotel's vast lobby. Jimmy was alone with Viggo, but the man remained staring down at the carpet, lost in his own thoughts. Jimmy watched him, not blinking, studying Viggo's face. He was searching for something – a familiar movement, a likeness, or even just a feeling that there was a connection. He was searching for any sign of himself.

Is this...? Jimmy couldn't even finish the question inside his own head. His mouth opened as if he might ask it aloud, but his voice was wrapped up in his chest, a long way from coming out. He was still staring at Viggo as Keays tapped away at a laptop on the hotel reception desk. Just next to it, a projector flickered into life. Jimmy would need more time if he was going to work out for himself whether he was looking at his father.

"What are you staring at?" Viggo hissed. Jimmy looked away.

"Here's a treat for you, Jimmy," announced Keays, raising his voice above the distant rattle of a subway train. He pointed up at the wall behind Jimmy. "Blueprints." The beam from the projector threw giant images across its entire breadth. It was showing detailed technical drawings of the layout of a building, against a bright red background.

"But these are red," Jimmy pointed out.

"Some names just stick, kid. Ha!" Keays exploded into a laugh and slapped his legs. "Last I heard, you folks were still calling Britain 'Great'." Viggo tutted and turned away.

"Now tell me, Jimmy," Keays went on, growing more excited, "Can you see a weakness?"

"What?" Jimmy exclaimed. "What do you mean?"

"You're looking at MoMA – the Museum of Modern Art," Keays explained. He flicked through a series of images, tapping a key on the laptop every few seconds to move to the next one. "It's all here in front of you – schematics for the whole place. Construction, ventilation, power lines – everything. These are the sightlines" He traced the cursor across the blueprints. "These stars are the principal security posts." He walked across the room and pointed out dozens of them, but way too fast for Jimmy to follow. "And this..." He reached the wall and patted a point on a blueprint. The red light was painted across his body and face, making him look almost demonic. "...is where the President will be standing."

Jimmy was so bamboozled by all the information, Keays could have been telling him the President would be standing on the ceiling. That's how little sense it made.

"A press conference at MoMA?" Viggo asked softly. "That's a bit unusual, isn't it?"

"Security," replied the Colonel. "We use a different location each time the President makes a public appearance. We have to keep the terrorists guessing." He was deadly serious.

Meanwhile, Jimmy's eyes darted all over the blueprints. It made him dizzy.

"So can you see a weakness, Jimmy?" barked Keays.

"I–I—" Jimmy stuttered. "I don't know. I'd have to study these plans I guess." He forced himself to keep staring at the wall, but there was too much information to take in. As soon as he thought he'd worked out what a line meant, it seemed to shift into a totally new position, and then Jimmy lost it.

"These plans look pretty thorough to me, Jimmy," said Viggo. "Should you be showing us this, Colonel? Isn't it classified information?"

"Ha!" Keays roared. "Of course it's classified. These are top-secret documents. But you guys are with me now, aren't you?"

Jimmy and Viggo shot each other a quick glance.

"Of course we're with you," Viggo said hurriedly.

"Yeah, of course," Jimmy muttered, though it took a lot of effort.

Keays moved back towards the beam and tapped more keys on the laptop. The blueprints disappeared from the wall. It was dark again. Jimmy tried to cling on to the maze of lines and symbols, but the more he tried, the less he could remember. It was as if the lines of the schematics twisted into a net that wrapped round Jimmy's brain and cut off the blood.

"You're still not sure, are you?" Keays asked. Jimmy didn't react. However much Colonel Keays worked to convince him, there was still that terror gripping Jimmy's heart. The images from his dream hardly left his head now. It felt almost as if death itself had made its way inside him to share its secrets.

"Hey, listen," Keays went on at last, "if you're still convinced that something is going to happen to the President, then I'd be a fool to ignore your warning. So I tell you what – I'll review every security precaution personally over the next few hours. Even better than that – I want you to come to the press conference yourself to keep an eye out for anything you think is suspicious." He reached into the top pocket of his jacket and pulled out two laminated security passes on black cords. "Will you take one of these?"

"You want me to come?" Jimmy was stunned. He was pleased that the Colonel was taking his premonition seriously, but he had never expected this.

"You too, Viggo," the Colonel announced, offering a security pass to him as well. He held one in each hand, waiting for Jimmy and Viggo to take them.

"Look," Viggo said cautiously, "we appreciate all your help, but I don't think we should be the ones protecting the President."

"Ha! You won't be protecting the President." Keays' gleaming smile stood out in the gloom. His arms were still stretched out in front of him. "That's my job. You two will be my guests. That's all. But if you do spot anything you think I've missed, you'll be doing America a great service by pointing it out."

Viggo hesitated. Then he said, "What I mean is, it's not safe. We're here to hide. The sooner the CIA can relocate us, with new identities, the better. Meanwhile, we should stay out of sight and out of trouble." He looked at Jimmy, his eyes almost pleading him not to agree with the Colonel.

Jimmy tried to make his decision rationally. Of course, the safest thing was to go back to Chinatown and hide. But the strength of his desire was compelling. He forced himself to think through all the consequences of him being at the press conference, but it was all shoved aside by an overwhelming urge taking control of his muscles. It was as if his hand reached out by itself. Even if he'd tried to hold back, the movement was stronger than Jimmy's willpower – he could do nothing to stop himself taking the security pass. His body wanted him to be there. Somehow, the images in his head made it impossible for him to go anywhere else.

As soon as Jimmy's fingers touched the plastic, Viggo gasped.

"Jimmy," he exclaimed, "think about it. NJ7 will be all over the place. We shouldn't even be in the same city."

"Rubbish," scoffed Keays. "They'll have a couple of agents acting as bodyguards – nothing more. And I'm in charge of the operation. I can make sure any British agents are posted somewhere they'll never see either of you."

Jimmy watched as his arm drew the security pass towards him. He was no longer responsible for any movement his limbs made, but it felt good – as if, at last, he was in control.

"Jimmy, stop," Viggo urged again. But Jimmy couldn't stop – and he didn't want to. He knew exactly what Viggo was going to say next.

He looked Viggo in the eye. It was almost a challenge. *Say it*, Jimmy was thinking. *Tell me my father will be there.* There was a tortured delight in Jimmy's heart when he saw the reluctance on Viggo's face to say what he had to. *You know it's a lie, don't you?* There was a twist in Jimmy's stomach. It sent a shiver up through his body and tears to the corners of his eyes. *Say 'father'.*

Viggo's voice was barely a whisper:

"Your father will be there."

CHAPTER EIGHTEEN - STRIPS, SPLASHES, 53, K

From the top of the Cranberry Tower in Brooklyn Heights, the view of Manhattan was spectacular. But nobody ever came up to see it. According to public records, the building didn't even exist – despite the fact that it was pretty hard to miss. All seventy-eight floors of it. Among the exclusive residential enclave, this was the only building that was strictly business – and it was Government business.

Zafi picked it out from over a mile away – it was the only building in the area without 'Keep Clear' signs covering every fire door. But Zafi had the benefit of an aerial view, in restricted airspace. She pointed at the building out of the side of the helicopter as the door slid open. The pilot nodded patiently. He'd seen it too.

They buzzed down like a bee circling a flower. The more the tiny helicopter rocked, the more Zafi smiled. To her left sat Uno Stovorsky, a senior agent in the French Secret Service. He'd turned green as soon as they left the ground in Paris. In contrast, Zafi loved flying and found it hilarious to listen for Stovorsky's groans over the white noise of the flight.

As well as Zafi, Stovorsky and the pilot, there was a fourth man. He was posing as a diplomatic attaché, but really was just cover to get Zafi into the country as his daughter. He'd be watched closely for his whole stay in the US, while Zafi would be left to move through the city unobserved. The Americans were never smart enough to suspect that a child would be on a mission.

And Zafi was on a most vital mission.

The helicopter landed with a bang and bounced up a couple of times. The three passengers jumped out even before it had come fully to rest. Zafi ripped off her helmet and walked with her 'father' across the asphalt, following Stovorsky. She attempted in vain to smoothe her hair down and tried not to think about the horrific outfit she was wearing as part of her cover – white frilly socks, a tartan skirt and a white blouse buttoned all the way to the top.

A woman was there to meet them. She was in her thirties, wearing a black business suit, too much make-up and her hair in a tight bun. She ushered them as far from the helicopter as possible – right to the edge of the roof. The noise of the chopper, combined with the blustery wind, made conversation almost impossible, so it was understandable that this woman didn't waste time on niceties.

"The President was upset when he read your message," she yelled. "Britain is an ally. Why go to war with them?"

"It must be the season," Stovorsky barked back. His long grey raincoat wrapped around him in the wind. "If the President is on Britain's side, why did you arrange for us to meet with you?"

"Just because we are friendly with them in public, it doesn't mean we can't hear arguments from both sides – in private, of course." The woman's face still revealed no emotion.

Stovorsky looked back at Zafi. She smiled sweetly, as if she hadn't heard a word. Stovorsky smiled too, knowing that she had understood everything. He turned back to the American, his expression serious again.

"So can we count on the President's support?"

"President Grogan has considered your position," the woman announced. "I've been instructed to tell you that current US policy is not to intervene in foreign conflicts. However, the President places great importance on the historical friendship between our two nations." She reeled off her speech as if the words meant nothing to her. "Therefore, he would like to offer you a package of the finest military hardware the US industry has to offer."

"How much?" snarled Stovorsky, without missing a beat.

"Eighty billion dollars."

"Tell Grogan that if I'd wanted to go shopping I would have landed at Bloomingdales."

Before the woman could even draw breath, Stovorsky spun round. He winked at Zafi and marched back towards the helicopter, signalling to the pilot to start it up again. Zafi fluttered her eyelashes at the American woman, but didn't move. Nor did the man next to her. They stood together as Stovorsky issued one more instruction. His words were almost lost in the wind.

"Look after my new attaché and his daughter!" he hollered, taking his seat in the helicopter. He was quickly several metres off the ground. "Show them the sights – especially the art galleries."

Jimmy felt the rumble of a helicopter in the air. He instinctively ducked his head and sidestepped into the shadow of a doorway. Then came the swish of a rotor overhead. Jimmy kept his face down towards the pavement so that it was invisible from above.

"Ha! Don't worry," chuckled Colonel Keays. "It's one of ours. You'll find nothing but CIA choppers in the air round here today. Even the birds are scared of us."

Jimmy trusted what the man was saying, but still couldn't bring himself to step into the open until the helicopter was gone. He watched it pass across the crack of sky between the skyscrapers. Unfamiliar judgements throbbed in his head: *Looks like a Bell 450 armed reconnaissance helicopter*, he thought. *Definitely US army*.

"Nobody from NJ7 is anywhere near here," Keays added, reading Jimmy's expression. "I made sure of that."

"Come on," urged Viggo. "Let's keep going. You're the one who insisted on being at this press conference." He looked as nervous as Jimmy.

The three of them marched down 6th Avenue, hunching their shoulders against the furious wind. The power of Jimmy's obsession had drawn him here. Something inside was forcing him to follow this overpowering sensation of doom. It could lead to Jimmy preventing the murder of the President or it could lead to nothing at all. Either way, he had to find out – the torment of the images in his head made it that way.

They crossed 51st Street, then 52nd. Apart from them, the place was deserted, despite it being the middle of the day. These few blocks in midtown Manhattan had been ringed by a security cordon for hours.

"Don't people want to come and cheer the President when he arrives?" Jimmy asked, kicking at an empty can. The clatter echoed against the buildings.

"Sure they do," Keays replied. "That's what we have a team of actors for."

"Actors?" Jimmy thought he'd misheard because of the wind.

"Yeah – they cheer when I tell them to cheer, and they cheer right."

"What do you mean they cheer right?"

"You know, they cheer so it looks good on Fox News. Normal people don't do it right."

Jimmy was about to question him further, but Viggo cut him off.

"You won't understand how they do things here, Jimmy," he said. "This is a real democracy."

"And soon," Keays added, "you and your friends will be able to enjoy it. Preparations are under way. We'll relocate you and you'll be able to live almost as if you were American." He looked very pleased with himself, then he quickly added, "You could never be completely American, of course. That's not the way things work in a free country."

Jimmy didn't fully understand what Keays was saying. He tried to feel happy about the chance to escape to a new life, but inside him his thoughts weren't connecting with his emotions. It felt wrong. He didn't want to be American or even nearly American. The more he thought about it, the more he realised that he didn't even want to go into hiding. What sort of life was it to pretend to be someone else and live every day in fear of being discovered?

Jimmy wanted to be himself, but it was becoming harder and harder to work out who that was. Suddenly, he stopped dead. It was as if his legs had been frozen. He stared up at the street sign.

"This is it," he gasped.

"What?" asked Viggo, but he didn't need an answer. He followed Jimmy's stare and knew instantly what was wrong.

It was the same as any street sign in Manhattan. They all have the same design: white lettering on a green background. But to Jimmy, this sign was more chilling than having a gun in his face. They were standing on the corner of 53rd Street. Above them, on the sign, was a white 53 surrounded by green. It could have been a precise copy of one of the pictures Jimmy had drawn over and over in his notebook. Even the way the light reflected off it seemed familiar to him. It was already inside his head.

"Let's go," Viggo ordered.

They turned together into 53rd Street. One feeling gripped Jimmy's muscles: determination to find the assassin who was here to kill the President. He was convinced now more than ever that there would be one hiding somewhere in the Museum of Modern Art. He had to stop them.

53rd Street was lined with CIA agents. Jimmy thought to himself how similar they looked to the men and women of NJ7 – the lean physiques, close-cropped hair and black suits. Only the green stripes were missing. To Jimmy, it was just one more way that Britain and America were more alike than he would have guessed: the dirty streets, the cameras tracking every move, the Security Services controlling what was seen on TV. He tried to remind himself that instead of the Green Stripe, the Americans had freedom.

Jimmy flashed his pass at the team on the door. Keays and Viggo followed him in.

"Where now, Jimmy?" Keays whispered. "Where is your sixth sense leading now?"

Jimmy ignored the man's mocking tone. Why did he seem to be enjoying this so much?

The lobby of the Museum of Modern Art was a large white hallway leading to a reception desk and a staircase up to the main part of the museum. Jimmy wandered towards the stairs, looking around him all the time, searching for anything that would give him a clue about where to go.

"I don't recognise any of this," he whispered, almost to himself. Then he noticed a line of CIA agents all eyeing him suspiciously. Jimmy shuddered at the thought that any one of them might be connected to NJ7 somehow.

"It's all right boys," Keays reassured them. "Show them your pass, Jimmy."

Jimmy did, breathing deeply. It felt good to know that Colonel Keays was protecting him.

"Sir," replied one of the agents, a huge man in a black suit, "the press are ready to take their seats and the President will be arriving in four minutes. We need you in position to greet him and your guests need to clear the lobby." He nodded his head respectfully, then walked away. When he turned, Jimmy noticed a wire coil coming out of the back of his jacket and into an earpiece. All of the agents had them, along with radio sets clipped to their belts. Almost immediately, Keays was handing a set to Jimmy.

"Take this," he ordered. "The second you see anything I should know about – send out a general alert. You just push this button." He showed Jimmy and gave a set to Viggo too. "Go upstairs and look at where the President and the Prime Minister will be speaking. Then stay in one of the service stairwells so the Prime Minister doesn't see you. He'll have his personal security team with him – you don't want them seeing you here either."

"Thank you, Colonel," said Jimmy. He clasped the radio handset. It was much smaller and lighter than he had expected – only just bigger than his palm in fact. After a few seconds, he was aware of a voice in the back of his mind. *Icom F-Series*, it said. *Looks like an upgrade.* He turned the handset over and saw the maker's logo on the back: Icom. He would never be able to escape that relentless voice in his head. Right now, he wished it would just shut up. He made his way up the main stairs with Viggo.

"Looks like this is it," Viggo said in an undertone. "Anything you recognise?"

At the top of the stairs was a much larger hall. The ceiling was way above them, and the bright white walls made it look like they'd got lost inside a massive fridge. CIA dogs were leading agents between the rows of chairs on a final sweep for explosives. On the far side of the hall were two lecterns, each with a single microphone. This is where the two heads of state would announce what they'd been talking about all day at the United Nations. There were two huge flags as well – a Union Jack and the Stars and Stripes. But Jimmy looked straight past them.

His eyes went directly to the wall behind the lecterns. It was covered by a long abstract painting that sent panic into Jimmy's heart. The pace of his breathing tripled. Even his programming couldn't put him at ease – the assassin in him was as excited as the boy was terrified. The painting was a dull beige canvas covered in bold splashes of red and yellow. Every one of them could have been plucked from inside Jimmy's head.

"It will happen here," Jimmy announced, his voice struggling to get out.

Viggo was too shocked to say anything. They both hit the alert buttons on their radio sets. Within seconds, Colonel Keays was back with them.

"What is it?" he asked. "The President is about to arrive."

Journalists and photographers filed past to take their seats. Jimmy had to ignore them. He pointed to the painting.

"What does it mean?" asked Keays.

"There's an assassin in the building. The President is the target. I'm sure of it."

The Colonel's face didn't flicker, but his eyes were pinched at the edges. He wasn't laughing now.

"Find him," he ordered. "I'll send you back-up."

He spun round without waiting for an answer and barked orders into his radio set as he jogged down the stairs. The applause and the cheering had already started. President Grogan was close. Would Ian Coates be far behind?

"Where do we start?" Viggo asked.

Jimmy looked around the hall, moving through it, scanning for anything familiar. It was an amazing building – sleek and modern. This central hall went right up the middle for the entire height, with balconies overlooking it from every floor. Everything was white except the flags and the painting.

By now, Viggo was surrounded by six CIA agents, all poised for action, awaiting instructions. They looked to Jimmy, but Jimmy had nothing to tell them. All he knew about the Museum was from a thirty-second glance at the blueprints and the images that had been pounding in his head.

That's when he realised – he didn't have to search the building. The images were giving him precise instructions. He closed his eyes and searched his mind instead. He didn't have to look very hard to recall the images one by one. 53 and the coloured splashes had already appeared in real life. There were three left: rainbow stripes, black K and the President's face.

"K," Jimmy blurted out.

"What?" said Viggo.

"Where's there a K? A black K on a white background."

Viggo shrugged and looked around him, but the CIA team was already running towards an adjoining hallway. Jimmy followed, his limbs buzzing with anticipation.

There, by the base of the escalators, was a service door. It, like the walls, was pristine white, but in its centre a sign stood out: STAIR K. The writing was big and black, with the K larger than any of the other letters.

Jimmy didn't hesitate. He clattered through the door, a line of Secret Service agents behind him, with Viggo rushing after them.

Jimmy found himself at the bottom of a narrow stairwell. The neat design of the rest of the place was gone. This was a service area – not meant to be seen by the public. It was still white though, and when Jimmy looked up he could see the silver banister glinting at him from the very top, ten floors up.

Jimmy dashed up the stairs. The hammering of the agents' boots nearly drowned out the cheering that was coming from the lobby. *The target has arrived*, thought Jimmy.

The next floor up he barely paused. There was

nothing out of the ordinary there – just a door out into the gallery and more stairs. So Jimmy kept running. With each flight of stairs, he felt his confidence rising. Was it his programming drawing him closer to the assassin or was it Jimmy – the real Jimmy – boosted by the company of half a dozen agents? They were following him, trusting him, relying on him.

But then Jimmy had to stop. There were no more stairs. He'd reached the top floor sooner than he'd expected, and though he was barely out of breath, he felt that lurch of doubt again. There was nothing here.

"Rainbow stripes," he announced quickly. "That's the next thing. Where are they?"

There was nothing to see. The walls were as white here as they were everywhere else.

"Where are they?" he yelled.

"Jimmy, calm down," Viggo panted, resting with his hands on his knees. "There's nothing here. You must have made a mistake."

"No!" snapped Jimmy. But one of the agents was already murmuring into his radio.

"There's nothing up here," he was saying. "You can let the President into the main hall. Proceed as planned."

Jimmy spun round, desperate for the next clue. Nothing was going to stop him. There was no time to wait around and no chance of him giving in. Inside, his programming was crying out, hungry to move on. But where was there to go?

"What's up there?" Jimmy asked, frantic. He was pointing above his head, to the light embedded in the ceiling panels.

"I take it you're not asking whether there's a heaven," Viggo replied, raising an eyebrow. "But otherwise, you're just pointing to the ceiling."

"There's nothing up there," one of the CIA agents cut in. "You can unscrew the light fitting to access the wiring, but it's nowhere near big enough for a person to fit through."

Jimmy looked around at the agents. They all had broad shoulders and muscles that looked like bridges across their chests – even the women. But recently, Jimmy had come to know that sometimes the deadliest packages are also the smallest.

"What about a child?" he snarled.

CHAPTER NINETEEN - RATS IN THE ATTIC

Jimmy slipped his radio into his pocket and climbed on to Viggo's shoulders. Balancing on his knees, he reached up to the light fitting. The light beamed into his face. It was so strong he had to look away, but he felt round its edges.

"Ah!" he cried, pulling his hands away. "It's hot."

"Of course it's hot, you idiot. What did you expect?" Viggo's voice came out strained. Jimmy was obviously heavier than he'd expected.

Jimmy took a deep breath and went back to the task. He was just going to have to shut out the pain. He summoned his programming from within. It quickly swirled round his head, and now when Jimmy reached for the edges of the light fitting, the burning was reduced to a tingling. With one tug, the fitting came loose and Jimmy unscrewed it until the light was dangling from its wire. That left a hole about fifteen centimetres across – not anywhere near big enough for Jimmy to fit through.

He slipped his hand into the hole and reached for the edges of the ceiling panel. His fingers brushed over a screw at the corner.

"How about going a little slower up there?" Viggo called out sarcastically.

Jimmy responded by digging his heel into Viggo's chin. Gradually, one by one, Jimmy was able to undo the screws that held the panel in place. Then he carefully lifted the whole thing off its resting place. The square hole was still only about thirty centimetres by thirty centimetres, but just as Jimmy had expected, it was now possible for a child to crawl into the ceiling.

Jimmy hauled himself up. It was a tight squeeze. He went head first. He had to wriggle and push to get his shoulders through, but he made it.

"Looks like you're on your own, mate," said Viggo, his face red from holding Jimmy up for so long. "When you've realised there's nothing up there, I'll be waiting here."

Jimmy nodded, refusing to let Viggo's doubt get to him.

"And if you do find anything," added one of the agents nervously, "use your radio."

Jimmy didn't even wait to nod again. With only enough room to lie flat on his belly, he shuffled away.

It was much darker up here. The air was dusty and hot. He was closed in on either side by metal struts that created a narrow path, barely wide enough for him to crawl through. He moved himself steadily onwards with his elbows, not even knowing which direction he was going in. Yet the more he thought about it, the more certain he became.

There was no evidence to back up his premonition, but it made absolute sense to him that somewhere up here there was an NJ7 assassin waiting for the chance to kill the President. And it had to be Mitchell. Who else from NJ7 could fit through these small spaces?

Jimmy wiped his face with the back of his hand. The dust was getting up his nose. He tried to see what was waiting for him up ahead, and his night-vision helped to enhance the shapes, but there were too many obstacles in the way – metal struts, wires, pipes and all kinds of debris. It was like a maze that nobody was ever meant to wander into.

Jimmy kept going, breathing hard. Sweat dripped down the back of his neck and his muscles started throbbing from his awkward position. Then something in the dust caught his attention.

If nobody had ever crawled around up here, how come there was an area where the dust had been wiped away? It looked like a trail. Jimmy pushed more strength into his arms, picking up his pace, but remaining silent. The noise and lights of the Museum seemed like a different world from this. There was only silence up here. Once he thought he could hear Viggo shouting to him, but it was impossible to make anything out clearly.

Jimmy followed the trail, a smile breaking out across his face. Mitchell had thrown him into an industrial shredder and nearly strangled him on top of a taxi. Both times Jimmy had been taken by surprise. *Your turn now*, Jimmy thought. The idea of getting his own back sent a gleam to his eyes. They flashed in the shadows.

Then, up ahead, he saw the silhouette of a figure. *Definitely a child*, Jimmy said to himself with delight. The figure was outlined against a grate of some kind. It threw strips of bright light onto his back. Jimmy realised that Mitchell was looking out over the main hall, watching the press conference – waiting to kill.

Jimmy felt a warm surge of confidence. He had been right to trust in his programming. It had led him to the assassin and he was going to save the President's life. For a second, he thought about using the radio to send out an alert. But he immediately realised that would be the worst thing he could do. The noise would tell Mitchell he'd been discovered and he'd shoot straight away. There wouldn't be time for the agents on the floor of the hall to pull the President to safety.

Jimmy inched closer. But as he did, he saw that the silhouette wasn't Mitchell at all. Jimmy gasped. He couldn't help it. As soon as the sound escaped his lips, the assassin in him regretted that momentary lapse of control. The figure turned to look at him. It was Zafi.

She didn't hesitate for even a fraction of a second. Her speed took Jimmy by surprise. She rolled to the side, grabbed one of the metal struts and swung herself round it, launching both feet at Jimmy's head. They landed with an awesome crunch in his jaw. Jimmy's head rocked back with the impact, jarring his neck.

He wasn't going to let that finish him off though. Far from it. Jimmy used the impetus of Zafi's kick to pull himself out of her reach. He flipped on to his back and grabbed the wires that ran along the ceiling. Zafi kicked out at him again. Just in time, Jimmy pulled himself completely off the floor. Zafi's legs swept beneath him, hurting nothing but the air.

The next second, Jimmy dropped himself down. He caught Zafi's ankle and skilfully redirected it towards one of the support struts. Bone clanged into metal.

"*Zut!*" Zafi exclaimed, wincing at the pain in her ankle. She quickly brushed it off and the pair of them swung round the struts. Sometimes they used them for protection, then the next moment they would launch themselves off them into their opponent. It was a horizontal acrobatics display, with the pace and power of fireworks on fast-forward.

Jimmy ducked behind a strut. For a split-second he was sheltered. He reached into his pocket, clutching at his radio set, fumbling for the alert button.

"That won't work up here," Zafi announced in a scolding tone. "These are structural supports." She crawled towards him, tantalisingly slowly. "We're surrounded by so much metal and concrete that the only signal that makes it through is from the cellphone mast on the roof. And that's only because it's right above our heads, and it's about ten thousand times bigger than the aerial on your radio."

Jimmy mashed the alert button over and over, but he knew Zafi was right. Nothing was happening. Then, in the instant that Jimmy's fingers were occupied on his radio set, Zafi launched a devastating attack. She swooped between the struts. Jimmy swerved to the side. He thought he was out of Zafi's way, but she twisted in a zigzag and landed with her head in Jimmy's midriff.

Jimmy crumpled in half. *How does she put so much power into a single blow?* his mind cried out. He pushed away the pain, letting his programming swallow him up. Zafi shoved him against the side and pulled his hands behind him. Jimmy's face pressed up against the grate. He could feel Zafi's breath on the back of his neck and the warmth of her body squeezed up against his. Her hair smelled of coconut. He wrenched his shoulders round to shake her off him, but Zafi had him locked down.

While he was blinking at the dazzling white on the other side of the grate, Zafi sent two sharp kicks at one of the iron supports. The top of it snapped like it was made of chocolate. Then Zafi heaved on it with all her weight, bending it down and twisting it, still managing to keep Jimmy in place with her thighs. She crushed his hands under her knee. Finally, she pulled the metal strut over Jimmy's wrists.

He could wriggle and shout, but he was stuck.

"Nice to see you, Jimmy," Zafi cooed. "But don't disturb me at work again."

Jimmy didn't bother struggling any more. He pushed his hands apart to try to break the metal, but his arms were behind him and that made them much weaker. He twisted his shoulders, trying to loosen the metal. His wrists grated against the sharp edges.

A centimetre from his eyes was the lattice side-panel, and beyond that a perfect aerial view of the press conference. The hall was packed with journalists, all fighting to get their questions answered before anybody else's. Dozens of bald heads bobbed up and down for attention.

Security agents lined the walls and the area in front of the two heads of state. Jimmy immediately recognised Paduk, He was a lot taller than any other agent, with a skull that looked as if it was constructed out of industrial scaffolding.

Behind him stood Ian Coates. They weren't directly above him, so Jimmy could see the man's face. He gulped at the sight of his ex-father, expecting to be overcome by sadness, or anger, or even relief – anything. But everything inside him was numb. His gut contorted, desperate to grab hold of any emotion. But Jimmy's head refused to feel. *He doesn't deserve that*, he thought. *He's nothing.*

A click pulled Jimmy out of his thoughts. He looked up at Zafi. Her attention was focused on a black metal rod nearly a metre long. She carefully screwed it into something shaped like the handle of a revolver. The light shimmered off it. Zafi was building her assassination weapon. Her slim fingers worked efficiently, covered in those black leather gloves she had been wearing last time they met.

When the rod was in place, she reached to her side and from a brown leather satchel she produced a coil. It was about half a metre of thick metal and the silver shone out of the shadows. Zafi placed it over the metal rod and secured it in place. If this was a gun, it wasn't like any one Jimmy had ever seen.

"How's Felix?" Zafi asked, without even turning to look at him. Even so, Jimmy knew there was a hint of a smile on her face. Clearly, all this was still amusing to her. She flicked her hair back behind her ear.

"You don't have to do this," Jimmy replied, choking back the dust in the air. "There's no reason to kill anybody."

"What if it avoids a war?" Zafi shot back immediately. "Killing could save lives."

Jimmy didn't know how to answer. "But, but..."

"Stop snivelling," Zafi ordered. "This is nothing to do with us."

"What? So who else is there up here?"

Zafi giggled.

"You're cute," she mewed. "But you know what I mean. This isn't our responsibility." Her hands were busy mounting her weapon on a tripod that she'd put together out of the pieces in her bag. Then she detached the leather strap of her satchel and fastened it to her weapon, tying the other end round the tripod. Everything was held in place perfectly. "Nothing we do is up to us. It's in our blood. It's in our instincts. Don't you feel it too?" At last she glanced at Jimmy.

Her eyes caught the light. The sight of her, so calm, almost smiling, with one gloved hand wrapped around the handle of her weapon, sent a ferocious anger through Jimmy's veins.

"Take control!" he yelled. "Of course it's your responsibility. Who else has their finger on the trigger?"

"Oh, Jimmy," Zafi sighed, smiling sweetly. "That's just the last moment in a chain of events that started a long, long time ago. It's not my fault. It just happens to be my finger. My actions obey my programming, and my programming had nothing to do with me."

She turned back to look down the length of the metal rod. She took aim.

"Stop!" Jimmy pleaded. He writhed against his makeshift handcuffs, squirming with all the strength he could muster. But there was nothing he could do.

Zafi pulled the trigger.

CHAPTER TWENTY - MARS

As Zafi's hand squeezed the handle of her gun, Jimmy winced. He felt a shudder up his entire body. When he opened his eyes again, he looked through the grate to witness the carnage.

But below him, nothing had changed. The journalists were still waving their pens in the air, the lights from the TV cameras were still glaring and the security guards stood their ground. Most important of all, the President was still standing, fidgeting with the microphone in front of him, taking yet another question.

Jimmy looked back at Zafi. What had gone wrong? There had been no sound when she pulled the trigger, but Jimmy had expected that. Any gun as fancy as hers would have an inbuilt silencer.

"Did you miss?" he whispered in shock.

A flicker went across her face. "I don't miss," she snapped, still in that light, girly tone. "This isn't a gun."

Jimmy stared at her blankly.

"Does it look like a gun?" Zafi asked. She maintained her steady gaze down the black metal rod, watching, waiting. But what for? "This is MARS – the *Magnétism Appareil Rigolo Super-Spécifique*. I invented it." There was a proud smile across her face. "What do you think?"

Jimmy shrugged. "What does it do?" he asked meekly.

Zafi giggled softly. "The first time I pull the trigger, it locks on to the resonance of the specific metal object it's aimed at. The second time, it attracts that object towards it with an electron-boosted magnet. It's incredibly powerful." She flicked her hair behind her ear again and a haughty expression came over her face. "Any object up to the size of a *pétanque* ball will be pulled towards it at nine times the speed of a machine-gun bullet."

"What's *pétanque*?" Jimmy asked. "Never mind," he added quickly, shaking his head. He stared at the weapon, awed at the contraption that this girl had designed and built.

"Oh, you're impressed," Zafi squeaked. "I like it when you're impressed, Jimmy Coates." There were shadows across her face from the grate, but Jimmy was sure her eyelashes fluttered at him.

"And that's not even the best part," Zafi went on. "He's wearing a metal pin on his lapel. I've locked on to that. Now all I have to do is wait for him to turn round.

When I pull the trigger again, it will look like he's been shot, but from completely the opposite direction, leaving me time to get away while everybody's running about in the wrong place." The light had left her eyes. This was the most serious Jimmy had ever seen her. "That Union Jack badge will rip straight through his heart."

Jimmy slowly absorbed everything she was saying. It was disgusting to hear it in such detail. He struggled harder against the metal round his wrists. The press conference would be over in a matter of minutes. Jimmy had to do something fast. But as the thoughts sunk in, Jimmy stopped dead.

"Wait," he whispered, almost to himself. "Why is President Grogan wearing a Union Jack lapel badge?" He peered down at the President, trying to make out any kind of badge on his suit jacket. But there was nothing.

"He's not, *mon cher*," Zafi replied.

"But you said that was what you locked on to."

"That's right. But President Grogan's not wearing it. The Prime Minister is." She turned to Jimmy, her eyes wide. Never had someone so dangerous looked so innocent.

"So how will that kill the President?" Jimmy asked. His brain was processing steadily, trying to work out what was really going on.

"Don't be silly, Jimmy," Zafi urged. "It won't kill the President. I'm not here to kill President Grogan. I'm here to kill Ian Coates."

Jimmy's head snapped back to the press conference. He'd been looking on the wrong man's suit. There it was – a bright Union Jack on Ian Coates' lapel. Jimmy's breathing quickened. He racked his brains, but all he found was doubt.

"No," he gasped. "The images – they were so specific. I was sure. It was definite: an assassin would be here to kill President Grogan." His voice rose up in his panic. "I saw Grogan's face," he insisted. "Why has everything else come true and not this? There must be an assassin to kill the President! Tell me the truth!"

Zafi looked at him for a long time. When Jimmy saw the pity in her eyes he hated her more than he ever had.

"Maybe there *is* an assassin up here to kill Grogan," Zafi whispered. Jimmy felt the air in his lungs freeze. He suddenly knew what she was about to suggest. "Don't you remember, Jimmy? You're an assassin too."

Jimmy tried to shout. But there was nothing inside to come out. He looked down at the President. The man's face merged with the image in Jimmy's head – the image of death itself. There *was* an assassin here to kill the President – but it wasn't Mitchell and it wasn't Zafi. It was Jimmy Coates.

Then came that searing pain in his head. Jimmy cried out, his whole body convulsing. It was the strongest attack he'd had yet. He writhed and screamed and kicked, knocking loose a panel in the floor by his feet.

At last the pain subsided. There were tears in Jimmy's eyes. When he looked along the floor to his feet, he saw something to complete the horror – thin horizontal strips in the colours of the rainbow. It was the final image from his nightmare. The panel cover he'd accidentally kicked away revealed a highway of electronic wiring.

At first, Jimmy couldn't look at anything else. He couldn't even blink. Then his programming seized his muscles. With no control, he turned back to the hall below. Inside came a flash of understanding. To him the hall was instantly transformed into a complex puzzle of structural engineering, yet he knew it better than he knew his own name. It was as if he could see through the walls. He'd seen the blueprints. Without even knowing it, his programming had memorised every line, every dot and every centimetre of the Museum's circuitry.

Now he leaned forward, closer to the grate. His eyes focused solely on Grogan.

"What's he saying?" Jimmy whispered, fighting all the time to regain control within himself.

"Oh, I gave up trying to listen," Zafi replied. "It's all lies about how America is going to make sure Britain and France let the UN sort out all their problems diplomatically. Blah blah blah." She gave a little laugh, but Jimmy was far from amused. "They're both saying they're best buddies and that they'll do everything they can to avoid a war between Britain and France. But they're both lying. Coates scratches his nose too much and Grogan keeps fidgeting with his microphone. Look, there, he did it again."

Jimmy saw it and it sent his mind spiralling into freefall. His eyes traced the lead of the President's microphone to the base of the lectern. From there it went into the floor and disappeared. But Jimmy kept following it. He knew the power lines. He ran his eyes along the floor to the wall and kept going – all the way up the wall, across the ceiling and right into the intersection at his feet. One damning fact combined with another, faster and faster, until the only conclusion was that the President would die, and by Jimmy's hand.

His programming had drawn him here. He knew that now and he knew why – to kill the President. The rainbow stripes – the wiring – that was the murder weapon. A misconnection here would send thousands of volts down the wires and into the only appliance plugged into that line – the President's microphone. And every time the President lied, he touched the microphone.

A quiet voice in Jimmy's head thanked his luck that Zafi had trapped his hands behind his back. He closed his eyes. *Stay like this*, he ordered himself. *Don't move and you won't kill.* Inside was an urge so strong he thought he was going to throw up. His mind was a furnace of contradictions, like a computer overheating and about to crash. The desire to kill had never been so strong. He clenched up every muscle.

"No," he cried out, tears running down his face. "Don't do it."

"You can't stop me, Jimmy," Zafi whispered, thinking he was talking to her. She leaned forwards over her weapon, holding it steady.

Jimmy peeled his eyes open just enough to see her. What could he do? If he didn't break free, Zafi would assassinate the Prime Minister. But if he did, he knew he would have a tougher fight – to stop himself killing the President.

It was that moment of distraction that weakened Jimmy's resistance. While he was grappling with his dilemma, the 62 per cent of him that was raw, unfeeling assassin forced more power into his arms than there had ever been. The constant drive to kill throbbed in his muscles, tearing at the metal strut that was bent round his wrists. After two seconds, it was loose enough for Jimmy to pull his arms free.

Zafi didn't even notice. Beneath them, the questioning was coming to an end. The press conference was nearly over. The photographers moved to the front as a journalist asked the final question.

"Come on," Zafi urged between her teeth. "Turn round."

Without making a sound, Jimmy bent down to the wires. An expert tug pulled them apart. Jimmy moved his hands with short, sharp movements. He was the model of efficiency. With his fingernail he stripped the plastic cover from two of the wires – one blue, one red. Nobody would notice that the President's microphone wasn't working until he tried to speak. As soon as he did, a single lie would kill him.

Jimmy's human voice was frantically calling out for help – but it was stuck inside his head and rolled into a ball so small it was almost lost completely. He held the two wires a centimetre apart. The assassin in him was waiting for the perfect moment.

"Turn round!" Zafi whispered, exasperated.

Jimmy looked at her out of the corner of his eye. Her hands were steady, just like Jimmy's. They were two professionals going about their jobs as if it were the most normal thing in the world. But inside Jimmy was screaming. Was Zafi too? Jimmy looked more closely. Why were her eyes glistening? Was that a tear? Suddenly, Jimmy felt like he could see deep into Zafi's heart. Her body might have been poised to kill, but Jimmy could see something more about her. Something that was terrified.

In that moment, Jimmy knew that Zafi had never done this before. Despite all her cocky behaviour, and all the pride in her skills and her gadgets, she was no more a killer than Jimmy was. He knew that in Zafi's mind was the same struggle that had been Jimmy's constant battle since the second he had found out he was designed to kill. Until today, he had been winning – would Zafi prove as strong?

Jimmy's fingers were moving towards each other, bringing together the two wires that would mean death. Beneath him, the President leaned towards his microphone to begin his answer. His hand reached up to grip the microphone. Another lie. He started to talk. When nobody heard him he leaned in closer and gripped the microphone tighter. This was the moment. Jimmy's fists trembled, squeezing tight. He was moving them together and pulling them apart at the same time. Then his hands crept towards each other. He couldn't stop them. The wires trembled, millimetres from each other, millimetres from killing the President of the USA.

Jimmy couldn't stop his hands now. They were too strong. He looked again at Zafi. On her face was the same fear that was in Jimmy's heart. Her expression connected directly with every contradiction that was pumping through Jimmy's veins. They were united. For a second, it wasn't a French girl crouching there by her weapon – in Jimmy's eyes, he could have been looking at himself.

A surge of warmth swept through his limbs. It felt like there was a suit of ice keeping his muscles locked in battle mode, but now at last it was melting.

One finger at a time his grip dissolved. The wires dropped to the floor. They sparked, but they never connected.

Jimmy had saved the President. Now he had to save Zafi.

CHAPTER TWENTY-ONE - REVENGE OF THE SON

A hundred metres below them, on the Museum floor, the journalists were laughing. The President's microphone had stopped working and he resorted to shouting his final answer. With a gloating smile at a job well done, Grogan nodded his thanks and waved. Then he held out his hand to the British Prime Minister, Ian Coates.

Up in the rafters, Jimmy knew that as soon as the Prime Minister's back was turned, his Union Jack lapel pin would tear through his body. All Jimmy had to do to save him was dive across and knock Zafi away from her MARS weapon.

So why was he hesitating?

It was then that one thundering truth hit him right between the eyes. He looked down at Ian Coates. Jimmy had a chance that might never come to him again – to let the man be killed.

Didn't Ian Coates deserve it? Didn't he, above all people, need to pay for the blood on his hands? He'd been a killer since long before Jimmy was born. Who knew how many innocent people he'd slaughtered to keep the tyrant Hollingdale in power? And now he was in power himself, how many more was he murdering or brutally intimidating every day just to stay there? And there would be even more massacred if Coates were allowed to take Britain and France into an unnecessary war. Maybe killing him now would save lives.

But Jimmy realised that wasn't why he was hesitating. There was only one reason Jimmy wanted that man dead. Ian Coates had betrayed him. As a father, he'd lied day after day, with every gesture that built up the fiction that they were a family, and with every act of false love. He'd gradually destroyed Jimmy's life. And then he had sacrificed his family for power over a nation.

It was time to pay. It was time for revenge.

The President clasped the Prime Minister's hand. Photographers bunched together at the front of the hall, bustling for the best shot. Jimmy could hear Zafi's breathing quicken. Ian Coates was still facing the front. As soon as the posing was over, he would turn to go and that would be the end of him.

Jimmy didn't move. *It's for what he's doing to Britain,* he thought. *For what NJ7 have done on his orders.* Tears rolled down his face. *For what he did to me.*

Scores of cameras flashed like a firework display. Then they stopped. The two heads of state released each other's hands. Ian Coates turned to leave. Jimmy watched, his whole body shaking. He couldn't hold back his sobs. He heard Zafi draw in a deep breath. His ears were so finely tuned, he could make out the creaking of the trigger as her finger clenched.

Suddenly, Jimmy dived to the side. He barged into Zafi, leading with his shoulder, and reached out with both hands to push her weapon off target. He landed on top of Zafi. They turned together to watch her specially designed and custom-built magnetic traction gun crash into the grating. The weight of the weapon forced a panel loose. Light from the hall streamed into their hiding place. The MARS weapon teetered for a second, then toppled over the precipice.

Jimmy jumped forwards quickly enough to watch the weapon and the grating swirling through the air. They seemed to be falling forever.

"*Non!*" cried Zafi.

Then, at last, with every face in the hall watching, the metal smashed into the floor. Tiny parts bounced up several metres. Some hit journalists, who held up their arms to protect themselves, shouting in panic. But one piece was strong enough to withstand the impact – the trigger. It clicked into place. The remains of the weapon gave an almost inaudible buzz. Then the Prime Minister's shoulder exploded in a shower of blood. The painting behind him was spattered with even more abstract red shapes. He fell to the floor.

"He's hit!" somebody shouted, before the rest of the room erupted into screams. The President was whisked away to safety.

"The angle was wrong," Zafi whispered in a fluster.

"What?" cried Jimmy, wiping the sweat and tears from his face with the back of his sleeve.

"It was meant to be activated up here, not down there." The words rushed out of Zafi's mouth. Her eyes darted from side to side as she tried to work out the geometry of what had just happened. "It was a hundred metres off. It pulled the pin in the wrong direction. Look, it's barely a scratch."

Journalists were rushing for the exits, while the security team drew their weapons and took up new positions. They were completely calm, as if they'd rehearsed this drill a million times. Several of them stared up at the ceiling, straight at the point where Jimmy and Zafi were hiding.

Jimmy watched the Prime Minister. The man was surrounded by Secret Service agents, but already Ian Coates was waving them away. Jimmy read his lips:

"I'm fine, I'm fine – it's just my shoulder."

Paduk was holding the Prime Minister's head. Then he peered upwards, looking for where the weapon had fallen from. For less than a second, he and Jimmy locked eyes. Paduk cracked his jaw and helped Ian Coates out of the room.

"Let's get out of here," Jimmy declared. He looked round. Zafi was already gone.

Jimmy crashed through a vent in the ceiling and crawled out on to the roof. Steam floated around him. The Manhattan wind buffeted his body. This was the only way out. He knew that the CIA would believe that he'd had nothing to do with trying to kill the Prime Minister, but if he'd gone back down to the stairwell there was too much chance that he'd be met by NJ7. Paduk had seen him and that meant Jimmy had to get away as quickly as possible. He could meet up with Viggo and the CIA later.

He staggered to his feet, but before he could run, or even work out which direction to go, he was knocked sideways by a piercing squeal. He clasped his ears, but it did no good. The noise was inside his head. It sounded like feedback. He rocked from side to side, trying to shake out the horrific sound. He wanted to tear at his own skull and physically remove whatever this was.

He reached out to steady himself and found a metal structure in the middle of the roof. It was a system of aerials, with five long, slim rectangles pointing in every different direction. Jimmy waited for relief, but the closer he got to this metal structure, the worse the screech in his head became. He tottered backwards, barely able to keep his balance. It was then that he realised this must be the cellphone mast Zafi had mentioned. Was it causing some kind of interference inside his head?

Jimmy should have run. He knew that. Any second there might be helicopters shooting at him, or Paduk's muscly grin charging through the vent on to the Museum roof. Instead, Jimmy launched an attack on the mast. His hands stayed firmly around his ears, but he kicked at the metal poles until they were bent out of recognition. Now there were sirens mixing with the already deafening noise. Jimmy was wasting time, but he didn't care.

"Get out of my head!" he screamed. "Get out! It's my head! It's my life!" Now he went at the phone mast with his fists, tearing at every corner of metal, twisting each element of the mast and ripping it off where he could. "You stole my life!" he screamed. "You deserve to die!"

At last, the din that was drilling into his brain subsided. A couple of sparks fizzled and died. However many millions of messages the phone mast had been beaming across New York City, the conversations were silent now.

Jimmy wiped his face. His tears were blown away in the wind. His screams had gone with them, lost in the air. It felt like every emotion he was capable of had flown away too, leaving only the thought of his father.

"Why did I save you?" he whispered.

The battered mast couldn't answer. Nor could the wind. But there wasn't time to wait. At last, the voice of sanity took control. Jimmy powered his limbs into a sprint. He dashed across the roof of the Museum, hardly even conscious of what he was doing any more. His survival instinct kept him moving.

In seconds, he was at the end of the block. He looked over the edge of the building and immediately had to pull back. He'd never been afraid of heights, but the distance to the ground made his head swirl. There was a mist clinging to the buildings that made it almost impossible to see the street. *There's no way I'm jumping*, he thought, yet at the same time he could feel his brain turning it over as a possibility, calculating the force of the impact, working out how he would land. He looked over the edge again. A rush of wind swept up into his face and took his breath away. *No way*, Jimmy commanded himself.

He wiped his hands on his trousers and crouched, ready to start his climb down. But then, in the corner of his eye, he caught sight of a shadow hurtling towards him. A grey shape loomed out of the fog. Jimmy dropped flat on his face, just in time. It swooped over him, without making a sound.

Jimmy flipped over to get a glimpse of it as it disappeared again. He instantly recognised the fragile outline of a twelve-year-old girl – Zafi. Was she flying, he wondered, aghast. Then he spotted it – emerging out of the mist was a huge crane. There were no construction workers in the area today – it had been evacuated as a security measure for the press conference. So there was nobody to stop Zafi swinging on the end of the crane's line like a fish caught by an angler. But Zafi was as deadly as a shark.

Jimmy bounced to his feet. Before he could move away, Zafi was back at him. She was holding on to the metal claw with one hand, twirling in the air like an acrobat. Jimmy recognised the moves of a master of Capoeira – a lethal brand of Brazilian martial arts. She landed a kick hard in the base of Jimmy's back. He stumbled forwards. The pain shooting up from his kidneys told him this was no play-fight.

Now Jimmy had a chance to move. He forced himself to ignore the sharp sting from Zafi's attack and climbed over the side of the building. Digging his fingers into the brickwork, he clambered downwards as fast as he could. He had to heave in every breath. Then she hit him again.

With the force of a missile, Zafi launched herself off the crane and landed right on Jimmy's back. She clamped her arm round his neck and squeezed. Jimmy twisted, but couldn't shake her off. He let go of the brickwork with one hand to try to prise her grip loose. His fingers were already white from holding the entire weight of both him and Zafi. Now they were numb, but still able to lock into the tiniest irregularities in the surface of the wall.

Below him, the earth seemed to loom upwards, making him dizzy. Then he glimpsed Zafi's other arm raised above her head. Any second she would deliver a vicious chop to the back of his neck. Jimmy knew that would be fatal for any normal human. He didn't care to find out how much damage it would do to him. He let go of the wall.

He felt Zafi gasp. She clung on to him even tighter. Jimmy's face was red – only a tiny amount of air was seeping through Zafi's stranglehold. They fell together for less than a second. Zafi kicked her legs forwards and caught a window ledge with her ankles, but she couldn't keep hold of Jimmy. As they fell, he sent a jab into her midriff to loosen her grip and grabbed hold of her arm. They hung there – Zafi upside-down, Jimmy beneath her, staring up, his rock-hard fingers now locked in position round Zafi's wrist, instead of digging into the wall.

"What are you doing?" he yelled.

"Feels like yoga," Zafi giggled. Jimmy wasn't in the mood.

"I'm not your enemy, remember?"

"You're NJ7," Zafi announced. "And you saved your Prime Minister."

"I might have saved the Prime Minister, but I was saving you too."

"Saving me?" Zafi scoffed.

"Yes – from being a killer." Jimmy was seething. "You don't have to be one."

Zafi tried to shake him loose, but his fingers were like bolts, drilling into Zafi's skin. However much she stretched and twisted her hand, she couldn't get rid of him.

"I saw you trying to kill the President," Zafi snapped. "That's the work of NJ7."

"You've got it wrong," Jimmy hollered. "That wasn't really me!"

"I don't blame you, Jimmy, but I'm going to have to kill you."

CHAPTER TWENTY-TWO - A WALK IN THE PARK

With a flick of her arm, Zafi sent Jimmy flying into the air. He hurtled upwards. The wind bit into him and it felt like he'd left his stomach holding on to the side of the building. He landed with a bump, back on the roof. The impact jarred through his body, but he rolled over, unhurt. He had to move.

He wished he could explain to Zafi that there was no way he'd ever work for NJ7. The injustice of the situation tore at his mind. There was no reason for Zafi to kill him, but she wouldn't listen.

Jimmy jumped to his feet, ready to run, but Zafi's fingers appeared over the edge of the roof. She'd climbed back up for him.

"You know it's not that easy, killing me!" Jimmy shouted, backing away. There was a light rain refreshing his face, keeping every sense tingling. He told himself to stand firm, though his knees were trembling. Was it because they wanted him to run or because of fear? Zafi crawled on to the roof and looked up at Jimmy. There was menace in her eyes.

"By the time this fight is over," Jimmy went on, "they will have found us. And there's no way past the security cordon. You won't kill me and have a chance to escape. You're trapped."

Zafi raised an eyebrow and hissed, "One thing at a time."

Then she pounced. She moved with such well-directed pace that even though Jimmy knew she was coming, he couldn't get completely out of the way. Zafi was like a tiger, her eyes flashing in the dying light.

Jimmy dived to the side, but Zafi's hand snatched his collar. She dragged him three metres across the roof, then jumped, bringing Jimmy with her.

Jimmy had no idea what she had planned, but he was in her control now. He'd never imagined that anybody could move as fast as she could. Even with his programming pumping through him at full volume, he was virtually powerless against her. She was the wrong girl to have made into an enemy.

Together, they left the ground, Jimmy dangling in Zafi's grip like a rag doll. With her other hand she caught the claw of the crane. Jimmy gradually realised how she was going to get past the security cordon – in her situation, he might have done the same.

They swung through the air, the world spinning by in a grey blur. Zafi's momentum carried them high into the air. To Jimmy, it felt like being on a huge swing, except that somebody else was in control. Jimmy flailed his legs up at Zafi, like a circus trapeze artist, but she dodged his foot with a graceful sway.

As the crane claw reached the top of the arc, Zafi kicked out, sending them swinging back down on their giant pendulum with even greater velocity. The roof of the building lurched towards them. Jimmy's insides were churning. *How does Spider-man do this without puking?* he thought.

He reached out with his legs to try and catch something he could use to pull himself free of Zafi's hold, but she yanked him closer. Then she let go of the crane.

Suddenly, the world went silent except for the rushing of the wind in Jimmy's ears. Even his heartbeat seemed to stop. For a few seconds, the beauty of it overcame all of the pain and the terror. This was as close as man could come to flying. Jimmy's heart swelled with amazement.

It didn't last long.

They soared over the heads of the agents manning the security cordon, but they were still well below the sights of the aerial patrol above them. Jimmy braced himself. They were falling now, and from a considerable height. What if Zafi tried to use him to break her fall? But she was smarter than that. She had planned her escape meticulously and judged their flight perfectly.

In an alley three blocks away, Zafi and Jimmy plunged to earth. They landed precisely in the middle of a dumpster, specially packed not with rubbish but with polystyrene foam. It was like landing on cushions. Jimmy couldn't help smiling at Zafi's attention to detail, but he had no time to waste.

He spat some foam from his mouth and clambered out of the bin. Zafi had lost her grip on him when they landed. This was his chance to escape. As soon as his feet hit the pavement, he ran. He was out of the alley in a flash, but Zafi's steps rang out close behind him.

The street was packed with people – they were outside the security cordon now. Jimmy ducked his head and dodged through the crowds. The noise of the city filled his head, but he filtered it out until all he could hear was the rapid-fire pace of Zafi's feet. For a second it sounded almost as if there were two people chasing him. He didn't dare look back. That would slow him down. But he knew that if they kept running, Zafi was bound to catch him. She was faster.

He strained every muscle to put some distance between them, but he knew it was just a matter of time before that chop came down on the back of his neck. At the end of the street he hurdled a low grey wall, hardly breaking his stride. He had made it to Central Park. Grass stretched out in front of him, with a wooded area about 200 metres away. Maybe on the less-even terrain he'd stand more of a chance. Or maybe not.

He powered his way across the field with new determination. His breathing was heavy but regular. His mouth was dry and the rain coated his skin, but he didn't care. Groups of tourists stopped to watch them, amazed at how fast they were running, but to them it looked like two kids playing games. How could they know that they'd seen two of the world's most dangerous assassins fighting for supremacy?

Jimmy kept running, changing direction at every opportunity to counteract Zafi's greater speed. He made it into the wood, weaving between the trees. It was no good. He could almost feel Zafi's breath on his back. Tears pricked his eyes from the effort, but his programming kept him going, always digging deeper for that extra energy that would keep him going.

Finally, Jimmy dived into the air. His body braced rigid and his arms stretched out above his head. He splashed down into Central Park Lake.

The water was ice-cold, but it felt like wonderful relief. He plunged several metres down, already kicking with the efficiency and power of a turbine engine. After a few seconds he drew a gulp of water into his lungs. It tasted disgusting, almost burning his tongue with its bitterness, but he couldn't let that stop him. He knew it was his body's mechanism to keep him breathing underwater.

Zafi followed him into the lake without hesitation. Now there was nothing else Jimmy could do. If she was faster on land and faster in the water, it was time to turn and fight.

Jimmy flipped over suddenly. Zafi was taken by surprise, but it hardly showed. Straight away she made a dive for Jimmy's neck. Jimmy spun out of the way at the last split-second and Zafi found herself lost in a school of shocked fish. She shook them off, her hair tangling up around her head, even trapping some of the smaller fish. She glared at Jimmy in anger and for the first time Jimmy began to suspect that he might stand a chance against her. There was only one way to find out.

Jimmy spun round, generating enough energy to lash out a devastating kick. But instead of dodging, Zafi caught Jimmy's ankle a centimetre from her cheek. Then she used his own pace to throw him off-balance. He was sucked deeper into the water in the mini-whirlpool he'd created. The further down he went, the darker it became, and the thicker this ancient swamp was with reeds and mud.

Jimmy looked up. There was nowhere for him to go now. Beneath him was the bed of the lake. If he went to either side, Zafi could easily cut him off. And above him was Zafi herself, silhouetted against the faint light coming from the surface of the water. With the agility of an eel, she flipped over, raising her arms – she was ready to strike.

Jimmy braced himself, his brain churning. How long could he fend her off before she destroyed him? Just then, his eye was drawn to something else in the water. It was behind Zafi and speeding down towards her, spinning through the lake like a torpedo. It stirred up the water, sending clouds of silt in all directions.

Zafi hesitated, noticing Jimmy's expression. She looked over her shoulder. The missile crashed into her. Jimmy didn't wait to see what happened. He kicked for all he was worth to get back to the surface.

At last his head broke through into the air and he choked up a lungful of water. Every time he did that it still felt like he was going to throw up the lining of his chest. He rolled on to the bank, lying flat on his back for a second to catch his breath. He knew he had to move, but the water next to him was stirring with amazing force. Something was happening down there; something violent. Jimmy peered down. That instant, two figures leapt out of the water, thrashing at each other's throats.

Jimmy ducked behind a bush, watching as Zafi and her opponent made it to the bank opposite. Zafi's arms were whirring like propellers, spraying Central Park Lake for several metres around her. But it wasn't her Jimmy was looking at – it was who she was fighting. What Jimmy had thought at first was a missile when it had pelted into Zafi's back was now a living, breathing boy – Mitchell.

Jimmy gasped. The two of them were half in, half out of the water. Neither one was backing down, but neither had the upper hand either. For all Mitchell's incredible strength and determination, Zafi was moving so fast that only one in four of his blows connected. Then suddenly, he bent double and barrelled into Zafi with his entire body weight. She was knocked back and fell to the ground on the opposite bank.

Jimmy's legs were twitching. His whole body was tearing him away. The assassin in him would never have waited by the side of the lake for even a second. Yet Jimmy had just enough control. His mind was much clearer now that those images were no longer tormenting him.

Watching Zafi and Mitchell was so compelling that he could hardly blink. Mitchell loomed over Zafi. He raised his fist above his head. Zafi cowered. There was nothing she could do now. In her fear, she looked across the lake – to Jimmy. In that instant, Jimmy saw in her the same expression he had seen back at the Museum. It was the look of someone trapped. Not trapped physically – although Zafi was certainly boxed in by Mitchell's imposing frame. But it looked as if she herself were the cage, and something inside her was crying out for freedom.

Hardly knowing what he was doing, or why, Jimmy snatched a stone from the ground and jumped to his feet.

"Hey!" he yelled, before he could stop himself. Mitchell turned to look at him. Jimmy bent low and snapped his arm by his side, sending the stone fizzing across the surface of the water. It bounced on the lake three times, then jumped up, cracking into Mitchell's knee.

He didn't cry out, but even at a distance Jimmy saw him wince and list slightly to one side. In that moment, Zafi crawled backwards, out of Mitchell's reach and out of danger. She looked at Jimmy in disbelief. So did Mitchell. For less than a second the three of them stood absolutely still, sizing each other up, each one trying to work out the motives of the other two. Surely now Zafi must have understood that he wasn't working for NJ7, Jimmy thought. And did Mitchell realise that he had saved Jimmy from Zafi?

Before any of them moved, Jimmy looked directly at Zafi and called out, "If you need me, I'm a stone's throw away." His voice was low and calm.

Zafi smiled, then broke into a sprint. Mitchell hesitated for a second. His face was a picture of confusion, anger and disappointment. Jimmy had upset another of his missions. He headed quickly after Zafi, but Jimmy had no doubt that she would make it to safety – for now.

Finally, Jimmy dashed in the opposite direction. He didn't care where he was going, so long as he made it out of Central Park alive.

CHAPTER TWENTY-THREE - PROTECT THEM

Jimmy was sodden and shivering when he slumped against one of the park's low outer walls. It was only now that he remembered his radio set. He reached into his pocket and pulled it out. It too was dripping wet, but he had confidence that the Icom F-Series would still work after being underwater. He jammed his thumb down on the general alert key and waited.

Traffic buzzed along the road in front of him. There were tourists and businessmen waiting at the bus stop. He overheard one man in a sharp suit ask, "Do you think it's a conspiracy?"

"I heard it was a lone gunman," came the reply.

"That definitely means it's a conspiracy."

Jimmy deliberately shut out their words. It was the last thing he wanted to hear. He closed his eyes and revisited that moment – Mitchell and Zafi both staring at him. Didn't they realise they could fight against their programming? Didn't they *want* to?

Within six minutes a black Lincoln Sedan pulled up in front of him. The back door flew open even before it had come to a complete stop. Jimmy jumped in, not even bothering to shake off the rest of Central Park Lake that was still dripping from his skin and his clothes. Inside the car, pools of water gathered on the black leather.

Colonel Keays was next to him on the back seat, and sitting by the other door was Viggo. The driver was behind a perspex screen, guiding them smoothly through Manhattan.

"It was Zafi," Jimmy panted, before anyone could ask him anything. "She was going to kill my— She was going to kill the Prime Minister."

Should he tell them about how close he came to assassinating Grogan? Maybe that was best saved for later. Viggo grumbled something from the other side of the car, but Jimmy didn't catch what it was.

"Whoever this Zafi is," Keays croaked, "we can protect you. You have my promise."

"And my friends?" Jimmy asked. "And Georgie and Mum?"

Keays sighed, looking straight ahead out of the front of the car. "Of course," he reassured Jimmy. "You'll all be protected."

"Looked like you were protecting Ian Coates as well," Viggo snapped. Keays didn't turn to look at him, but Jimmy felt him tense up. "I saw your agents rush to him when he was hit," Viggo went on. "Whose side are you on?"

"Yours, of course," Keays barked.

"Then why don't you show it?" Viggo's voice filled the car. "Ian Coates is here, in New York – he's right in your lap. Are you just going to let him waltz back to London to carry on destroying Britain, and maybe even trample all over France while he's at it?" His fists were clenched and between each word his teeth ground together. But Keays was furious too.

"What do you expect me to do?" the American shouted.

"Kill Coates," came Viggo's whispered reply. "Then send agents to smash NJ7."

"There are laws—" Keays replied, but Viggo cut him off.

"Forget laws! What about what's right? NJ7 is an illegal organisation, and it's broken the law so many times you could easily get away with it. Anyway, nobody has to find out. Or doesn't the CIA do covert operations any more?"

Jimmy was stunned. He shifted uneasily. How different this Viggo was to the man Jimmy had first met, the man who believed in solving Britain's problems without violence.

The windows were steamed up now – it was the moisture from Jimmy's clothes mixed with the anger in the air. Keays took a deep breath. "One thing at a time," he groaned. "I'm not here to run your personal crusade against NJ7. For now I can only protect you."

"Protect me?" Viggo stormed. "I'm not some kid. I don't need protecting. Protect them." He waved his hand at Jimmy and turned to look out of the window. Jimmy felt his gesture like a bee sting. He owed Viggo so much. The man was right to feel angry. The only thing he'd had since Jimmy came into his life was pain and misery.

When Viggo turned back to them there was an even more intense anger in his voice.

"I left Saffron for your promises," he snarled. "I left her lying there, in a filthy back room in the middle of nowhere, with some dodgy doctor I hardly even know – and she was dying. I left because of your promises." Viggo choked on his words, hardly able to get them out. "I don't even know if she's still alive."

Jimmy wanted desperately to say something, to comfort the man or to bring him back to his senses. But Viggo's passion was overwhelming.

"Protection isn't good enough," Viggo went on. "I came to annihilate the people who harmed her."

Keays didn't know how to respond. He bowed his head and stared into his lap.

"There are bigger things going on here, Chris," he said, trying to sound calm. "Diplomacy, politics – there's a time for everything."

"Bigger things?" Viggo spat, his rage only building. "Don't talk to me about 'bigger things'. Don't you remember her being shot, Jimmy?"

Viggo's stare stabbed Jimmy like a syringe full of poison. Of course he remembered, but what could he say?

"Since the second it happened," Viggo stormed on, "I've thought of nothing else. We'd made it to the lift in the basement of the French Embassy, remember? There were dozens of NJ7 agents behind us, but we were going to make it. I really thought we were going to make it. You'd already made a hole in the roof of the lift. And I jumped up first." He clenched a fist and ground his teeth. His eyes glazed over, but there was passion running all the way through him. "I should never have jumped up first."

Jimmy felt his heart being crushed under the weight of Viggo's grief. He watched a tear brimming at the edge of the man's eye.

"Then you came up next," Viggo continued. "And you were so quick. I knew nothing could touch you." A smile flashed on to his face, but it was pure anguish. "She was right behind you. Do you remember the sound of the bullet when it tore through her muscles?"

Jimmy felt sick. He was pleading with himself to do something to interrupt the torture of reliving that event, but Viggo was unstoppable. Even Colonel Keays appeared mesmerised.

"That noise, Jimmy," Viggo sobbed. "It's been in my dreams every night. The feeling of her grip going weak when I caught her wrist – I can't wash it off."

"Miss Bennett was aiming for me," Jimmy whispered, hardly able to get his voice out of his throat.

"I know. But it's not your fault. It's NJ7. And I have to put it right. I don't care about diplomacy and politics. I'll crush them. Even if I have to do it on my own, I'll ring the neck of every last NJ7 agent on the planet, right up to Miss Bennett and Ian Coates."

Viggo wiped his face. He took a deep breath, then shouted, "Stop the car!"

"What?" Keays sat up. "But—"

"STOP THE CAR!"

The car slammed to a halt. Viggo pushed open his door, nearly thrusting it into a passing vehicle. Jimmy couldn't believe what was happening. He looked into Viggo's face, searching for something to say, some comforting words – anything that would make him stay. But nothing came. The noise and smell of city traffic flooded into the car. It was the perfect mirror of the conflict that wrenched Jimmy in two. *If he's going back to beat NJ7,* he thought, *I could go with him.* And yet his body stayed absolutely still.

"I'm sorry, Jimmy," Viggo whispered. Then his face was gone and the car door banged shut.

"Drive on, Kez," ordered Keays solemnly. "Get us back to Chinatown."

* * *

Jimmy stepped out of the car feeling like a bomb had gone off inside him. As soon as Keays had driven away, Jimmy rushed up the stairs of the Star of Manchuria and the story of everything that had happened poured out of him. But even while his mouth was moving and his words explained the events of the day, his head was buzzing with confusion.

"I can't believe it," gasped Georgie when he was done.

"Nor can I," Felix agreed, his mouth full of dried wontons and his fist rummaging in the packet. "The CIA is protecting me! It's awesome."

"I meant I can't believe Chris just left like that," said Georgie.

Jimmy's mother pushed herself up from the sofa and stepped over to the sink for a glass of water. The rush of the tap was the loudest noise in the room. Nobody knew what to say – Georgie and Felix on the floor, Felix's parents on the sofa. Jimmy was wrapped in a towel and leaning against the radiator.

"So what do we do now?" Felix's mum asked gently.

"We sit tight and wait," answered Felix's dad in his soft, deep tone. "That's all we can do. If this Colonel Keays says that he's going to protect us, then we should wait here until he's arranged where we're going and how we're getting there. That's right, isn't it,

Helen?" He looked up at Jimmy's mum. "I mean, I'm not a Secret Service agent, but that seems like the right thing to do."

"Do you think Chris'll be OK?" Georgie asked.

Helen Coates just downed her water, keeping her back to the others. She didn't reply.

Suddenly, the disasters of the day faded into the background for Jimmy. Nearly assassinating the President, hurtling through the air from a hijacked crane, being attacked and chased through Central Park by a French killing machine – at that moment, none of it seemed to hurt quite as much. But seeing his mother's expression was like digging a spike into his belly. For the first time she looked old. There was a sadness in her face that he had never seen before – even when his father had abandoned them.

"Come on," said Felix's mum, "we should all sort out what we're eating tonight."

The distraction was too late. Georgie and Jimmy glanced at each other. They'd both seen their mother's grief.

"That man's such an idiot sometimes," Helen sighed at last. "Does he think he can storm back into Britain and bring down NJ7 on his own? He's going to get himself killed. What a selfish idiot. I can't let him do it. I'm sorry. I have to go after him. He ran away twelve years ago and I'm not letting him do it again." She screwed up her face for an instant, then pushed away her anger. "You two stay here," she ordered sternly, looking from Georgie to Jimmy. "Don't move until I'm back or the CIA comes to get you. Hear me?"

"We'll be fine," Georgie insisted. "Won't we, Jimmy?"

Jimmy nodded.

"Whatever happens, I'll be back here by tomorrow morning," his mother promised. "OK? Even if I can't track him down."

"He'll be heading for the airport." Jimmy said. "Go now and you can catch him."

Helen looked to her friends, Olivia and Neil Muzbeke. She didn't need to say anything – her expression asked for their advice.

"We'll look after Jimmy and Georgie," said Olivia in a comforting voice. "Go. Bring Chris back."

"OK." Helen took a deep breath. "I can't believe he's making me do this." She hugged Jimmy and Georgie, then announced, "You're in charge, Felix. Look after this lot for a few hours."

Felix saluted, but his smile was uncertain. With less than ten minutes of preparation, Helen Coates was out of the door.

CHAPTER TWENTY-FOUR- AMATEUR REVENGE

"They've done it again," Felix exclaimed, tearing open his cardboard container of chicken chow mein. "Look how big the box is, then look at what's inside." He tipped it forwards for Jimmy to see. "It's only half full."

Jimmy dipped in with his chopsticks to steal a chunk of chicken.

"And getting less full by the second," he mumbled.

"Hey!" Felix pulled his box back. "You've got your own. I wasn't offering. I was just saying, you know, they fool you by making the box big. We should tell on them to the CIA. It's well unfair."

"Don't believe everything you see," Neil Muzbeke chipped in from the sofa. "Now where's ours? Don't make me come down there for it."

Felix had taken charge of fetching the food again. He was handing out the boxes from a plastic bag on the floor.

"But Mrs Kai-Ro knows me," he insisted, passing his father a box of chilli beef. "I'm a special customer now. She even showed me her stick insects."

Jimmy eyed his carton suspiciously.

"Not in the food, stupid," Felix reassured him. "She keeps them in a tank. Like pets. There was this one that looked dead, but it was actually just a stick. But then there was this other one and that was actually a stick insect, but that also looked dead. Then another one..."

"Is there an end to this story?" Georgie cut in.

"Wait, I'm not done." Felix was waving his chopsticks about frantically. Jimmy didn't realise anybody could get so worked up about stick insects.

"And this last one," Felix went on at a rapid pace, "I thought it was just a stick, but it was actually a stick insect, except it was, like, dead."

Jimmy laughed, almost snorting noodles up his nose. It was a wonderful feeling to have something to laugh about.

"Yeah," Felix added. "She had to take that one out of the tank."

"Sounds like you've gone out of your tank," Jimmy muttered with a smile. "So what else did you lot do all day – apart from flirting with an old Korean woman?"

They had spent so long that evening going over and over what had happened to Jimmy that he was relieved to be thinking about something else.

"First me and Georgie set up a rota," Felix began. "You know – to take it in turns to keep watch, in case those two guys who attacked you came back."

Jimmy felt another lurch of anxiety in his stomach. Just when he thought he was out of danger, Felix had reminded him that even this 'safehouse' was far from safe.

"But nobody turned up," said Felix, "and we got bored. So mostly we..." He stopped himself. Jimmy could never have known it, but what Felix was about to say was that he and Georgie had spent a lot of time discussing Jimmy – and the identity of Jimmy's father. After an awkward pause, Felix finally finished his sentence.

"...we gave up and watched TV."

Felix's mother rolled her eyes. "Sounds like America's already having an effect on you," she groaned.

Felix responded with a half-smile. Georgie reached out and hugged her brother round the neck. Jimmy was taken aback by the sudden display of affection.

In the background the news rumbled on. An expert from the American Government was busy explaining how a crazy gunman acting alone could have hidden himself in the roof of MoMA.

Two men marched through Chinatown together without saying a word, keeping their heads down. It was the middle of the night, but there were still a few people about and they didn't want to attract attention. They were dressed inconspicuously in jeans and hoodies – black is no camouflage when the streets of Chinatown are plastered with flashing neon signs. One was carrying an umbrella. They were both wearing black leather gloves.

When they reached the Star of Manchuria they stopped, not even needing to look at each other to know what the plan was. The one with the umbrella unscrewed the handle, a big tortoiseshell hook. It was attached to a thin black cord that extended from inside the body of the umbrella. The other man nodded at him now as they waited for the street to clear. A drunken couple tottered round the corner. Their steps echoed against the buildings and seemed to beat out every excruciating second. At last, they faded.

Then, in one swift movement, the man with the umbrella lobbed the hook up to the second-floor window. His aim was perfect. The cord reeled out from the rest of the umbrella in his hands and the hook caught on the window ledge. Neither man hesitated now. Any moment somebody could walk into that street and see them. They braced their legs against the building and, one after the other, pulled themselves up the cord.

In seconds they were at the window. The two tall wiry figures waited here, both checking that the street was still clear. Only now did they disguise their faces, pulling balaclavas over their heads. Neither said a word when he noticed the other man's hands shaking. Nerves were natural. They knew the power of the target that waited for them inside.

Jimmy wasn't sleeping. How could he after everything that had happened to him that day? And now he was worried about his mother too. He ached to hear that door opening and his mother coming back with Viggo, all smiles. Then the CIA would hide them and they could pretend to be a family. Or maybe, Jimmy thought, it wouldn't be pretending.

He wished he'd never let Viggo get out of the Sedan. No matter how furious the man had been, everything Viggo had said made sense, didn't it? Jimmy was certain that he was a good man, even if what he was doing didn't come from his sense of justice or belief in democracy any more, but from his anger. That didn't mean his actions were wrong, did it?

Maybe it *was* time somebody tried to crush NJ7. But Jimmy had already had his chance to take revenge on his ex-father. Something had stopped him then. Now the same feeling told him that perhaps attacking NJ7 the way they'd attacked him wouldn't be the best revenge. So what would be?

Suddenly, he sat up in bed. He'd heard a noise. At first his heart jumped – was it his mother coming back? He quickly realised that was just wishful thinking.

Next to him, Felix and Neil hadn't stirred. Neil Muzbeke's snores filled the room, but Jimmy had to listen past them, searching to identify whatever it was he had heard. Ever so gently, he shook Felix.

"Wha...?!" Felix clammed up immediately when he saw Jimmy's finger on his lips. Jimmy waited, listening hard, then he pointed at the window. That was where the noise was coming from – his senses screamed it at him, though he would never have been able to explain why. It was instinct.

Felix rolled over and elbowed his father. The man just spluttered and snored a little louder. Felix tried again, while Jimmy padded softly to the window. Neil Muzbeke wasn't coming round.

"Dad!" Felix whispered, way too loud.

"Shh!" Jimmy insisted.

"Wha...?!" Neil Muzbeke lumbered over, his eyes bleary. Felix clamped his hand down over his father's mouth before any more noise could escape.

The three of them mimed instructions to each other, Jimmy taking command. Felix and Neil backed into the far corners of the room, while Jimmy crouched under the window. His heart was thudding in his chest, but slowly, under control. Every bit of him tingled, right down to the ends of his fingers. His brain was held in that warm glow – his programming.

Fragments of information filtered through to his consciousness – assailants waiting outside. Two of them. Amateurs. Probably the same two he had seen off the night before.

The noise they'd made gave them away – these were no soldiers. Jimmy remembered how artfully Zafi had broken into the Bed and Breakfast place in England. Compared to her, these guys were a circus parade. But that didn't mean they weren't a threat. Anyone who wants you dead is a threat.

At last it came – the smashing of glass. Fragments peppered Jimmy's head, but he'd been expecting that. The intruders were smart enough to muffle the noise by holding up a blanket against the window, but now that same blanket was blocking their view.

Jimmy plucked two shards of glass from the floor – one in each hand. Then he swivelled, so fast that the two men were still standing on the window ledge. With both hands at the same time, Jimmy slashed the backs of two of the four ankles. He heard both men stifle their cries of pain. Blood spattered Jimmy's face. He dropped the glass and grabbed the men by their feet – without Jimmy catching them they both would have fallen to the pavement.

Jimmy yanked the men into the room, flinging them over his shoulders. They crashed on to the bed, utterly dazed. As soon as they landed, Felix and Neil pounced. They bundled blankets over the two masked intruders, smothering their limbs so tightly that they couldn't move. Felix had a bit more trouble than his father – he didn't have the advantage of Neil's body weight – so Jimmy wiped his face with the back of his sleeve and threw himself in as well.

It was barely a minute before the two intruders stopped struggling. They knew they'd been caught out. Jimmy reached out of the window again and pulled in their extending cord. Still without saying anything, he rolled the two men over and bound their hands. Finally, he sat them up on the mattresses, back to back.

"You better go and check the girls are OK," he instructed Felix. "Bring them down – just in case." Felix dashed out to do his job.

"Who are they, Jimmy?" asked Neil Muzbeke. "NJ7? CIA? Mafia?!"

Jimmy shook his head. "No way," he muttered.

"Who then?"

"Let's ask them."

CHAPTER TWENTY-FIVE- SILVERCUP

Jimmy reached forwards and peeled off the two balaclavas, revealing two red faces. The men were surprisingly young – probably early or mid-twenties, with hair crushed by their disguises and egos bruised by their speedy defeat. One was blond with a wispy beard. The other was dark with sharp features and looked slightly younger.

"You'll pay, Jimmy Coates," seethed the younger man. His accent was a polished English.

"Who are you?" Jimmy shot back. "And what do you think I owe you?"

Before they could answer, the door opened and in burst Georgie, with Felix's mother close behind.

"Oh my God!" Georgie shrieked. Jimmy was startled to see a huge smile on her face. "How's Eva? Is she here?"

"Eva?" Jimmy gasped.

"Eva?" gasped the two men on the floor. "Eva's dead."

Jimmy stared at them in horror. Everybody froze.

"You killed her," said the fair-haired man.

"What?" Jimmy felt like he'd been plunged into a bath full of ice.

"That's why we're here."

Jimmy was staggered. "I don't know what you're talking about," he pleaded, almost to himself. His blood was flooded with horror. What if he had killed without even knowing it? And killed someone who was a friend?

"Jimmy didn't kill anybody," Georgie said quickly. "And especially not Eva. Why would he do that? She's taking a massive risk to help us."

"Hey!" Jimmy shouted to his sister. "Careful what you say. We don't know who these men are yet."

"Of course we do," Georgie replied. "This is Quinn and Rick – Eva's brothers."

Jimmy stared at them. It felt like the cogs in his brain were struggling to churn through tar.

"I think somebody should explain what's going on," suggested Felix's mother calmly. "And can we put something over that window? It's freezing in here."

Neil rushed to hang the blanket over the empty curtain rail. It didn't make a huge difference, but at least now the wind wasn't blustering in everybody's faces.

"Right," Olivia went on. "Now one at a time."

Georgie was quickest off the mark. "These are Eva's brothers," she began. "But I've no idea what they're doing here. What *are* you doing here?" She turned to them. "Who told you Eva was dead? She's working for Miss Bennett at NJ7."

"What?" Quinn was disgusted. The hairs on his chin trembled. "But Eva was abducted by you, and then Miss Bennett said she was dead."

"Wait, wait," Jimmy interrupted. "First of all, Eva was not 'abducted'. She insisted on coming with us and we couldn't get rid of her."

"Hey!" Georgie protested. "That's mean."

"Well, it's true – I'm sorry."

"Yeah, it is kind of true," Felix agreed. "I couldn't stand her either." Then he quickly added, "But I can now – she's cool. Well, you know, for a girl."

Jimmy was thankful for Felix's support and carried on explaining.

"The only people who would kill Eva are NJ7," he said cautiously. "Maybe they've found out about her being on our side."

Rick was aghast. "So you're telling us Eva is still alive, and working for Miss Bennett at NJ7?"

Jimmy, Georgie and Felix nodded as one. Rick and Quinn peered over their shoulders at each other. Eventually, Quinn broke the silence.

"I can't believe it." There were tears creeping down his face.

"Wait," snapped his brother. "How come you're so sure this is true?"

"You'd rather trust Miss Bennett than these guys?" Quinn answered. "Georgie and Eva were best friends. She was always coming round."

"We *are* friends," Georgie corrected him. "I'm sure Eva's still alive. She's too clever for them to find her out."

"I hope you're right," whispered Quinn.

"Quick," Jimmy urged. "Get something to bandage their ankles."

He rushed to untie the two brothers, while Felix fetched two cushion covers from the sofa in the next room.

"I'll never forget what Miss Bennett told us," said Quinn. "We knew something was wrong. We hadn't heard anything about where Eva was or even who was looking for her. But nobody would answer our questions or let us get anywhere near Miss Bennett to find out from her. It was impossible. In the end, we had to threaten to chain ourselves to a pod on the London Eye before she agreed to meet us."

Jimmy listened closely as Quinn and Rick secured the makeshift bandages round their wounds.

"We met her in the lobby of the MI6 building," Quinn went on. "The *lobby*, Jimmy – they wouldn't even let us into an office." Jimmy could see the ferocity in his eyes. "We all went – us two and Mum and Dad. We were going to ask questions and stamp our feet. None of us was expecting bad news. But then she told us.

Straight out. I can still remember the words she used." There was a catch in Quinn's voice as he spoke. He was doing everything he could to hold his emotions back.

"She said, 'I have some terrible news' – that's when I knew. Even before she finished the sentence. It was in the way she spoke. So cold. And she wouldn't look any of us in the eyes. 'Nobody is to blame,' she said. 'It's a horrible tragedy. Eva is dead. She died in the name of her country.'" Quinn shook his head. His lips were trembling. Next to him, Rick held his head in his hands.

"Nobody said anything at first," Quinn explained in a whisper. "Just silence. It went on forever. Then Mum collapsed. She just fell down and Dad had to catch her. Then she started screaming. I think I probably did too. I don't know. It's all blurred after that. But I remember Rick standing frozen next to me and the unbelievable anger burning in here." He jabbed his thumb into his solar-plexus.

Rick nodded his agreement. "I remember shouting," he said. "But I don't know what I said. I couldn't control myself. I probably would have tried to rip that woman's throat open if Quinn hadn't pulled me away."

"She muttered something about counsellors, I think," Quinn added. "But we weren't interested. I just knew I had to get Mum home as quickly as possible, then do something to put things right."

"They told us Eva died for her country," Rick spat. His voice was twisted with bitterness. "So we decided somebody should die for her."

They looked up at Jimmy, but as soon as they saw him, their expressions changed from fury to confusion. They stared into Jimmy's face, completely fascinated.

"You're so human," said Rick. "I thought you were some kind of machine or robot."

Jimmy looked away. Hearing himself described like that still stung and he hated the way Rick was staring at him.

"We were going to kill you," Rick went on, his voice growing softer and softer. "How could we have been so stupid? We were going to kill a child?" He turned to his older brother.

"I'm so sorry," said Quinn, choking back his emotion. "We thought you deserved it. We were acting on what we thought was true – you can't blame us."

"He can blame us," Rick countered quickly, "and he should. We should have known better. I'm sorry, Jimmy."

Jimmy nodded uncomfortably. It was the first time anybody had tried to kill him and then apologised about it. *Better to apologise for nothing than kill me for nothing*, he thought.

"It's not your fault," Jimmy mumbled. "It's NJ7. Miss Bennett lies to everybody to get her own way – to get the Government's way. They're the real enemy."

Quinn and Rick nodded solemnly.

"Stay with us tonight," Georgie suggested.

"No, it's OK," said Quinn, wiping his face and taking a deep breath. "We've got a room at the hostel on East 14th. We'll stay there until we can get a flight back to London. If there's a chance that Eva's still alive, then we have to get back to England and find her."

"But if you ever need anything," his brother added, "you can call on us."

The two of them stood up wearily. The pain from their injured ankles and their confusion made them far less agile now than when they had taken Jimmy by surprise the night before.

They didn't stay long after that. As soon as they'd said a warm goodbye to everybody – and apologised again – they were gone. The others were left silent. To Jimmy, it didn't seem like there was anything left to say.

Neil Muzbeke soon found a big enough piece of discarded crate at the back of the restaurant to patch up the window. Jimmy swept up the glass. Soon he was shivering under his blankets.

He knew that he should have felt safer now. But if anything, he felt even more uneasy than he had before. It wasn't just Quinn and Rick's terrible ordeal that disturbed him. It was something tugging away at the back of his mind, like a dull pain, steadily increasing in intensity.

He finally fell asleep with one question swirling round his head: how come Eva's brothers had been able to find him, but, so far, NJ7 hadn't?

Jimmy's eyes burst open and his pupils rapidly dilated. His lungs hauled in a deep breath. *SILVERCUP*. What did that mean? The word buzzed round his head. Then he realised it wasn't the word – it was an image. Even with his eyes open, he could see it: SILVERCUP written in huge, old-fashioned red letters. The top of the word was flat, while the lower edge of the letters curved up to form an arch. Seeing it made his eyes burn.

Jimmy's despair churned inside him. Just when he thought he'd finished with the pain of having images in his head, this came along – and it was so much stronger than the K or the 53 or the rainbow stripes had been. He rubbed his eyes and clutched at his head. Maybe he was just overtired. But the more he tried to relax, the more clearly defined the letters of Silvercup became. And it wasn't alone. Within seconds, another image swamped his brain: four slim turrets, each one painted in three bands: red, white, then red again.

No, Jimmy urged internally. *Get out*. But his brain wasn't finished. There was one more image and it came with that intense feeling of dread. It was a ruin. It looked like a small castle, with brown stones and pointed gothic arches above the windows. Except in Jimmy's mind it was abandoned and overgrown. Grey tentacles of ivy attacked the brickwork. Jimmy felt like his brain was suffering the same way – these images grew within it, creeping into every corner, attacking his thoughts. He jumped up and shook out every limb.

"Come on," he hissed under his breath, and told himself over and over that it was just his imagination. But he didn't believe it. The images felt almost more real than the room around him. They swallowed up everything he saw and twisted it into the shape of his vision: SILVERCUP, four red and white towers, the ruin. Jimmy shivered.

"What's up?" It was Felix. "What time is it?"

Jimmy didn't answer. In silence he walked into the other room. Felix followed, leaving his father snoring. Jimmy paced the room, like a wild beast in a cage.

"You all right?" Felix asked, his face still bleary with sleep. The only light was from the neon signs outside the window. They cast weird shadows across the walls and gave both boys faces like demons.

"More images," Jimmy panted. They were so intense in his head that even speaking was difficult. Instead, he went back to grab his notebook and the pens he kept by the mattress. He came back scribbling frantically, his head cocked to one side and his eyes utterly focused.

As soon as one page was full he flipped over to the next one and kept drawing. Felix looked over his shoulder.

"SILVERCUP?" he asked. "What's that mean?"

Jimmy shook his head in desperation. "How am I meant to know?" he blurted. "Last time I thought my head was telling me an assassin was going to kill the President."

"It was right, wasn't it?" Felix pointed out.

"Yeah, but the assassin was me." He threw his notebook to the floor. "Who knows what this new stuff is going to force me to do?"

Felix tried to get Jimmy to sit down, but his friend was having none of it.

"You don't understand!" Jimmy whispered in a rage. "It's like there's somebody else in here." He pounded his head. "They're controlling me. Getting me to do anything they want. I'm not putting up with it any more." His eyes were turning red. "I have to stop it!"

Suddenly, Jimmy dropped to his knees and cried out in pain.

"What is it?" Felix asked desperately. "Are you OK?"

Jimmy's hand pressed against his temple.

"Another attack?" Felix rushed to the sink and fetched a glass of water. His hands were shaking, spilling large drops all over the floor. Jimmy took the glass and downed it in one, then threw himself forward on to his hands and knees.

"Thanks," he gasped. "Sorry."

"It's OK," Felix whispered. "It's not you. It's not your fault."

Jimmy wiped his face with the back of his sleeve and very slowly drew himself up on to his feet. He stared out of the window, taking deeper and deeper breaths. When he spoke, his voice was hardly audible. "Whatever it takes, I have to stop this."

Then, behind them, came a deep, clear voice. It was an old voice, but distinguished – and English.

"I think I can help you with that."

Jimmy and Felix spun round. The door of the apartment was open. In the doorway stood one man neither of them had ever expected to see again.

CHAPTER TWENTY-SIX - FAMILIAR FACE

Jimmy's stomach lurched. He felt like he was going to choke on his own breath.

"Aren't you..." gasped Felix. He couldn't finish his sentence.

Before them stood a tall man, whose frail body was wrapped in a thick tweed overcoat. It smelled like it was rotting. Round his neck was a long striped scarf, and a heavy cloth cap was pulled down nearly over his eyes. But it was unmistakably him – Dr Kasimit Higgins.

This was the scientist who had led the NJ7 team that designed the assassins all those years ago. Jimmy gathered his composure.

"Where's your white coat, doctor?" he asked bitterly.

"Don't blame me, Jimmy," Dr Higgins croaked in reply. "I thought I was creating something truly great. And I'm still not convinced I wasn't right."

His eyes twinkled, but the neon light cast up at his

face brought out the deep holes that had once been his cheeks, and the black bags under the caves of his eyes. Every wrinkle looked like an abyss.

"So NJ7 hasn't caught you yet then," said Jimmy, full of scorn.

"And they never will," Higgins replied. "They trained me. I'm uncatchable – a ghost."

His lips were almost white, but they creased into a narrow smile, revealing the black and yellow stones of his teeth. He took a step forwards.

"Stay where you are," Jimmy ordered.

Dr Higgins froze. "I'm not afraid," he whispered. "You can't harm me, Jimmy. You know that."

Jimmy kept his face rigid. It took so much effort. Inside him, his programming was spreading a weird warmth, dulling his anger. It was as if it was trying to make him feel happy – against his own judgement.

"But," the doctor continued, "you should know as well that I would never do anything to harm you. You're my proudest achievement."

"Get out," Jimmy insisted. *I'm not anybody's achievement but my own*, he thought. "Go and build more misery. I never want to see you again."

"I'm here to help. Don't you want to know what's happening to you?"

Jimmy didn't have anything to say. His heart leapt at the possibility of at last getting some answers, but he refused to show it.

"You're having visions," Dr Higgins went on. "Images. In your head. Am I right?"

Jimmy held himself absolutely still.

"And attacks," blurted Felix.

"I knew it!" Dr Higgins lit up. "And headaches, yes? They come like lightning bolts straight into your brain." He tapped his temple with the contorted bone that passed for a finger. His other hand stayed in his pocket.

"What's happening to me?" Jimmy rasped, his curiosity at last breaking through his anger. He fought back the tears.

Dr Higgins' eyes darted around the room. "Not here," he said under his breath. "They might be listening."

A chill juddered up Jimmy's spine. "You're paranoid," he insisted. "This is a safehouse."

Dr Higgins raised an eyebrow. "You won't think it's so safe when you hear what I've got to say," he announced. "What sort of safehouse can an old man break into with failing eyes and only one hand?" He took both hands out of his pockets. In his left hand he proudly displayed a length of wire, bent into a spike that he'd obviously used to pick the locks. But his other hand wasn't even visible beneath a huge ball of stained, yellow bandaging.

Jimmy looked away. He didn't need reminding of the time he'd witnessed Dr Higgins experimenting on Mitchell's brother. The old man's hand had been badly burned by his own laser.

"And what sort of safehouse is it," the doctor when on, "when two untrained boys can follow you here and attack you – not once, but twice?"

Jimmy gulped.

"Yes, I saw them," said Dr Higgins. "I've been watching."

"So if you can find us, and Eva's brothers can find us," Felix began slowly, "how come NJ7 can't find us?"

"Oh, they could," whispered Higgins. "If they were looking."

Felix and Jimmy looked at each other, growing more confused by the second.

"Now do you want to hear what I have to say?" the doctor asked.

Jimmy felt his head nodding even before he'd thought about the question.

"Good," said the doctor. "There's a taxi waiting downstairs."

"Felix," Jimmy said in a rush, pulling on some jeans and a sweater, "stay here. Look after your dad."

"What?" his friend protested. "You can't go!"

"I'll be back soon."

"That's what your mum said."

Jimmy paused. Was it crazy to go out alone into the night with Dr Higgins? Maybe. But Jimmy needed answers. What's more, he felt secure knowing that Dr Higgins was the one man in the world too proud of his own creation to ever cause Jimmy harm. Jimmy tried to smile at Felix and gripped his shoulder to reassure him. Felix shook his head, worry all over his features.

"Be careful," he whispered. "Come back alive."

"They're not trying to find you any more because they think they can control you." Dr Higgins announced.

"What?" Jimmy gasped, but even as the word left his lips, he knew that the doctor must be right. That's exactly what it felt like – somebody getting inside his head to convince him of something, forcing him to act in a way he didn't want to.

The taxi had brought them a few streets north, to Grand Central Station. After that, Jimmy had had to stay sharp to keep up. The old man might have been withered and hunched over, but he moved well. They'd come straight to the underbelly of the whole station complex – Grand Central Oyster Bar. It was two floors down, beneath the main hall, well out of sight of satellite surveillance, and the tiled walls would make it almost impossible for anybody trying to eavesdrop on their conversation.

"And as soon as they think they've got you controlled," Dr Higgins went on, "they'll go to Chinatown and pick up your friends. That safehouse is no hiding place. Too many people coming in and out all day. After we're done here, go back to your friends and get everybody out of there."

Jimmy didn't know how to react. Dr Higgins was speaking so casually, but his words stabbed like daggers at Jimmy's heart. He started frantically thinking about where they could all go. He cursed the CIA for being so slow at organising their protection, but at the same time he realised it was a big task to create new lives for all of them from scratch.

"Are you going to eat those?" Dr Higgins asked, pointing at the plate of a dozen raw Rockaway oysters in front of Jimmy. Jimmy wasn't even hungry – especially not for food that looked like it had been sneezed out of a giant's nose.

The Oyster Bar resembled an ancient cavern, with tiled domes low over their heads, as if any minute there might be bats flapping about them. It was dark, with rows of white tables bouncing what light there was straight up into people's faces. There were only a few customers. *Who comes for oysters in the middle of the night?* Jimmy wondered to himself.

The doctor reached across and plucked one oyster at a time off Jimmy's plate.

"I love these. I have to – it's the easiest food to eat with one hand." He waved his bandages in Jimmy's face.

"Yeah, well, it's a bit early for my breakfast," Jimmy muttered. A knot was forming in his stomach. He didn't want to waste time before he could get his friends to safety.

Dr Higgins eagerly wolfed down another oyster, tearing at the sachets of ketchup with his teeth, then slathering Tabasco sauce and lemon juice all over his plate.

"When I noticed the power cuts across parts of the UK and America," he explained, keeping his voice so low it was barely audible, "I thought something was up. Then there was the interference with vital radio networks, grounding so many commercial flights. I realised something must be disrupting the grid. And usually that something is the Secret Service." He wiped his mouth on the back of his sleeve, then guzzled another oyster. Drips of lemon juice oozed down his chin, but he didn't care. He was too excited about what he was telling Jimmy.

"Then when I heard about what happened this afternoon, I realised you must be in town and connected the two. But why try to kill the Prime Minister? That's the only thing that confused me. I thought, surely NJ7 wants the *President* killed to try and get a new administration more sympathetic to supporting them against France. Why would they kill the Prime Minister? But then I realised something must have gone wrong. You weren't there for the Prime Minister, were you?"

Jimmy just blinked, dazzled by the overload of information.

"I knew it!" exclaimed the doctor. "You were there for the President! Once that fell into place I was almost certain – I thought to myself, what if NJ7 has been sending out a signal to try and influence Jimmy's actions? It's very clever really."

"A signal?" Jimmy was trying to keep track of Dr Higgins' thoughts, but they came so fast and so quietly, it was like being lost in a snowstorm.

"I just haven't worked out how they would transmit a strong enough signal across an area large enough to make sure you were in its net. You'd need a subsystem of transmitters."

"The cellphone mast..." Jimmy gasped. At last he was catching up. He remembered the mast on the roof of MoMA and what it had done to him.

"Yes, yes," Dr Higgins hissed, "that's so obvious. That's how they did it."

"They're still doing it," Jimmy announced.

"I'm sorry, Jimmy, I'm a little deaf. Did you say they're still transmitting a signal?"

Jimmy pulled out one of his pens from his pocket. He grabbed a napkin and in red felt tip he drew the four long columns, with their distinctive colouring: red at the base, white in the middle, red again at the top.

"These images are new," Jimmy explained, "and I can't get them out of my head. What does it mean this time?"

Next to the turrets he sketched the ruin, then wrote SILVERCUP in that old-fashioned lettering – he had never been able to draw lettering so carefully before.

His grip on the pen was tense enough to rip through the napkin in a few places.

"I don't know what this means, Jimmy," the doctor sighed. "And this is a fresh signal?"

"Look," Jimmy replied, nodding. Full of frustration, he pulled his notebook out of his back pocket and slammed it down on the table. "I saw nothing but these for days." He flicked through the early pages. "And I realised almost too late that they were telling me to..." he dropped his voice right down, "you know – kill President Grogan. So, like, what do all these mean?" He flipped to the newest drawings in the book. "I have to find out before I..." He tailed off, not wanting to even contemplate what the images might force him to do this time.

"Relax," Dr Higgins urged. "You've managed to overcome your programming several times now. You can do it again." He looked at Jimmy for a long time. His eyes were grey discs, flashing with mystery. "You won't be able to do it as you get older, but do you realise how amazing it is that you've done it at all? You're a remarkable boy, Jimmy. The hardware in you is a thousand times more complex than a super-computer. It's controlling organic materials and growing them according to a specific formula. It isn't manipulating an easy, clean material like metal. There's no metal in you."

Jimmy thought for a second. That didn't fit in with something he remembered.

"What about the chip?" he asked.

"The chip?" said Dr Higgins. "You mean the chip that programmed the laser when it adjusted your DNA? Sure, there were metal components in that, but that's not you, is it?"

"But my mum told me the chip was implanted in me as an embryo to oversee my development and then it was absorbed into my body."

"Ah, your mum." The doctor sighed again and leaned back, looking far off into nowhere. "Well Jimmy, I'm afraid that was a small lie I told her nearly twelve yeas ago. It's important for every mother to feel like her child is unique."

Another lie, thought Jimmy. *Why am I not surprised?* A bitter taste rose in his mouth. *38 per cent human and 99 per cent lies.*

"Your body wouldn't assimilate a metal chip," Dr Higgins went on. "It would have ejected it. And what would be the point? It's your DNA that controls how you grow and that was already pre-programmed."

"So the chip isn't in me?"

"No."

"So where is it?"

The response was only silence.

CHAPTER TWENTY-SEVEN- TIME AVENGES

For a second, Dr Higgins had the expression of a lost toddler. Was his massive intellect slipping away, Jimmy wondered. This was a man who could remember so much, and yet now he had no idea about the location of this vital piece of military hardware. The old man shrugged off the question and picked up Jimmy's notebook again, diverting attention from his failings.

"I can't work these images out, Jimmy," he muttered, then finished off his last oyster. "But it's almost definitely a trap. They'll lure you somewhere to finish you off. You're better off not knowing what all this means."

"You're useless!" Jimmy yelled. "This is in my head!" He rose from his stool and it clattered to the floor behind him. His words echoed round the bar. The two lone customers at the other end of the room raised their eyes for a second and both shook their heads. The waitress lumbered over, wiping her hands on her apron. She was a short, middle-aged woman, with a pencil sticking out of the bun at the back of her head and an attitude hanging round her neck like a medal.

"Everything OK over here?" she croaked in a New York accent so thick it could have insulated a bomb shelter. Jimmy smiled, trying to look innocent. He set his stool up again and took a seat.

The waitress gathered their plates, pausing when she picked up Jimmy's napkin. "You draw this?" she snapped.

Jimmy nodded.

"So you like Big Allis, huh?" asked the waitress.

"Alice who?" Jimmy shrugged.

"You know," the waitress replied. "This place with the funnels." She held up the napkin and pointed to the red and white columns in Jimmy's picture. "It's the big power station over in Brooklyn. But it looks like you drew this from the tramway heading to Roosevelt Island. Am I right? Is that where you drew this?"

Jimmy nodded very slowly, bemused.

"Yeah, I knew I was right," the waitress beamed. "Every New Yorker knows this view." She was about to leave, but then she noticed the other side of the napkin. "Hey," she exclaimed, a look of delight on her face, "you've drawn the ruin down the south end as well. I knew you'd been to Roosevelt Island." She winked as she turned away. "Cute kid."

Jimmy took in a sharp breath. Roosevelt Island. That's where he was being led.

"You go there and you'll die," whispered Dr Higgins, reading Jimmy's face. Jimmy stared across the room, not focusing on anything.

"Maybe that's the only way this will end," he croaked, his voice suddenly not working properly. Dr Higgins said something in response, but Jimmy blocked it out. In his head the word SILVERCUP flashed over and over, like the signs over those noodle bars in Chinatown. He saw the ruin. He saw the towers that he now knew were the funnels of Big Allis Power Station. The images danced behind his eyes, scorching the inside of his head.

"It will never end," Jimmy said under his breath. "We'll always be on the run. Every day – always in danger. Even in hiding with the CIA, we'd live the rest of our lives in fear. In pain. They could torture me with *this* for the rest of my life." He put his head in his hands and rattled his skull.

"Jimmy..." Dr Higgins tried to interrupt, but there were too many thoughts shouting for attention in Jimmy's ears.

"My friends," he muttered, "my family. I have to put this right. It's all my fault." As soon as he heard the words, he flinched. "No, wait." He pulled himself upright and turned to Dr Higgins. He stared at him. "It's not *all* my fault, is it?"

"Jimmy," the doctor began, a sudden grief oozing from his eyes. "If I'd known..."

"That's no excuse," Jimmy interrupted. "You *should* have known."

"You're cruel."

"But I'm right." Jimmy's face was clenched in quiet anger.

"Yes," Dr Higgins admitted. He hung his head, exposing the back of his neck, where his skin was sallow – almost grey. "They say that time avenges," he whispered, "but sometimes it needs a helping hand." He paused, staring into the table. "You should kill me. I deserve it."

"Who'd be sorry?" Jimmy snapped.

"The women." Dr Higgins raised his head slightly and peeked at Jimmy out of the corner of his eye with a glimmer of delight. It made Jimmy feel physically sick. How could he joke like this when there were lives at stake?

With renewed energy, Dr Higgins knocked his head back and downed the last drop of his apple juice.

"Ahh," he sighed. "Nothing better with oysters than a cool apple juice."

Jimmy was so furious he was ready to slam the man's head on to the table. He could feel his rage feeding his muscles. But then Dr Higgins wiped his mouth with the back of his sleeve and Jimmy froze. He replayed the action in his imagination and studied the man's face.

"Who's my-my—" Jimmy couldn't get the muscles in his throat to let the words out. "Who's my father?"

Dread beat in Jimmy's chest. Dr Higgins stared at him, taken aback by the question. It was a few seconds before he spoke. They were the longest seconds of Jimmy's life.

"I see," the doctor said, incredibly quietly. His eyes widened. "I didn't think this time would come."

"Is it... Is it..." Jimmy stammered.

"It's not Ian Coates," Dr Higgins said quickly. "I presume you know that and that's why you're asking."

Jimmy nodded. He could feel his bottom lip trembling and he hated himself for it.

"Your biological father is dead," the old man announced.

"Don't lie to me!" Jimmy shouted and he snatched the doctor's collar.

"It's the truth, Jimmy. It is."

The power drained out of Jimmy's arm.

"What about my mother," he murmured. "Is she..." He stopped. He could feel that heat rising in his chest. If he said any more he knew he would cry and he didn't want to give Dr Higgins that power.

"She is your mother," said the doctor quickly. "Yes, yes, don't worry. Of course she's your mother."

Jimmy slumped forward on the table. He didn't dare imagine what might have happened to her. He could only hope that when he made it back to Chinatown, she would be there waiting for him.

"So who is he?" he demanded, lifting his head from the table and trying to piece back together his tough outer layer. "Who is my father?"

Dr Higgins said nothing. Instead, he picked up Jimmy's pen and pulled another napkin from the rusty dispenser. He wrote something down, shielding it from Jimmy's eyes. Then he folded it over and pushed it across the table. But his fingers didn't release it .

"Your father is dead, Jimmy," he said again, more slowly. "I've written his name on this napkin. It's up to you whether you look."

Jimmy had no patience for this; he reached out for it. The doctor pulled it away.

"Wait," Higgins insisted. "There will be a danger in reading this name, Jimmy." He took a deep breath. Jimmy stared at him, uncertain whether to listen or to grab the napkin and run. "You've overcome your programming so many times," the doctor continued, "and in such difficult circumstances, that you've shown me something I never thought could be true."

"What's that?" Jimmy's voice came out meek and small.

"It's that you have the potential to be your own man. You're not like Mitchell. From what I've seen and heard, he's succumbing to his programming more and more every day. You, though – you've torn up the rule book, Jimmy. But it's going to get harder for you from now on. Your programming has already developed so far, so quickly, and it will keep growing inside you, taking over. If you're going to keep it at bay, the only way to do it is to fight every day to control your own destiny."

His stare scorched Jimmy's eyes.

"Take responsibility for your actions," Dr Higgins urged. His whisper seemed to cancel out any other noise in the place. "Seize control. If you do, you've shown that you might have a chance to escape the destiny that I programmed into your genes."

He paused and looked down at the napkin. The tips of his fingers had turned white, pressing harder and harder, nailing the identity of Jimmy's father in its place.

"Will you be able to do that, Jimmy," the doctor asked, "if you know the name of your genetic father? If you're always looking over your shoulder, checking yourself to see whether you're turning into him? If you're chasing your father's shadow?"

Very slowly, he lifted his fingers off the napkin. It sat there, folded in two. The lettering showed through as a red blur, ever so faintly – too faint to be legible. It looked like a bloodstained bandage. Jimmy couldn't take his eyes off it.

"Take some time," Dr Higgins told him, a sadness in his face. "Think about it. But take responsibility for your actions. Only read this if you need another man's identity to define who you are."

Jimmy picked up the napkin in the tips of his fingers and turned it around. The material was coarse and cold to the touch. Jimmy couldn't believe he was holding this in his hands and not reading the name inside. But he was still weighing up what Dr Higgins had told him. He could be his own man. And if he managed that, the identity of his father wouldn't matter. *I shouldn't need to know*, he thought to himself. *So why do I feel like I do?*

His hand trembling slightly, he slipped the napkin into the back pocket of his jeans. He could feel it, suddenly hot, burning through his pocket. Then he grabbed the pen from Dr Higgins and scribbled something quickly in his notebook.

"Dr Higgins," he said in a business-like tone. "Do one favour for me."

"So we're doing each other favours now, are we?"

"Take this back to Chinatown," Jimmy ordered. "Give it to Felix. It's very important."

Jimmy stood up suddenly and handed Dr Higgins his notebook, dropping his pen on the table. He was about to dash away, but checked back and stuffed his hand into the dish of ketchup sachets.

"What are you doing?" asked Dr Higgins.

Jimmy grabbed a fistful of the small plastic packets of ketchup and ran.

"Where are you going?" the doctor cried out after him.

Jimmy's response echoed through the underground caverns long after he was out of sight:

"I'm taking responsibility for my actions."

Dr Higgins tapped his bandaged hand on Jimmy's notebook, listening to the boy's steps fade. He was deep in thought.

"Wait," he whispered, to nobody in particular. The waitress tutted and shook her head. To her, the grey man with his cloth cap was just another senile old coot.

"If they're using phone masts," Dr Higgins went on under his breath, "it would work in England, but here they'd need access to the US networks and..."

Suddenly, horror attacked his face. He jumped up, more lively than he had been for half a century.

"Jimmy, wait!" Dr Higgins' words echoed around the room. It was too late. Jimmy was already gone. He never heard the old man's final warning:

"It's them!"

CHAPTER TWENTY-EIGHT - TERMINAL MEETING

Jimmy raced across the spectacular main hall of Grand Central Station. His trainers squeaked on the oversized tiles. He wished he had time to stop and admire the place with its high, rounded ceiling and the orange glow of the walls, but inside him was a new urgency. The images pounded in his head. Hatred of them drove him on. He was desperate to get rid of them and now he knew exactly how to do it – let them take over. If Miss Bennett wanted to lead him into an NJ7 trap on Roosevelt Island, then that's where he'd go.

There were people scurrying across the floor – busy, even though it was still the early hours of the morning. Jimmy wove a path between them. At the information desk in the centre of the hall he hardly even slowed down, but reached out and plucked a city centre map from the rack. He glanced at the four-faced golden clock as he passed, but it had stopped.

How would he know when NJ7 were expecting him, he wondered. All he could do was give himself over to his instincts.

He burst into the street. It was eerily quiet. The dampness in the air soaked into the map as he unfolded it. To Jimmy it felt like it was coating his very bones as well. He quickly found Roosevelt Island – a sliver of land wedged between Manhattan and Queens. The shape of it looked like a large submarine about to submerge into the East River.

Straight away, Jimmy worked out how to get to the tramway that would take him over the water on to the island. But there was somewhere else he needed to go first. Instead of heading north to the tramway, he dashed west, along 42nd Street. The wind gusted in his face. He leaned into it, running with his body at an extreme angle to the ground. The map flapped behind him like the tail of a comet. He let it go. He didn't need it. He knew now that the Manhattan grid would be scored in his visual memory – it was far simpler than the schematics of a museum.

His feet sprang off the pavement, throwing him forwards. The rhythm was frenetic but regular. Every few strides he felt a fog creeping over his brain. It was doubt in himself. It urged him to stop. *Look in your back pocket. Read the name.* Jimmy tightened his shoulders and increased his pace. He had to keep moving. It was the only way to stop himself crumbling.

In barely a minute he reached Times Square. Any other boy in the world would have slowed down and craned his neck to gawp at the spectacle. Jimmy ignored it. Times Square could wait. He charged into the station and down the steps. There was still money in his jeans. He bought a ticket from the machine, then clattered through the turnstiles and into the maze of tunnels.

For some reason, it was busier below ground than in the street, as if New York disappeared beneath the earth after dark. A drunk bellowed out a song. His voice filled the tunnels, surrounding Jimmy until the rattle of a train drowned it out.

Jimmy kept running, though he wasn't trying to catch a train.

KNICKERBOCKER – the word called out to Jimmy. Looking at those time-weathered letters, he felt for an instant that stab in the back where he'd been shot by the CIA's laser-blanks, and that terror when he'd believed it would kill him. He brushed it all aside and leapt up to tweak the grimy white box that unlocked the door.

There was no mystery this time when he barged through into the lobby of the abandoned hotel.

"Colonel Keays!" he shouted into the expanse of darkness. He gathered a deep breath to settle his panting. "Colonel Keays, it's me, Jimmy Coates. I need your help."

At first the only response was his own words echoing back to him. Then, "What is it?"

Jimmy looked up to where the voice had come from. In a fuzzy blue haze, he made out Colonel Keays peering down at him from the balcony.

"I need to borrow some equipment," Jimmy declared.

The Colonel marched down towards him. He was wearing a night-vision headset that made him look like an alien.

"Whatever you need, Jimmy," he said when he was close. "I can trust you with any of our kit. We're on the same side now, remember?"

Jimmy hesitated a moment, then brushed off his anxiety.

"It's not for me," he announced. "But if I tell you what to do, can you do it?"

Colonel Keays pulled a pen and a black leather notebook from the inside pocket of his uniform.

"Make a shopping list," he instructed, handing them to Jimmy. "We'll deliver."

In minutes, Jimmy was back on the street. Even when his breathing grated in his lungs he didn't stop running. The city was still now. Jimmy felt like he was moving through a ghost town. Indistinct noises floated down from a few windows high above him, and he could hear the whirr of the street sweepers never far away. But nobody was around.

New York was only a network of shadows and pools of neon light diffracted by the drizzle.

Eventually, Jimmy rounded the corner of 60th Street on to Second Avenue to see the giant concrete construction that dominated the block. It held the terminal for the tramway over to Roosevelt Island. Above Jimmy's head the building spat out half a dozen super-thick cables – although it had been named a 'tramway' by New Yorkers, it was actually what Jimmy would have called a cable car.

That moment, the fat red cabin swung down along the cables to dock in the terminal. On its side, in big white letters, was 'Roosevelt Island'. Jimmy peered up at it. Through the reflections in its windows, Jimmy made out the silhouette of a single passenger. Who would possibly be travelling across into Manhattan at this time?

Jimmy dashed up the concrete steps, listening to the doors of the cabin sliding open on their ancient runners. A lone set of footsteps emerged. Jimmy reached the top of the stairs. When he saw who it was that had just stepped off the cable car, he thought his heart would stop.

Paduk spun round. His expression reflected the shock in Jimmy. Clearly, NJ7 hadn't expected Jimmy to arrive so soon. Maybe he wasn't meant to work out the clues in the images for a few more hours, allowing them to send him closer and closer to insanity the longer the day drew on. But here he was. And seeing the sculpted bulk of Paduk in the same place confirmed it for him – nothing was waiting for him on the island but a battalion of NJ7 agents. Yet Jimmy knew he had to get to them. He had to end this lethal cat-and-mouse chase or it would carry on forever.

Paduk reached under his suit jacket. Jimmy didn't wait to see what would emerge. He dived to the floor and rolled forwards. A bullet blasted into the concrete behind where he had been standing. Paduk adjusted his aim, but Jimmy launched himself off the ground. In mid-air, he kicked out with both feet. His first kick connected with Paduk's gun, which jumped out of his fist and clattered to the floor. Jimmy's other leg followed, aiming straight for Paduk's head, but the agent was quick. He raised his arm to block the blow and parried Jimmy over his shoulder.

Jimmy twisted in the air to land on his back, while Paduk lunged forwards to pick up his gun. Jimmy swept his foot across Paduk's ankles to bring the man down. Then Jimmy dived into the cable car. Without hesitating, he slammed his palm down on the control panel twice. One red button started the doors sliding back together. The second jolted the whole cabin into life. It creaked and wobbled, then shifted awkwardly out of its dock.

Just in time, Paduk thrust out his foot. He jammed it between the doors and the cabin dragged him along the floor of the terminal. As he moved, he took aim at Jimmy through the cabin windows. Jimmy dropped to the floor and kicked Paduk's foot away. At last, the doors shut and the tram was out of the dock. It lurched through the air, swinging for a few seconds, then settled. Jimmy was alone in the cabin. NJ7 must have somehow made sure that the usual staff weren't manning their posts that morning.

He looked back at the dock expecting to see Paduk shrinking into the distance. But nobody was there. That instant, something blasted a hole in the floor of the cabin. A hand burst through and grabbed Jimmy's ankle. Paduk was hanging off the underside of the cable car.

Felix kicked his father gently in the belly.

"Get up," he insisted. "Come on!"

Neil Muzbeke groaned and rolled over.

"Come on!" Felix urged, louder. "Get up! Jimmy's not back."

His father's eyes shot open. "Not back?" he asked. "What do you mean, 'not back'? Where did he go?"

"I shouldn't have let him go," Felix replied. "But he said he'd be OK. He went with Dr Higgins."

"Dr Higgins?" Neil pushed himself to his feet and rubbed his hands over his face. He was suddenly wide awake. "Helen back yet?" Felix shook his head. "This isn't good."

Then they both heard a noise from downstairs – a click. They stared at each other. Felix had never felt his blood pumping so hard through his veins. He waited to hear either Jimmy or Jimmy's mother coming up the stairs. Nothing.

He ran out of the room and down to the front door. Waiting for him on the mat was Jimmy's notebook. He grabbed it and yanked the door open. The wind wrapped around him and squeezed out all warmth. He stepped out and peered up and down the street. It was deserted.

"Well?" asked Neil Muzbeke, appearing in the doorway with a blanket pulled around his shoulders.

Felix turned round and shrugged.

"Just Jimmy's notebook," he said, turning it over in his hands. Then he saw the front cover. He shivered, but it wasn't from the cold. He ran back into the building and slammed the door behind him.

"Get the others," he ordered. "We're leaving."

"What?" Neil exclaimed. "Calm down."

"I'll calm down as soon as we're out of Chinatown." Felix held up the notebook in front of his chest. On the front was a message, scrawled in red capital letters, but very shakily, as if somebody had written it with his wrong hand, or it had been written by someone very old – or both. It read:

"THEY KNOW WHERE YOU ARE. GET OUT."

CHAPTER TWENTY-NINE - TRAMWAY CROSSING

Jimmy looked down through the hole in the cable car floor. Paduk's fist squeezed so tightly around his ankle that he lost all feeling in his foot. For a few seconds they stared into each other's eyes.

A hundred metres beneath Paduk, the street rushed past. Then the tramway took them off the edge of Manhattan, over the surging waves of the East River. In the darkness, it looked like they had gone off the edge of the world.

Paduk's other hand dangled beside him. In it he held his gun. Slowly, he lifted his arm and took aim at Jimmy's head. Jimmy's programming had never reacted so fast. He moved with such power and precision that he didn't even know what position he was in until he'd already moved on. In a flash, he raised his leg and Paduk with it. Then he slammed his other foot down on Paduk's forearm.

Jimmy felt the impact of the man's bone. It didn't

crack, but Paduk's grip gave way immediately. He caught the edge of the hole in the floor and started tearing at the metal, to claw his way into the cabin.

Jimmy didn't wait for him. He jumped up, grabbing the handrail that ran through the carriage. In the middle of the ceiling was a small perspex square – a skylight. Jimmy swung his body upwards and smashed it open with both feet. It snapped off in one piece, flying away with the wind. Jimmy swung up again, this time hooking his legs through the skylight.

The wind whipped round the cabin. It tore at Jimmy's cheeks. In his chest was a panic struggling to make itself felt above the discipline of his programming.

Paduk pulled the top half of his body through the floor. He was barely two metres away. He steadied himself on his elbows, then took aim. Jimmy hauled himself through the skylight, upside-down, swerving his body out of the way just as Paduk's bullet ripped into the ceiling. Jimmy thought his ears were going to burst with the power of the shot.

He crouched on top of the carriage. Above his head was the squealing wheel and cable system. To his right he could see the skyscrapers of downtown Manhattan getting smaller and smaller as the tram approached Roosevelt Island. His view was cut into chunks by the rusting scaffold of Queensborough Bridge.

It was less than a second before he had to move again. He heard the click of Paduk's gun. The man wasn't climbing up to get him. It was more straightforward to shoot through the roof.

The first blast tore through just a centimetre from Jimmy's right foot. A splinter of the metal jumped up and hit him in the face. He turned away instinctively and that's when he saw it. Straight ahead of them, rising out of the mist, way out past Roosevelt Island and on the other side of the river, were four slim towers, each one painted red at the base, white in the middle and red at the top. Big Allis Power Station.

The muscles in Jimmy's eyes locked. He couldn't look away. It was like when two strings on a guitar play the same note and they're exactly in tune. He had a perfect view of the towers and it set off an involuntary surge of joy in his brain. He couldn't control it – it was a chemical reaction.

Move, he heard in his head. It was a tiny voice at first, swamped by the powerful emotion of his mental vision connecting with the world. Then he forced it through his brain's confusion: *MOVE!*

Another shot ripped through the roof. Jimmy jumped backwards just in time. But there was hardly any space left on top of the cable car. In a few seconds Paduk would have shot up the whole thing and Jimmy with it.

Felix quickly roused his mother and Georgie, while Neil Muzbeke collected as many items as he could that he thought might be useful, including a couple of blankets and some leftover food. When they were all together he shared the rest of the dollars out equally between them.

"What do we do about Helen?" asked Olivia Muzbeke. "She said she'd be back by the morning." They all looked at each other.

Georgie knew without anybody saying a word that they had to leave. The message on the notebook said it all. There was no time to wait for her mum. They had to get out now.

Felix's father marched into the bedroom and removed the crate from the broken window.

"She'll see that from the other end of the street," he announced. "It should be enough to warn her. Don't worry." He took Georgie by the shoulders. "I know she's coming back and I know she'll be fine."

Georgie looked into his big comforting eyes.

"How will we find her again?" she asked.

"We won't need to." Neil's voice was confident and encouraging. "She'll find us. She's a top agent and a strong woman. Remember that."

Georgie didn't smile and didn't nod. But she pretended there was a core of strength inside her taking control. "Let's get out of here," she urged.

Neil grinned.

"We don't know where we're going yet," Olivia pointed out.

"Show me Jimmy's pictures," Georgie ordered. Felix flipped open the notebook to the four towers and the ruin. "This is where we should go." Georgie paused, then added, "Any idea where it is?"

Felix shrugged at first, but then he dashed for the door.

"Back in a sec," he yelled. He tumbled down the stairs, limbs flailing everywhere, and burst into the street.

"Felix, wait!" cried Neil Muzbeke. He dropped the batteries he'd found under the sink and ran after his son. Olivia and Georgie quickly followed. When they got downstairs. Felix was hammering on the door to the restaurant beneath the apartments.

His face was pressed up against the glass. There was a light on somewhere in the back of the restaurant, and after a good thirty seconds of Felix hammering, a shadow lumbered towards them across the restaurant floor. The door swung open violently and out flew a tirade of Korean.

Mrs Kai-Ro was not pleased. She hadn't been asleep – that much was obvious. She was dressed and alert. But her hands were full of pak choi, and there were shouts ringing from the kitchen in the back. They were obviously unloading that morning's delivery.

"Where's this?" Felix demanded, opening Jimmy's notebook up to the right page. The only response was a blank look. "Come on, please? Do you know where this is?"

"Insect?" Mrs Kai-Ro blurted in her thick Korean accent. "Come back later."

"No, no!" Felix cried. "Where is this?"

"Saying it louder won't help," Georgie pointed out. "Didn't you pick up any Korean when you were hanging out with her?"

"Jimmy would know what to say," Felix mumbled.

In desperation, he performed a ridiculous mime. He bashed the paper with his finger, then walked around in a circle in the street with his hand shielding his eyes, as if he was very obviously looking for something. Georgie laughed, despite her tension.

"Stop messing about," sighed Felix's father. But then at last Mrs Kai-Ro's expression changed.

"Oh!" she exclaimed with a smile. "You want to go Roosevelt Island?"

"That's it!" Olivia shouted. "Where's that?"

"Roosevelt Island!" Mrs Kai-Ro shouted.

"Yeah, like I said," groaned Georgie. "Louder isn't clearer!"

Mrs Kai-Ro gave a sprightly spin and disappeared again into the restaurant.

"You offended her," Felix whispered. "No, wait, maybe she's getting us some dumplings for the journey."

Georgie let out an exasperated squeal, but a second later, the old woman had returned with something in her hands. A map of Manhattan.

"Roosevelt Island!" she declared, pointing to the sliver of land in the East River.

"Thank you," said Felix's father. Then he turned to Felix and Georgie. "You two wait here." He took the map from Mrs Kai-Ro's hands with a smile and a nod of gratitude, and thrust it on Felix. "Your mother and I will fetch all the stuff from upstairs."

"Be quick," Felix urged.

"We'll be two seconds," was his father's reply. "Don't move."

Neil and Olivia rushed back into the building and up to the apartments.

"Thanks, Mrs Kai-Ro," said Felix, very slowly and a little too loudly. The Korean woman nodded, clearly unsure of why these people were so grateful to her. But then she looked up and her face changed. Where there had been bewilderment there was now intense fear.

Felix and Georgie spun round to see what she was looking at. Horror tore into their hearts. Round the corner, creeping like a nightmare, came a long black car. It had no number plate. It might have been the contrasting neon lights that flooded the street, but Felix flinched when he thought he saw, just under the front grill, a green stripe.

"Mum!" Felix squeaked. "Dad!" He tried to shout it, but his voice emerged as a throttled whisper.

"Quick," said Mrs Kai-Ro. "In!" She pulled Felix and

Georgie towards her and clattered the restaurant door shut behind them.

"What do we do?" Felix panted.

Georgie peered through the glass. The car stopped right outside the Star of Manchuria. The inside of the restaurant was dark though, so there was a chance they could hide.

"Do you think they saw us?" Georgie asked.

The car doors opened. Out came two huge men in dark suits. The driver straightened his tie and looked the building up and down. Together they strode straight towards the restaurant door.

"They saw us," gasped Felix.

"Out back!" Mrs Kai-Ro shouted.

Felix and Georgie swivelled and hurtled across the restaurant, stumbling over the forest of chairs. When they made it to the door of the kitchen, Felix paused and turned back. Mrs Kai-Ro was waving them on, her face a picture of panic. But beyond where she was standing, on the other side of the glass, Felix could see why the two men hadn't yet burst into the restaurant.

His parents had arrived in the street. Felix ran back towards the front window.

"Felix, come on," urged Georgie. "What are you doing?"

Felix didn't even answer. He charged to the door, but froze when his hand touched the handle. He was too late.

However much Neil and Olivia struggled, it was no good. Peeking through the slats in the venetian blind, Felix watched his parents being violently pushed to the pavement, face down. His mother looked up as one of the agents pulled plastic hand ties tight around her wrists. For a second, she was staring straight at Felix, but there was no fear in her eyes. Instead, she gave a tiny shake of her head. The agent would have thought it was from the cold of the ground, but Felix knew what his mother was telling him. He shrank back into the protection of the restaurant's darkness.

"Let's go," Georgie called out behind him.

One of Mrs Kai-Ro's kitchen workers pointed the way out and towards a truck, loaded with Chinese cabbage. Somebody else started the engine.

The last thing Felix saw before he spun round and ran for his life through the restaurant, through the kitchen, out of the back door and into the back of the truck, was his mother mouthing simple instructions:

"Go. Get to Jimmy!"

The next shot ripped through the roof of the cable car. Jimmy pulled his face back. He could have sworn he felt the bullet grazing the tip of his nose. He looked above him, searching for a way out of Paduk's shooting gallery. The wheels of the cable car screeched on the cables. If he tried to catch hold of one, he'd surely get mangled up in the complex pulley system.

So instead he looked down. It was too far to jump. Way too far. And it wasn't water below them any more. They'd reached the island. The water's edge was lined with rocks, then it was pure concrete. Jimmy gulped. He had less than a second to decide which way to go – staying on top of the carriage was not an option. Through the immense noise of the wind and the screeching of the cables, Jimmy's ear picked out the click of Paduk's gun. The next bullet was in the chamber. The man was picking his spot.

Suddenly, Jimmy saw his chance. Without thinking, he snapped his legs straight, pushing himself forwards off the roof of the cable car and into the air. The screech of the cables vanished. Wind took its place, rushing through Jimmy's head. He closed his eyes, trusting himself completely to the instinct that had made him jump.

His fall seemed to last forever, as if time didn't apply any more. He hurtled through the air. The speed of his fall made his whole body go numb as the air blasted into it. A million thoughts whirled round his mind all at once. He let the bad ones fly out as soon as he'd thought them. There was no time to regret this decision. No time to consider what else he could have done. Only time to beg that he'd survive.

CHAPTER THIRTY - ROOSEVELT ISLAND

Helen Coates moved slowly through Manhattan, keeping to the shadows. Overhead, the lights of a plane disappeared into the clouds. For all she knew, Viggo could be on it, heading back to London. But for now she had to put that out of her head.

She stepped off the pavement to cross Canal Street, but a truck loaded with crates of cabbage rattled past. She pulled herself back violently to avoid getting knocked down. She took a deep breath and jogged on, back towards the safehouse.

When she reached the corner of the street she stopped. She knew immediately that the safehouse had been breached. The discreet sign that Neil Muzbeke had left was clear – leaving the broken window uncovered. But Helen didn't need it because in the middle of the road was a long black car. With a lurch of dread, she saw two of her best friends being ushered into the back, their hands secured behind them with strips of white plastic.

Her first instinct was to run and try to help them. But she knew there was nothing to be gained from barging in and getting captured herself. She held herself in a doorway, watching, waiting. Gradually, panic crept over her. Where were the others? Where was Jimmy? Where was Georgie? The car drew away like a rat scurrying through the gutter.

Helen could feel herself shaking, but she couldn't stop it. Every day for thirteen years she had known what it was like to fear for her family. This was worse. She tried desperately to clear her thoughts. But her heart was being attacked by guilt. *I should never have left them alone*, she thought. Tears gathered in her eyes.

Even once the car was out of sight, Helen held herself back in the shadow of the doorway. She could feel a buzz rising up inside her. It was the terrible thrill of being in danger. It was time to recall everything she had learned all those years ago, before she was a mother, when she had been on active duty as an NJ7 agent, a servant of her nation. *Time to do what I should have been doing every day since then*, she told herself. *Time to serve my family.*

Though tears were running down her cheeks, she felt stronger. Then a picture emerged in her head: Neil and Olivia being forced into the back of the car. Something wasn't right. With everything else burning through her mind – the guilt, the panic, the excitement – she couldn't see anything clearly. Then it hit her. The white plastic hand ties round her friends' wrists. NJ7 used metal cuffs.

Whoever had taken Neil and Olivia Muzbeke, it wasn't NJ7.

When Jimmy opened his eyes he still couldn't see. The wind buffeting his face had made his eyes water so much that a constant stream of tears flew up to the sky behind him. With a mammoth effort he brought his arm to his face to wipe them away. At last he could see where he was heading – just in time.

A wave of relief sent a new power through his muscles. He had judged his jump perfectly. He was heading for the domed plastic roof of the Roosevelt Island Tennis Club courts. He turned his shoulder to cushion the impact, then,

SMACK!

His whole skeleton clattered inside his skin. It was the kindest landing he could have hoped for. Hitting the dome at its peak would have splattered his body into a thousand pieces, but he landed just below that. He slid and bumped down the side of the dome. The friction allowed him to slow down more gradually. Effectively, it was like putting the brakes on. Then Jimmy hit the ground with a nasty thud.

He groaned and rolled over, clutching his shoulder. He looked up to the sky, and could just make out a tiny face peeking through the glass of the cable car, way above him. Even from this distance, Paduk did not look pleased.

Seeing him was a chilling reminder. Jimmy hadn't got away yet. But he'd made it to the island. From here he would be going deeper into the centre of the NJ7 trap – and that was exactly what he wanted. Today was the day he settled this.

Jimmy bulldozed his pain to one side and staggered to his feet. Hardly pausing for breath, he clambered over the low railing of the Tennis Club and broke into a run. At first he had to clutch his shoulder and his running was unbalanced – he'd landed on his right side and it wasn't ready for any more action yet. But Jimmy forced his way through that. He could already picture the cable car docking at the terminal and Paduk coming after him. In seconds, Jimmy was running normally again.

He ran down the side of the island, heading for its Southern tip. That's where the waitress at the Oyster Bar had said he'd find the ruin. The image of it blasted at him from the inside with all the force that the wind had put on him in his fall. He ran on as if he could run away from what was inside his head.

To his right was a slim railing separating the walkway from the river. There were posts every few metres along it and on top of each post was a fat seagull. Jimmy raced past them and they each in turn launched themselves into the air, giving Jimmy a fanfare of feathers as he ran.

Manhattan was just across the river. In the corner of his eye Jimmy could see the giant buildings squeezed into every possible space. But Roosevelt Island was completely different. There were no skyscrapers. Just a single road winding through a deserted medical centre, and the walkway along the river that Jimmy was on.

He closed his mind to the surroundings. All he could see were the two remaining images: the ruin and SILVERCUP. All he could hear were the squawks of the seagulls. They were like sirens warning him of the danger. Then came the first gunshot – Paduk was behind him. But the man wasn't giving chase. Instead, when the shot missed, Jimmy heard the crackle of Paduk's radio. Jimmy knew all he'd find at the tip of the island would be scores of NJ7 agents. And they'd be ready for him.

The end of the path came quickly, but Jimmy knew he wasn't at his destination yet. Ahead of him was a high metal fence, with a sign saying SOUTH POINT – NO TRESPASSING NO LOITERING. Jimmy didn't have time to pay attention to that. He knew what was waiting for him on the other side of the fence. He leapt up and caught the metal. In under a second he had scrambled to the top. This was no obstacle to him – and NJ7 knew it. But they had to make it seem like it had been difficult for Jimmy to get there. A trap that's easy to walk into is easy to spot.

Jimmy jumped down on to the other side. Here the island was a wasteland – just a rubbish tip surrounded by weeds and discarded Christmas trees. Jimmy ran on past the rubbish. The wind whipped around him, swooping in off the river. And then, at last, there it was: the ruin.

It was exactly as he'd pictured it. A crumbling brownstone building with holes where there should have been windows. Jimmy couldn't have known, but it was actually the remains of a nineteenth century smallpox hospital for children. Thousands had died there. This morning, NJ7 planned to kill one more.

Jimmy heard the metal fence rattling. Paduk was catching up. But that was the least of his problems. Suddenly, from out of the silence of the early morning, there came the buzzing of motors. Jimmy turned to look across the water and straight away saw the foam tracks of six military speedboats jetting towards him, against the stunning backdrop of Manhattan. One building stood out: the United Nations.

The boats scythed through the water. Jimmy had reached the ruin and sprung the trap, but for a second he couldn't move. He was imagining the lies that had filled that building this week: Ian Coates pretending to negotiate for peace, while all the time preparing for war.

The boats reached the shore. From further down the river came six more. Jimmy didn't need to see them to know that on the other side of the island there would be another six. Each boat carried two riflemen, with their long black barrels loaded on their shoulders. Jimmy was startled into action.

With a desperate glance at the sky, he pushed off his heels and made for the ruin. It was the only protection from the guns. He clambered over the rubble – the roof of the place had collapsed almost a century ago. Then he hauled himself up the inside of the wall, gripping the dead ivy. So far, this was not how he'd planned for things to go.

"Jimmy!" The shout echoed through the ruin, then was lost in the open air. Jimmy kept moving, trying to work out where the voice had come from and who it could be.

"Jimmy!" it came again. "Give up. You're surrounded." Only now did Jimmy realise it was the shout of a thirteen-year-old boy.

"Is that what you'd do, Mitchell?" Jimmy yelled back. He found a ledge where there used to be a floor and edged his way round it. There was nothing in the middle of the 'room' but a big hole. A single floodlight illuminated the place as if it was some kind of tourist attraction. Long corridors of light beamed up from ground level. Jimmy kept to the shadows.

He could hear the rustling of the long grass outside the ruin. The snipers had him encircled, but as long as he stayed within these walls, they couldn't shoot him. However, the walls held other dangers.

Mitchell's shadow appeared on the wall next to him. Jimmy jumped across to it, catching the brickwork. Broken rocks pattered down to join the rubble below.

"I hear you, Jimmy!" Mitchell cried. "Better get out of here while you can."

Jimmy kept moving. "You're on the wrong side!" he yelled, throwing his voice to try and confuse his opponent, though he knew Mitchell would be doing the same thing. "NJ7 tricked you. I told you that: they have your brother."

"I know," Mitchell countered straight away. His shadow shifted again. Jimmy moved with it, on the ledges around the barren spaces that had once been second floor rooms.

"So you should be attacking them, not me!" Jimmy yelled. "Take your revenge."

"Everybody wants revenge!" Mitchell bellowed, so loud Jimmy thought the whole ruin might crumble away. But Mitchell followed it with a whisper: "I already got mine."

Suddenly, Jimmy pinpointed the source of the voice. He whipped his head round. Mitchell was in mid-air, looming down at him, arm raised, ready to strike. Jimmy caught Mitchell's wrist a centimetre from his throat and lurched backwards. He dropped on to his back – there was barely enough space on the ledge. He used Mitchell's momentum to hurl the boy away, over his head.

Mitchell caught the ledge on the other side of the hole and swung himself to his feet again.

"I hated my brother," he grunted between gritted teeth, then jumped back at Jimmy. Jimmy spun on his back and pushed his legs against the wall. That sent him hurtling into Mitchell's midriff like a battering ram. He twisted in the air and the two of them, locked together, fell through the hole on to the pile of rubble right in the centre of the ruin.

Mitchell slammed two fists into the small of Jimmy's back. Jimmy felt it like a bomb going off inside him, forcing out all the air. For a second he lay face down on the rubble, helpless. But his programming lurched up a gear.

He rolled to the side just as Mitchell's hand chopped down, splitting a slab of stone. Jimmy pushed himself to his feet. The two boys circled each other, their postures identical, arms spread, ready for action.

"Because of you I failed another mission," Mitchell sneered.

"So you didn't catch Zafi?" Jimmy smiled to himself.

"She's crawled back to France. But I'll get her. Right after I've killed you."

Jimmy glanced quickly up at the sky again, as if any moment he expected to sprout wings and be able to fly into the heavens. It was getting lighter all the time. The shadows were fading as the floodlight gave way to natural light – the sun would be up soon.

"Expecting help from above?" Mitchell quipped.

Jimmy ignored him. Then, at precisely the same moment, they both drew their arms in and wiped the sweat from their faces with their sleeves.

Mitchell didn't even notice what he'd done, but Jimmy felt like he was looking in a mirror. It hit him harder than any of Mitchell's blows and made any pain in his muscles seem insignificant. Realisation flooded through him.

"Your brother," Jimmy gasped. "Is he your..."

Mitchell didn't flicker. His eyes were steady, waiting for that opening in Jimmy's defences. Then he mumbled, "NJ7 wheeled him away to be a human guinea pig. That's what I call revenge."

"But he was only your half-brother," Jimmy whispered, as if explaining it to himself.

Mitchell's confusion showed now, but he was still just as lethal. He dipped his shoulders to the left, then ducked down and grabbed for Jimmy's waist.

Jimmy was quick and alert. He gave a small skip, planting his foot on Mitchell's neck and launching himself off again. Mitchell controlled his fall, and rolled back to his feet.

"My half-brother?" he shouted.

Jimmy nodded. "And so am I."

Just then, the ruin shook with the noise of a helicopter. Jimmy smiled and dashed for the other end of the ruin. Mitchell was frozen to the spot.

Jimmy threw himself out of the ruin so fast that he had made it twenty metres before the snipers even took aim. The helicopter roar grew louder and a cloud of dust rose from the ruin, sucked into the whirlwind of its blades. He cemented the memory of Mitchell's confused expression in his mind. The same man had to be the father of both of them, he thought. But they were so different. And if the same man could produce two such different sons, did it matter who the man was?

He hurtled towards the very tip of the island. The sun was creeping up over Queens, turning the UN building into a dazzling orange monolith. It was the first real sunshine of the year. Jimmy felt it warming his cheeks. Then he heard the click of a sniper's trigger behind him. A noise like that cuts through everything else. He threw himself into a roll, avoiding the bullet, but he wouldn't be so lucky with the next shot. There were too many agents behind him, all expert marksmen.

Finally, Jimmy ran out of island. He reached the flimsy gauze fence between him and the water. He turned to face the snipers. For a split-second, the sun almost blinded him. Then he made out dozens of crouching figures, all with their guns pointed at him. As one, they all pulled their triggers.

Jimmy's programming was processing information so fast, he could see the bullets spinning towards him, glinting in the sun just as brightly as the UN building. *Is this it?* he heard a voice ask in his head. It asked without fear, without indignation. It felt like his entire body was as empty as the universe was large. *Is this how I die?*

But the bullets never reached him.

The helicopter plunged down, hovering centimetres from the ground, right between Jimmy and the gunmen. The bullets tore into the side of the chopper.

There were only two people inside. Two masked men – a pilot and a passenger. They both picked up machine guns and now it was their turn to shoot at Jimmy. Nobody could get in the way this time.

Jimmy raised his hands, but too late. His chest reverberated with the repeated pounding and blood spurted into the sunlight. Jimmy's eyes widened. He staggered backwards, leaning on the gauze fence. Then he toppled over it. The last thing he saw as he fell into the East River was a huge advertising hoarding overlooking the water from Queens. It was decades old, and the arched red letters were accentuated by the sun streaming through them from behind. *At last*, thought Jimmy. The prophecy of his final image had been fulfilled. He'd seen SILVERCUP.

CHAPTER THIRTY-ONE - PROFESSIONAL REVENGE

Georgie and Felix jumped out of the back of the truck before it had even come to a complete stop. They waved their thanks to the driver as he sped off again and brushed the cabbage from their clothes.

"Come on, let's go!" Georgie insisted, sprinting away.

"Wait, I think I've got cabbage in my shoe." Felix half-ran, half-hopped after her.

"OK, great, so we'll be killed by the British Secret Service," Georgie mumbled, "but at least your shoes will be free of pak choi."

Felix put in a burst of speed and caught up.

"I'm sorry," Georgie said, her tone changing. "I didn't mean your mum and dad would..."

"It's OK." Felix shrugged and tried not to look sad. "I know."

There wasn't time for being miserable – that could wait. The last thing Felix wanted to think about was the look on his mother's face as his parents had been dragged away.

"How did they find us?" he asked, sneaking a look over his shoulder.

Georgie didn't answer straight away. She and Felix exchanged a glance, both thinking the same thing. If the CIA had been protecting them, how had NJ7 found the safehouse?

They ran on like they never had before, not only because there could be agents chasing them, but because they feared for Jimmy. What was he trying to do at Roosevelt Island and why hadn't he told them? Now finding him was their only chance of finding safety – neither one trusted the CIA any more than they trusted NJ7.

They reached the corner of the block and Georgie grabbed the map from Felix.

"Give me that," she ordered. "I know what you're like with maps."

"Hey," Felix protested. "I can find anything on a map. I just can't find things in real life."

"This way." Georgie stuffed the map into her pocket and set off again, not waiting for either of them to catch their breath. It wasn't long before they reached the edge of Manhattan.

"There it is," Georgie announced, bending double and pressing a hand on the stitch in her side.

Felix shielded his eyes from the sun as it rose over the river. The island was only a short distance away across the water. He peered towards it.

"Hey!" he gasped. "There's Jimmy!"

Georgie followed where he was pointing. Together they saw a fleet of military speedboats close in on the island. They watched in silence as Jimmy emerged from the ruin. To them he was a tiny figure, silhouetted against the rising sun, but they gaped at his speed.

His speed wasn't enough.

"NO!" Georgie screamed. "JIMMY!"

Felix couldn't even speak.

They saw the helicopter swoop down and cut off the sniper fire. Then they watched, helpless, as the masked men in the helicopter opened fire and Jimmy's chest spattered a shower of red into the air. Georgie's face was white. Her hands clamped over her mouth. This time, her scream came out as nothing but a desperate wheeze of air. As her brother hit the water, she broke down. Her sobs wrenched her whole body and she collapsed on the pavement.

"Didn't you see...?" she panted. Felix was as still as a lamp-post. "Why aren't you...?"

"Wait, no," Felix protested. "It's not..." He couldn't finish his sentence. Instead, he held up Jimmy's notebook, open to the last page. On it, in bold red capitals, was written:

DON'T BELIEVE EVERYTHING YOU SEE. REMEMBER THE STICK INSECTS.

"Remember?" Felix asked, his eyes lit up with excitement. "Some of the stick insects looked dead, but they weren't."

"What?" Georgie sobbed, trying hard to control herself until she knew exactly what Felix was talking about.

"That's what he's telling us. He probably didn't think we'd see it in real life. He probably meant for us to see this on TV or something, but if everybody thinks he's dead, NJ7 will stop chasing him. And, wait..." He looked out again at the island. "I don't know how they did it, but I think I know who was in the helicopter. I think Jimmy planned this." He turned back to Georgie and hauled her on to her feet. "I think he's going to be OK."

Georgie looked at him, then over to the island. She replayed in her head the horrific scene she'd witnessed. She couldn't stop herself wincing, then she read Jimmy's message again. Her tears stopped. She wiped her face and blinked hard. At last, a tiny smile made her lips quiver. Then she said, "Look's like my brother's not such an idiot."

"Smartest guy I know," Felix agreed. "But now we have to look after ourselves."

Georgie nodded. "What do we do?" she asked. "Go to the CIA?"

"Do you trust them?"

They looked at each other for a long time, neither one knowing what to say. Then they held each other's shoulders to gather their strength. Each of them took a huge deep breath and ran.

* * *

Jimmy pulled himself up on to the rocks that ran alongside the promenade at the other end of Roosevelt Island. He flopped on to the walkway with a desperate lurch. Black water gushed out of his lungs and his body convulsed, thrusting a massive gulp of air down in place of the liquid. Before he could move, a strong hand clamped on to his shoulder.

"Good job, Jimmy," came a deep, American voice. "Don't worry. You're with the CIA now."

Jimmy wanted to say "thanks" but he didn't have his breath back yet. The current in the East River had been stronger than he'd expected. Instead, he rolled over on to his back and reached into his shirt. One by one, he pulled off the burst sachets of ketchup that he'd stuck all over his chest. He laughed when he noticed that he'd accidentally used one mayonnaise sachet as well. He gathered the wrappers together and handed them to the CIA agent, who dropped them into a litter bin. He was a big broad man, but in casual clothes, not military uniform.

"We'd better move," he announced.

Jimmy stood up and ran unevenly to a long black car that was waiting with the door to the back seat open. All his energy dropped away when he slumped into the seat. There was a towel waiting for him and he buried his head in it. He didn't know what to feel. The emptiness hadn't gone away yet. His friends and his family would watch him being killed on the next TV news bulletin. But his enemies had already seen it, and that was what counted.

The CIA man followed him to the car, but paused to pick up a ragged scrap of white paper that had fallen out of Jimmy's back pocket.

The helicopter tipped from side to side, buffeted by the wind. The pilot's crash course in how to fly wasn't much good now because his hands were on a machine gun instead of the controls. Even after Jimmy tumbled backwards into the water, the two men in the chopper kept firing for several seconds. Then at last, the peal of their bullets died away, and only their joint war-cry rang out:

"REVENGE!"

Before the word was even completely out of their mouths, the team of NJ7 agents stormed the aircraft. The two men were bundled out of the cockpit and found themselves with their faces pressed into the Roosevelt Island mud. Each one had an NJ7 knee in his back. Eventually the helicopter was brought safely to rest.

"SECURE!" yelled one of the agents. That was the signal for their commanding officer to step off one of the speedboats and approach the scene.

"Take off their balaclavas," Miss Bennett ordered. "Let's find out what's going on."

She stayed a safe distance away, and tried to maintain her composure, but when she saw the faces of the gunmen, she bristled and pulled her long black coat tighter around her.

"Quinn and Rick Doren," she announced. "Playing with toys for bigger boys than you, no?"

"He killed our sister," Quinn said bitterly, spitting mud out of his mouth. "If we'd let you kill him, we would never have had our revenge."

Miss Bennett thought hard, examining the two young men on the ground in front of her. She nodded to the surrounding agents to let them up. Then, from Miss Bennett's boat, came a teenage girl, wrapped in a thick black coat.

"Quinn! Rick!"

She was already crying, clearly distraught at the events she had watched unfold in front of her.

"Eva!" shouted the two men, running to embrace their sister. They suffocated her in a muddy embrace. All three wept. For a few seconds they were huddled together.

"You killed Jimmy!" Eva sobbed quietly. The boys didn't reply, but Rick slipped a small piece of card into her coat pocket.

"What are you...?"

Eva discreetly pulled it out, using her two brothers as a shield so that nobody else saw. In her woolly gloves she grasped what looked like the torn-off corner of a small cardboard box. On it was a lot of technical information she didn't understand, but one word stood out: LASER-BLANKS.

"Blanks?" she gasped. Quinn quickly pulled her towards him and smothered her before she could say anything else.

"I'm so glad you're OK," he whispered. "I'm so glad *everyone's* OK."

He held on to his sister for several seconds more. He could feel that, wrapped in his arms, she was squealing with delight and laughing.

Meanwhile, Rick confronted Miss Bennett. "You told us she was dead!" he bellowed.

"Oh, look," Miss Bennett said blankly. "We found her. Hooray."

"But we only killed Jimmy because we thought he'd killed our sister."

"I know." Miss Bennett was eyeing Rick and Quinn suspiciously, sizing them up. "Such an unfortunate turn of events. But at least the outcome is happy. In the end you've done your country a great service. Even if you thought you were doing it for personal reasons."

Rick and Quinn stood on either side of Eva now, waiting for Miss Bennett's judgement.

"Well, look at you," the woman cooed, deep in thought. "A family affair." Then she added, "Eva is doing very well in my office, you know." She looked from Quinn, to Eva, to Rick, and back again. "You'll need training, but if you can all keep a secret from your parents, how about adding two more Doren recruits to NJ7?"

All three broke into huge smiles – though for very different reasons than Miss Bennett believed. Quinn and Rick shook her hand, then Eva escorted them back to the boat.

Meanwhile, Miss Bennett had a clean-up operation to run.

"Get me divers!" she screamed. "Bring me charts of the currents. Show me the exact spot where his body is going to be washed up. I want divers trawling every miserable litre of this river. Bring me the body!"

"Miss Bennett, this isn't London!" Paduk yelled back, marching up to her. "We don't have jurisdiction here. We're lucky we haven't all been arrested already."

Miss Bennett scrunched her fists in her hair. "I need confirmation," she insisted.

"Confirmation?" Paduk whispered, so that none of the other soldiers could hear. "What more confirmation do you need? Didn't you see that little boy's body being torn apart by machine-gun fire?"

"Are you implying something, Paduk?"

"It's not right," Paduk hissed. "What we've done here today. It's not right."

"You were protecting Britain," Miss Bennett barked back.

Paduk marched off, not daring to contradict his superior officer, but he muttered under his breath, "I'm beginning to wonder whether Britain is still worth protecting."

Miss Bennett drew in a deep sigh. Her brow was furrowed in thought. She never imagined quite these sorts of tribulations facing her when she took on the role of running Britain's most powerful and secret intelligence agency.

She walked right to the edge of the island, to the very spot where Jimmy had fallen. She looked out across the river, narrowing her eyes against the wind. It made them water a little and blew her hair into a flame behind her head. There were so many shadows shifting beneath the surf. She wanted to examine each of them in turn, but as soon as she looked at one, it was gone again. The waves lapped around the island while behind her, Paduk commanded the NJ7 unit.

It was several minutes before Miss Bennett turned away from the water, away from the wind, and walked back towards the ruin. Her eyes were still watering.

CHAPTER THIRTY-TWO - NEW VISION

Union Square bustled with traffic and people. In the centre of the square, near where everybody was rushing in and out of the subway, there was a small collection of stalls. Some were selling home-made products like cheese, bread and jams; others stocked trinkets and carriage clocks. This was Union Square Market and plenty of people slowed down to browse what the stallholders had to offer.

One of those people was Colonel Keays. He looked strangely uncomfortable in jeans and a faded leather jacket. No more than two metres behind him, at all times, was one of his agents, also dressed so that he blended into the crowd.

In fact, all around the square, on every corner and on the roof of every surrounding building, there were more CIA agents in constant communication with each other. No member of the public would have noticed them, even as they moved among them. What's more, that morning the square was packed with NJ7 agents too. Each of them also looked like a perfectly normal member of the public – shopping, dashing back to work or meeting friends for a coffee.

Miss Bennett spotted Colonel Keays straight away and marched right up to the stall where he was browsing for second-hand watches.

"You've got a lot of explaining to do, Keays," she snapped, quietly.

"And so have you, Miss Bennett."

Neither of them looked directly at each other. Anybody observing from a distance would have had no idea that they were even in conversation.

"Well, you're starting," Miss Bennett ordered. "What were Quinn and Rick Doren doing in a US military helicopter, with American army machine-guns?"

The two of them moved along the stalls together, worming through the crowds.

"How do I know?" Keays sighed. "This army seems to leak hardware all over the world. They could have bought the stuff off eBay. There'll be an enquiry, but it won't find anything."

"Don't give me that—" Miss Bennett started, but the Colonel cut her off sharply.

"And don't you forget your place. I won't have the head of the secret police of some insignificant dictatorship thinking she can treat me the way she treats her prisoners. Keep that in mind when you speak to me, Miss Bennett, and we'll continue to get along fine." He glanced up for an instant and shot Miss Bennett a huge grin. It quickly vanished.

"I went to a lot of trouble for your 'Reflex Plan'," the man continued. "I arranged for you to transmit covert signals over the United States cellphone mast network on the understanding that it was a joint operation."

"It was," Miss Bennett insisted. "We wanted the President dead and I thought you did too."

They both looked around, uneasy, and walked along to another stall.

"Of course I do," Keays whispered.

"So what went wrong?"

"What went wrong? I'll tell you what went wrong. *You* did." Keays was having trouble keeping his voice down. "My side of the operation went perfectly: *I* showed Jimmy the schematics of the building. *I* gave him his security pass. *I* diverted three whole police divisions so that only my handpicked team was on site. The President had no protection. *I* cleared security from the rooftops so the assassin could get away. It was perfect. Except that the assassin forgot to do any assassinating. Where was the NJ7 back-up?"

"The French had an agent in place to take out the Prime Minister," Miss Bennett explained. "We couldn't have foreseen that. The PM's life was our priority."

"And yet this mysterious French agent has completely disappeared. Then, to top it all, I find out that you started transmitting a new signal – still using *our* masts, of course – and kept it secret from me. What were you thinking?"

"It worked, didn't it? Jimmy Coates is dead."

"Some of us didn't want Jimmy Coates dead," Keays snarled.

"Oh, really? And what did you plan to do with him if he had survived? Use him to get you into the White House?"

Keays pulled himself up to his full height and for the first time they stared at each other.

"If Jimmy were alive," the Colonel rasped, "that's exactly what I would do." There was a sharp glint in his eye. Against his will, his face threatened to crack into a smile, so he turned his back on Miss Bennett, pretending to inspect the cheeses on the stall next to him.

"Alphonsus Grogan is a money-obsessed chump," he muttered. "He thinks this place is his private company, not a great nation. He only takes advice from the heads of big business, and most of them are his uncles, aunts or cousins. His only principle is 'How much money can I make today?' He's selling America to the highest bidder." Keays looked over his shoulder to make sure even his own agent couldn't hear him. Miss Bennett leaned in closer so her ear was right next to the man's face. The smell of the cheeses was overpowering, but so were the Colonel's words:

"I won't sit back and watch the USA being run like a market stall. Grogan needs to go. Then I can declare a state of emergency and step in to run this country efficiently."

Miss Bennett nodded sagely. "I look forward to seeing the end of old-fashioned democracy in the United States," she announced with a soft smile.

"Ha! Old fashioned democracy died a long time ago – if it ever really existed. People here might be allowed to vote every now and again, but that's just because we know they like to feel free. Really, a vote means nothing unless you're rich. In America, only those with money have any power."

"And in Britain, only those with power have any money. I suppose that's the difference between us." Miss Bennett smiled, then asked, "Can we count on your support if Britain and France..."

"Until I'm in the White House, that's up to Grogan. And he will act according to his business interests. That could either mean backing France to punish Britain for not trading in US goods, or it could mean backing Britain so he can blackmail you into putting a Starbucks on every corner again." He hesitated and finally added, "Good luck, Miss Bennett."

They made eye contact and nodded to each other discreetly, before Miss Bennett strolled away, blending into the Union Square crowd.

Colonel Keays' assistant chose that moment to step forward and hand him a palmtop. Keays stared at the screen. His future was a green dot travelling fast along a map of New York, heading for a secret military airbase just outside Piscataway, New Jersey. At that he chuckled, then slipped the gadget into his pocket.

Jimmy knew he was surely being tracked. But in these circumstances, it was reassuring. He was with a powerful organisation now and he knew they were only tracking him to protect him. The car was speeding out of the city. The driver had told him a private plane was waiting to whisk him into the clouds and several thousand miles away.

It was such a relief to have his head clear of those visions. They'd invaded every thought and now, at last, they were gone. But in their place was a heavy anxiety. He still didn't know what had happened to his mother. And until he received word from Colonel Keays, he couldn't be sure that the others were in protection with their new identities.

Nevertheless, Jimmy's future looked a lot brighter now than it had for a long time. Even though he had no idea where he was going, or who he was going to see when he got there, he had a chance at living a life. His only battle now would be with time and the progress of the powers inside him.

He couldn't help wondering whether he'd made the right decision. Thinking about it made his insides feel heavy. He didn't want to feel sad because he was sure that this was the best outcome – NJ7 wouldn't be looking for any of them any more. But how could he be happy, when he didn't know if he would see his mother, his sister or his friends again?

He sniffed, pretending the cold from the river had made his nose run, so the driver wouldn't notice he was holding back tears. He covered his eyes with his hand. What would it take for him to go back to a normal life, with Georgie, his mother and Felix? There was only one way that was going to happen: if the Neo-democratic British Government fell and NJ7 became a force for good.

Jimmy laughed at the idea. But then, after a minute or two, he started thinking about it more seriously. *It could happen*, he told himself. And if he really wanted to take revenge on his ex-father, maybe the way to do it would be to turn Britain back into a true democracy, with Ian Coates as just another citizen.

Jimmy stared out of the window, watching the unfamiliar landscape rush past – vast industrial estates with occasional spring flowers pushing through the concrete. Bubbling inside him he could feel a new strength. It wasn't his programming, and it wasn't some vision that had been forced on to him by a phone network. It was determination. He gritted his teeth, picturing himself with Georgie and Felix in the Prime

Minister's office putting together a new government. It was so ridiculous it made him laugh again – but there was something in the back of his mind that didn't find it so funny.

Suddenly, his thoughts were interrupted.

"Oh, by the way, Jimmy," the driver called out, "this fell out of your pocket."

With a look of intense concentration, the man had one hand on the wheel while the other hand was picking apart the sodden leaves of a white paper napkin.

"No!" Jimmy cried. "Don't read that!"

It was too late. The agent was already rotating the paper this way and that, trying to make out what it said. He glanced round when he heard Jimmy's protest, then turned back to watch the road.

"Oh, I'm sorry, Jimmy," he said with a smile. "But it's OK..." He held up the napkin to show Jimmy, who shrank away, not wanting to see. "I think the water made the ink run, or something."

He threw the paper on to the front passenger seat, but carried on examining it as he drove. The faint red smudge puzzled him. *Does that say what I think it does?* he thought. *Didn't he used to be Prime Minister of England?* He shrugged, then muttered, "It's almost illegible, anyway."

Jimmy dropped his head back and breathed a massive sigh of relief.

"It doesn't matter," he whispered with a confident smile. *It really doesn't*, he thought to himself. *Whoever's name is there, I'm not going to be him. I'm going to be me.*

SABOTAGE

If you think it's over, think again

Sneak preview...

BANG! The plane gave a massive jolt. Jimmy was hurled sideways, slamming his head against the side of the cockpit. If it hadn't been for the helmet, he would have been knocked out cold. He heard both agents yelling through his headset, but he couldn't make out what they were saying. He was suddenly aware of the whole plane violently shaking. His stomach rolled around, and he cried out without even knowing what he was doing. His head was still reeling from the impact. Then he heard the first clear words through his earpiece.

"It's there!" the pilot shouted. His reedy voice came as a shock. Jimmy strained against his strap to see what the man was talking about.

"On your DS!" said Froy urgently, reaching over to shake Jimmy's shoulder. "Your display station!"

Jimmy looked down at the screen in front of him. There was a green outline of jagged straight lines surrounded by blue, representing the coastline beneath them. The whole screen was criss-crossed by thin blue and red lines, but it was hard to make anything out because of the furious vibrations of the plane.

"It's sprung out of nowhere!" the pilot cried. "They won't

miss next time." Then Jimmy saw it – first the black aeroplane icon that represented the EA-22G Growler he was sitting in. Then, barely two centimetres away on the screen, the flashing red dot that could only mean trouble.

"They've found me!" Jimmy gasped, barely able to get the words out. "How did they find me?"

"Hold on tight!" the pilot screamed.

For a second Jimmy felt like the plane had disappeared from under him. The pilot had sent them into a rapid dive, then he swooped out of it almost immediately. The massive reversal of the g-force thrust Jimmy deep into his seat, and the blood rushing to his head made it feel like his brain was about to burst.

"I don't know how they found us," Froy shouted, peering behind him through the glass. "I'm sorry Jimmy." Jimmy looked over as well. With the intense shaking and the limited view, he only caught sight of it for a split-second, but it was enough – the wing-tip of another plane. It was behind them, it was fast, and it could only be NJ7.

The plane surged onwards, back up above the clouds. The vibrations calmed a little and the pilot kept deploying what countermeasures he could. Instinctively, Jimmy knew that first would come a hot flare to divert heat-seeking missiles, then chaff – debris which would disrupt any missile that automatically sought the nearest solid objects.

Jimmy closed his eyes, searching for that power inside him. He had to forget that he was terrified – that was only the human part of him, the 38 per cent that was a normal, frightened boy. He willed the assassin to take him over. He knew that somewhere within him was enough strength, resilience and expert knowledge to survive this crisis.

At last, he felt a rush up the side of his neck – like a rising flood taking over his brain and energising every muscle. His breathing slowed. The panic in his chest crumpled into a harmless ball.

"Can't we fire back?" Froy shouted.

Jimmy didn't wait for the pilot to answer. His voice came out low and calm.

"Check your DS," he ordered, punching a couple of keys. Schematics of the outside of the plane appeared, with the rockets highlighted. "Raytheon HARM High Speed Anti-Radiation Missile, AGM-99," he announced, thrilled at his own conviction. "This is an Electronic Countermeasures plane, not an attack plane. Our missiles can take out anti-radar artillery systems and surface-to-air missiles on land or on ships over 100 kilometres away. But we've got no way of attacking another plane."

The plane rocked again and the noise in the cockpit escalated. "We're losing control!" the pilot screamed above the rattle of the metal struts that were barely holding the cabin together.

CRASH!

It felt as if the plane had been hit by a sledgehammer. A direct hit. Jimmy was thrown to the side, slamming his helmet against the wall of the cockpit again.

Then the plane went into tailspin.